THE EXPAT

A Novel

HANSEN SHI

PEGASUS CRIME
NEW YORK LONDON

THE EXPAT

Pegasus Crime is an imprint of
Pegasus Books, Ltd.
148 West 37th Street, 13th Floor
New York, NY 10018

First Pegasus Books edition July 2024

Interior design by Maria Fernandez

Library of Congress Cataloging-in-Publication Data is available.

ISBN: 978-1-63936-677-4

10 9 8 7 6 5 4 3 2 1

Printed in the United States of America
Distributed by Simon & Schuster
www.pegasusbooks.com

To my parents,

Jason and Mandy

1

Nostalgia as a pathology was first defined in 1688 by the Swiss physician Johannes Hofer, who, as a young medical student at the University of Basel, observed its prevalence among Swiss mercenaries serving in the lowlands of France and Italy. For these hired guns, the condition manifested as fever, fainting, anxiety, insomnia, stomach pain, cardiac arrhythmia, and death, among other symptoms. The disease was taken so seriously that whistling one particular milking song called "Khue-Reyen" became punishable by death. So, for a while the disease came to be known as *mal du Suisse*.

These days I often find myself thinking about Hofer's mercenaries, stalking through the lowlands with a permanent whistle in their ears. I like to imagine them as an army of Werther's, yellow-panted and blue-jacketed, each clutching an identical, damp notebook in their breast pockets. When I first learned about Hofer's study in my freshman year of college, I used to think that a band of hired guns was a strange sample to select for the scientific study of homesickness. Now, nearly a decade later, I think I understand. Only a mercenary could contract such a fatal heartache, because he is further from home than a regular soldier. He has cut himself off from the heart.

Since I relocated to Sydney three months ago, I have experienced many symptoms of chronic nostalgia. At night I lie awake listening to NPR podcasts. I have lost weight, which I am secretly thrilled about. I have become obsessed with, consumed by, the news in America.

Nostalgia also torments me during my waking hours. Sydney is perpetually flooded with sunshine, a cultural export of California. If I close my eyes while walking through the farmers' market in Pyrmont Bay Park, the scent of strawberries and saltwater teleports me to the San Francisco Ferry Building Marketplace. Like a famous ex-girlfriend, America is everywhere I look, in the form of movie trailers, advertising jingles, franchise restaurants, and cereal boxes. Here is what I have learned: as an ex-American, nostalgia is as inescapable as gravity—not a perfect analogy, I am aware, since an American flag flies on the moon.

To protect myself from inflammation, most days I just stick to my apartment. For those of you familiar with Sydney, I live on the nineteenth floor of a new development called Opera Residences in Bennelong Point. The place came fully furnished after the taste of someone I knew well. It's not uncommon for me to spend the whole day here in the living room looking out into the harbor, making coffee, and aimlessly jotting things down, like I'm doing today.

It's not that I can't go back to America, or that there'd be men in uniform waiting for me at the airport if I returned. It's just that I no longer have anything there to go back to. To be clear, I'm not in Sydney to hide. In fact, I'm actively putting myself in harm's way by being here because this is one of the only places in the world people know to look for me. But I promised myself I would stay until I finished this book and hopefully cured myself of nostalgia.

I say "cure" because the warmth of these feelings toward a country that never embraced me strikes me as suspect. How can you feel nostalgic for a place or person you knowingly betrayed? I've learned recently that my feelings, in general, should not be trusted. I started to wonder if this sudden flare-up of nostalgia was masking a more chronic condition, something deeply rooted I haven't come to terms with yet. That's when I realized that in order to cure myself of this disease, I needed to investigate its etiology.

To begin, here is something that you must know about California. Its allure is simple. For centuries, gold has drawn the Chinese to California like mayflies to lamplight. Like iron shavings to a magnet. We flooded into the ports of Jiu Jin Shan (Old Gold Mountain—what the Chinese called Herb Caen's *Baghdad by the Bay*) first on barges, then on planes. After gold, steel. After steel, silicon. That brings us to the present. Remember: we've always been looking for gold in San Francisco.

2

I don't consider myself to be particularly spiritually attuned, but one thing I do know is this: if you want to really disappear, move into an ethnic enclave.

My adult home in San Francisco was at the corner of Stockton and Clay, in the upstairs loft of a Chinese restaurant called Club Mandarin. From the street, the Club Mandarin looked like an abandoned temple, with its portal-like moon gate and sloping double-eave rooftop resting on chipped red plaster pillars three stories tall. On the inside, twenty-five tables draped in faded white tablecloths dotted the vast dining room, ringed in by an ornate mezzanine on the second floor. There were usually no more than two or three families seated for dinner when I came home from work every day. Black-and-white *San Francisco Chronicle* clippings from the Mandarin's golden era hung on the walls, evoking bygone days where the tables were pushed out to the perimeter to make space for a dance floor, and a band was stationed on the mezzanine. A tight spiral staircase tucked away in the back corner of the kitchen led to my loft, a nine-hundred-square-foot space with sweeping ocean views through five bay windows that I almost always blocked out with thick, light-proof blinds.

I don't think it would've been an overstatement to call myself discerning. I subscribed to four different furniture magazines. I could (and did) spend two, three hours at a store in a single afternoon contemplating the slight difference between two nearly identical coffee tables. When it came to décor, I did not believe there were inconsequential decisions.

Here are some of the things that I had: a high-end Italian road bicycle I never rode, suspended perilously on the wall; a metallic, miniature replica of a Chinese scholar's rock; three shelves of books from college; a GameCube; two different coffee tables; an aqua-blue Egg Chair designed by Arne Jacobsen for the Radisson SAS in Copenhagen; tarot cards; a brown leather Danish mid-century modernist sofa; an Indian tapestry; an ultra-high-performance La Marzocco GS3 espresso machine; a desk made from a single piece of California redwood.

The landlady, Madame Suyi, leased this apartment to me at $2,500 a month. The space, I am told, used to board eight or nine restless, hungry, fresh-off-the-boat kitchen workers at any given time back in the restaurant's prime, before city officials shut the practice down. Unlike them, I'd arrived at the Club Mandarin's doorstep not from the Port of Guangzhou, but Newark Liberty. This was my first and only home in San Francisco since I moved from New Jersey nearly five years ago. I remember how confused my friends and relatives were when they found out where I had signed my lease. Based on their collective grimace, they probably thought of me as some destitute street urchin from an Amy Tan novel. What they didn't understand is my reasons for choosing to live in Chinatown were as conventional as could be. In real estate, people paid millions for vast lots and privacy hedges that protected them from wandering eyes and ears. In my view, it was much easier to simply pick a place where people wouldn't be looking for you.

⟜

My usual Sunday routine involved pulling a double shot, putting on my sand-colored Bang & Olufsen over-ears, and booting up Samarkand.

Samarkand was the world's most sophisticated online marketplace for hackers and those who needed their services. What set Samarkand apart was that all of the freelancers on the site had to pass a difficult timed coding challenge to register an account, and the challenge was constantly modified by an algorithm so there was no way to cheat. This weeded out the amateurs and obviated the need for bias-ridden human processes like job interviews. Statistically, it was actually harder to get approved to work on Samarkand than to get hired at Google. As a result, the user base was probably ninety percent psychos from the Indian Institute of Technology. All activity was completely anonymized, so you never knew who you were working for (or who was working for you). The site used a reputation system based on customer feedback, and an algorithm aggregated those reviews to set your hourly rate. I had accumulated a high enough reputation score to bill my time out at $150/hour, which was in the 99th percentile of all users. And since I worked approximately fifteen hours per week, my activities on Samarkand allowed me to effectively double my yearly income.

Not that I saved any of it. I was a single, twenty-six-year-old college graduate with no desire to own an apartment or start a family in the foreseeable future. So I spent as quickly as I earned—on DoorDash omakase; premium productivity-enhancing adaptogenic mushroom powder marketed on Instagram; a nine-piece Le Creuset kitchen set, even though I didn't know how to cook; and a small but growing family of Bearbrick figurines in various sizes and skins that lived in my bedroom. I found a masochistic pleasure in depleting myself and refuting the frugality that had been drilled into me throughout my childhood.

This, of course, gets us to the question of why I didn't just quit my day job and freelance full-time. I still haven't sorted that one out. I'm sure it had something to do with American notions of maturity, Protestant work ethic, and whatnot. Maybe I was just keeping up appearances, something I've more recently discovered I have a talent for. Just the other day, I was reading about this guy from Los Angeles who is the face of a movement called Nomadic Lifestyle Design. He's this twenty-nine-year-old white dude who "quit his boring corporate job" to run a twenty-hour-a-week "internet business" that gives him the flexibility and funds to shuttle between sandy Southeast Asian beaches drinking rum cocktails and bedding local women. I realized with a shock that in financial terms, I could easily manage a move like that these days. In fact, many similarly exotic isles were only a short flight from Sydney. But something about it—maybe just the decadence and escapism of it all—triggered my disdain reflex. As a principle, I believe it's best not to run from reality. Unless it chases you.

Usually when I was "on the clock," so to speak, I was wired because I found the work highly engaging. The night all of this started, I was working on a cryptography project for what I guessed was a prop trading firm. The job was intellectually complex, but the implementation was simple; once I figured out the broad strokes, it only took me an hour or two to get the code working. After I sent in the deliverable, I got a cold Trumer Pils from the fridge, put a record on, and waited. A few minutes later, the familiar Samarkand notification tone sounded from my laptop, accompanied by a five-star review and a credit in my Bitcoin wallet. I took a deeply satisfying swig.

That was one thing I liked about Samarkand. It was disruptive in this pure, almost utopian way—capitalism without the capitalists. There was no obnoxious tech monopoly looming over it collecting rents. Everything was decentralized so that the platform's take rate–the gap between what the customer paid and what you got paid—was essentially a rounding error, just enough to cover the platform's AWS costs. The work that would've once occupied the entire week (forty hours at approximately $60/hour) of a complacent, second-rate engineer was now compressed into a couple of hours and reallocated to a hungrier, more talented, and deserving candidate. This wasn't even some problematic outsourcing arrangement like those mega call centers in Delhi and Mumbai where you were exploiting people for pennies on the dollar. Samarkand was a pure meritocracy—equal pay for equal work, and competition on the basis of quality and efficiency.

Which was all great. But Samarkand also maintained an active community forum for its freelancers, called SamarChat. Imagine Reddit meets Stack Exchange. Usually after I finished my contracting work, I spent the rest of the night wandering in and out of threads. There was a fair bit of "talking shop," and I'd say about forty percent of the posts were about arcane topics such as how to write an optimal search algorithm or generate a topographical analysis. As a mod, I contributed frequently to these technical discussions. But I'll let you guess what the most common topic of discussion was.

That's right: dating. Perhaps because of the total anonymity offered by the platform, there was nothing that the average Samarkite loved to fixate on more than his (and I do mean his) relationships, or, more accurately, lack thereof. Page after page of agonizingly detailed personal narratives describing a pivotal moment in a Samarkite's budding romantic life, tales of anxious struggle and epic humiliation. I loved consuming these narratives, for reasons I'd rather not spell out but that should already be obvious to the reader.

That night, I was reading a long post by a user called Soren387 titled "Why Asian Women Won't Date Men from Their Own Race." In a pithy thirty thousand words, Soren387 laid out his argument as follows: because Asian men were emasculated by the American mainstream and Asian women were hypersexualized, the latter often abandoned the former to climb the social ladder by dating white guys. Questionable stuff (and totally unoriginal), but the post was climbing to the top of the "popular" page. Suddenly, a ton of users I had interacted with previously started to comment on this thread, critiquing and praising the framework. I had never seen such a frenzy of activity on the forum before.

After a few minutes, the dopamine rush from my espressos and Samarkand sesh wore off. I suddenly realized it was only eight o'clock and I still had about six more hours to kill until I could fall asleep. I was thinking about boiling some water to make instant noodles when my laptop made a familiar sound. It was a Samarkand DM from someone I didn't recognize, a user named viv798.

viv798: I think it's about time for us to meet. Don't you agree?

I clicked into viv798's profile. There was no profile picture, just a status message that said, "On the run." The account had approximately two years of activity associated with it—they'd been liking threads (including some of my own) dating as far back as 2016, but hadn't made any posts of their own. I saw that viv798's status bubble was green and sent a quick reply.

Who are you?
viv798: My name is Vivian. Do you believe in the possibility of a psychic connection?
What do you mean?
viv798: Through your work. I feel like I have known you for a long time. The way you think, the way you write, are beautiful.

Seemed sketchy. I took another swig of beer and responded.

What do you want?

The ellipses graphic showing that the other user was typing appeared, then disappeared, on the chat window. And then:

viv798: To talk. In person, as soon as you are able.

viv798: 415-910-7352. Leave me a voicemail. I want to know what your voice sounds like first.

Then she (or he, who knew) signed off. I stared at the screen for another couple seconds, then got a second beer from the fridge. I reread the conversation three times. Something about the cadence of the messages made me think of a blinking Morse code transmitter. Without fully understanding why, I saved the number into my phone.

I decided to go for a smoke. I floated through the restaurant dining room as invisibly as possible and slipped through the moon gate into the chilly evening. Turning at the corner into my usual spot, I ran into the same group of waiters from earlier taking a smoke break. They had their sleeves rolled up and bowties undone, the two flaps resting carelessly across the fronts of their shirts. Three of them were leaning back against the alley wall, the other two curled down in that particular squat position that seemed natural to many men of East Asian descent. From my position fifteen feet away I could make out the low murmur of Cantonese. The tallest man, Daniel, spotted me and nodded in my direction. I took my place in the alleyway and Daniel offered me a crumpled Lucky Strike. I lit up and inhaled.

My first ever cigarette was with these guys, about a month after I moved in. I ran into them by accident at the end of a long, lonesome walk around Sutter Street—I hadn't really spoken to anyone since graduation—and after a split second of awkwardness, Daniel, whose name I didn't yet know, held a single cigarette out toward me wordlessly in the alley light. I accepted it like a rescue line.

Now that I had joined them the linguistic register of the conversation shifted slightly from pure Cantonese to Chinglish. I didn't know Cantonese—Chinese schools in Bergen County only taught in Mandarin—so I missed a lot, but the conversation, which unfolded over four or five cigarettes, seemed to be about how much each of the men had saved to send to their extended families in Guangdong, which American movie stars they would cut off a finger to have sex with (Halle Berry, Uma Thurman), Daniel's plans of buying a motorcycle, Tony's problems with his *bingliang* (ice cold) girlfriend, and Jeffrey's idea to open a BBQ shop on Grant Avenue.

After about twenty minutes, Jeffrey snuck a bottle of house red out of the kitchen and we started passing it between the six of us. As the conversation flowed, my mind wandered back to the strange message I had received half an hour ago. I wondered if it was possible. During all the isolated hours I had spent writing code and posting it on the Samarkand message boards, I had always hoped that hidden somewhere in that digital vortex of upvotes and downvotes was a spark of genuine human connection. Hear me out. At the fundamental level, writing code is not so different from, say, building a cabinet or writing a poem. The creation bears the signature of its maker. So it was a craft, and thus like any craft, a foundation for human connection. The darkness of the alleyway and my waxing intoxication put my spirit in an expansive state. Did I believe in the possibility of a psychic connection? I certainly wanted to. I fixated on the 798 at the end of her username and pondered the mystery of those three numbers. An area code? I googled it: somewhere in Illinois. I imagined a blinking computer terminal hidden away in a darkened corn silo. I exhaled, and the smoke gave form to my resignation. For me, Illinois was as far as China. What I needed was proof or a sign.

The staff and I were on our sixth or seventh smoke of the night when my ex-girlfriend Jessica and her boyfriend Nick walked by. I had hoped that they wouldn't notice me, but they did.

"Michael?" Jessica's shrill voice rang out from across the street. I waved back awkwardly, hoping they'd sense my energy and just keep walking. Unfortunately she was now crossing to my side, dragging Nick with her.

"Michael, oh my God! I haven't seen you, since, like, Lawn Parties my junior year! What are you up to?" Her face was tomato-colored, which usually happened after one or two drinks.

"Just working," I said.

"Ha ha, do you work at a Chinese restaurant?"

"No, but I live in one," I replied. Fuck. That didn't sound as cool as I thought it would. Jessica frowned for a second and gave Nick a look, as if to say, *is this some kind of joke*?

"So yeah, what's new with you?" I continued.

"I just started a new job! Was getting kind of sick of New York and wanted something more relaxed. Seriously, though, do you work here? Who are these guys?"

"No, of course not," I said, taking a step away from my friends. "Actually, I'm working on developing cutting-edge autonomous driving technology."

"Ooh! Self-driving cars! Love it. So where are you working these days? Google? Uber?"

"No, General Motors," I said.

Immediately Jessica started laughing as if I had just told a hilarious joke, then stopped abruptly when she realized I wasn't kidding. "Michael, you remember Nick, right?" she asked.

I looked at Nick for the first time since they came over. He was in my freshman dorm at Princeton and had put on a few pounds since his days on the lacrosse team but still looked tall and broad, powerful, and, above all, very proportional in his dark wool coat. Of course I remembered Nick, but I was equally certain he didn't have the faintest idea who I was.

"No, actually, I don't think we ever got to meet," I said. I extended a hand.

"So, Michael," Nick began. His voice had an annoyingly friendly, almost patronizing ring to it. "Do you really live here?"

"I do. In a loft on top of the restaurant."

"That's awesome, man! You know, San Francisco has such a big problem with gentrification. All those big tech companies just gobbling up all the land, putting Blue Bottle Coffees on every block. It's really hard to find an ethnic neighborhood as authentic as this one just about anywhere anymore."

Perhaps out of instinct I looked back at Daniel, Tony, and Jeffrey, who were still dressed in their authentic waiter uniforms, leaning against the cracked brick wall, covered in authentic graffiti. For some reason, they had put out their cigarettes.

"Hey, these are my friends Dan, Tony, and Jeff," I said. I wasn't sure why I shortened their names; they never did. Daniel gave them a short, awkward wave while Tony and Jeffrey settled for a stiff nod.

"Oh, cool. Nick is a social entrepreneur," Jessica gushed. "His company provides microloans to low-income entrepreneurs in Oakland, the Tenderloin, and Bayview." I hummed my approval in what I hoped was a slightly but not overbearingly condescending way—like "oh, how wonderful, good for you." It pleased me that Nick's social prowess at Princeton hadn't translated to eminence in the real world; now he was a nonprofit nobody who'd resorted to "social entrepreneurship" as a sort of consolation prize.

"And he's going to Stanford next year! Graduate School of Business. Which worked out *so* perfectly for us," she added. An involuntary pang of envy flashed across my face before I could catch it.

"Anyway!" Jessica said. "Unfortunately we have to run, meeting some friends in the Marina. Jordan and Karim? Maybe you remember them, they were at Princeton too. In Cap and Gown. Actually, do you wanna join us?"

"No thanks. Work's piling up," I lied. A split-second frown rippled across her features, and I remembered how bad Jessica had always been at hiding her emotions.

"Well, how about dinner in the next couple weeks?" she asked, softening a bit. "With me and Nick, our place. I can cook."

So they were living together.

"I don't know, maybe. I've got so much on my plate these days . . . "

"Okay, okay. Just call me, alright?"

I nodded and Jessica came in with one of those awkward half hugs, her nose wrinkling a bit at the smell of cigs as she got close to me. Then Nick wrapped his arm around her waist and they walked off together. I turned around, ready to explain the whole thing to my friends, but when I looked back they were already gone, so I had a smoke by myself. Then I took out my phone, which was still on the screen with Vivian's number saved, and hesitated. My thumb lingered over the CALL button, but then I put the phone back in my pocket.

So much for a sign.

3

I just want to preface this by saying that I have no problem with brutally honest feedback. I've always thought of myself as someone who puts his craft above his ego. In fact, as I've already mentioned, I make a habit of uploading my work to online communities of credible experts and actively soliciting criticism. What does irk me, though, is when people who have no idea what they're doing dismiss my work without engaging with it.

The morning after my run-in with Jessica, I waited outside my boss's office for an important meeting. This was four days after our head of research, Alan, quit to go teach high school math in his hometown of Toledo. So now the position was open and I was, by any standard, his clear successor.

My boss, Lucas, was the junior VP overseeing the tiny twenty-person division of General Motors that employed me. Ours was a moonshot team working on the very early prototype (though "prototype" might be generous) of what was to be GM's first self-driving car, and we called ourselves GMX, a code name so cringeworthy I'm embarrassed to repeat it here. Autonomous driving—it was the holy grail of engineering, the grandest worldwide technological competition since the space race. Every advanced economy in the world had a national champion in the arena—Google, Tesla, Baidu, BMW, Toyota, and us. General Fucking Motors. The Sick Man of Detroit.

Here are some numbers. In 2014 Google invested two billion dollars into a driverless car research center staffed by two hundred of the world's brightest engineers. Baidu was backed by government money and had access to a pipeline of talent from the best universities in China. BMW had opened new research centers in Munich and Berlin, each with hundreds of employees.

Meanwhile, at General Motors, twenty of us sat in a second-tier corporate center in SoMa. Our shitty "SF office" was sublet from a much sexier, equity-rich(er) start-up, and we only had half of one floor; there was no escaping the penny-pinching Rust Belt ethic in our company DNA. There were no zero-gravity nap pods, shuffleboard tables, afternoon yoga classes, in-office massages, catered lunches, or any of the other amenities my generation of yuppies has come to expect from their high-tech employers. We still worked in cubicles. The odds were immensely against us, but in my mind (at least when I started) that was exactly the reason why we would eventually prevail and the foundation of my once-indefatigable hope. Like the Shire versus Mordor.

Only even Frodo had a Samwise to appreciate him, administer emotional support, and even help out with a few low-level tasks. At GM, I had no one. Obviously with the level of HR competition in the Bay Area, GMX had a difficult time attracting anything close to top-tier talent. The other engineers on my team were complacent, bumbling amateurs who'd struggle to assemble a LEGO Mindstorms set without supervision. They were a truly homogeneous, vanilla tribe—all married with families, each at least five years out of the Zone of Optimal Creativity and Disruptive Potential. I had always wondered how such ordinary people found their way out to the technology center of the world, until one day I heard that they had actually all been stationed out here, more or less voluntold for the new division, by Detroit. I imagined them somberly packing up their neat, midwestern lives in caravans and riding the Oregon Trail out to the Wild West.

Lucas: thirty-three years old, UC Irvine undergrad, Kellogg Business School. A four-year stint selling snake oil at one of those boutique consulting firms before latching onto the underbelly of the bloated whale that is General Motors upper-middle management like a lamprey eel. Lucas was one of those guys who looked like they learned how to dress from an article called "How to Make a Good First Impression" on eHow.com—the same cheap gray suit every day, a needy, brightly-colored tie, sometimes even a pocket square. His current role leading GMX in the remote satellite of San Francisco was to be his proving ground before being inducted into the corporate pantheon of the imperial capital in Detroit, like when the Chinese Communist Party sent Xi Jinping to govern the rural backwater of Fujian Province. To see if he could make something out of nothing.

As I paced in front of Lucas's office, I couldn't help but notice that my hands were shaking. The final push of preparation for this meeting had cost me three straight nights of sleep. My shirt was badly wrinkled and my hair was in even worse shape.

Still, I was more excited than nervous. I had delivered—via email, at four thirty that morning—what I had been working toward single-mindedly for the past year: a module that solved (more or less) one of the most difficult technical problems relating to how self-driving cars "see." The module, my magnum opus, existed in the form of roughly 100,000 lines of heavily commented code, in a secure folder on the General Motors cloud. But because I knew that Lucas was, as they called it, a "nontechnical," I had also included in the body of the email a three-thousand-word manifesto outlining my vision for the implementation of the program and the possibilities (technological, commercial, civic) that it opened up. No doubt Lucas was carefully studying the contents at that very moment. I thought it was pretty clear that my breakthrough would win him glory from the higher-ups and guarantee my own position.

I knocked on the door. "You may enter," he said.

When I let myself in I found Lucas leaning back in his chair, hands folded across his lap, staring intently at a brand-new Newton's cradle that he had acquired for his desk like some caricature of a corporate philosopher-king. He pretended not to see me, so we both watched the balls at the end of the cradle knock each other back and forth for an agonizing five seconds.

"Michael," he said. "Thanks for coming in. Let's get started." He pulled a manila folder with my name on it from his drawer and reviewed the contents privately for about thirty seconds. Then, with a sigh, he put the folder back in the drawer, which made me tense up a little.

"The team appreciates your contributions this year and we're excited to see what you come up with next," Lucas said. "You are a reliable engineer who gets the job done. And like I've often said, Lord knows you work hard."

I nodded, eagerly awaiting the next words.

"Alan mentioned before he left that he thought the stuff you were working on was going well. So, that's good. Now, onto development areas." Lucas took his steel-colored Oakley glasses off and leaned back in his chair. "Michael, do you know what the secret to GM's success is?"

"Technology," I said.

"No," Lucas said, lifting his index finger. "No, Michael. Not technology. Culture. Values, a way of being with each other. That's what sustains our success."

I stared blankly while he kept his finger hanging for a dramatic pause. "You know, Michael, when I hired you out of college—Princeton, right?—four years ago, I knew you were something special. Smart as hell. I mean, you're the only engineer in this office without a graduate degree. But at some point, Michael, you've got to realize that around here it's not really about this computer stuff at all. To be a leader at this company, you have to live and breathe the culture." Lucas got up from his seat, walked over to the whiteboard, and wrote CULTURE + TALENT = SUCCESS.

"This is something they taught me at Kellogg," he said, pausing a little to let the hallowed name sink in, "and I wanted to share it with you. Now, what does culture mean? Let's break this down." He picked the marker back up and wrote CULTURE = LEADERSHIP + TEAMWORK + RELATIONSHIPS.

"Culture equals leadership plus teamwork plus relationships, Michael. Brainstorm with me for a minute on how you can improve in those areas."

At this point he sort of paused, but I couldn't tell whether it was one of those rhetorical pauses or if he actually expected me to say something. I didn't know what to say. All of this babble about culture and leadership I thought was just HR boilerplate from the first week. It wasn't real, like my code. So I said nothing.

"Okay. One aspect of your performance we think you can improve on is leadership," Michael said. "For example, during our Monday morning check-ins, your voice is often missing from the discussion. I'll bet you have some great ideas, so why not speak up more?"

"I think it could just be a matter of working style," I said. "I see myself as having more independent work habits, which means—"

"Ah, but that's just the thing, Michael," Lucas cut in. "Actually, this gets me to my next point." He tapped the word TEAMWORK with his marker. "We really need you to be more of a team player. We hardly see you during the day, but then we find out you've been here all night. I spoke with the other guys around here, and some of them don't even know what you're working on," he said.

"Oh, I put it all in my memo to you this morning," I said, "I've been developing a cloud protocol that combines input from existing vehicle-mounted cameras to create a highly accurate 3D map that outperforms LIDAR, all using 5G technology that should be readily available within—"

"Michael. Let's not dwell on the computer stuff here, focus on the big picture with me for one second. Where do you see yourself in five years?"

I stared at the Newton's cradle, which was now inert. "As a leader at GMX," I lied.

"Ah," Lucas said. "But you've got to realize, GM isn't just a company, it's a family. And what do families do?"

"Spend time together," I regurgitated. Lucas nodded and tapped the word RELATIONSHIPS.

"That's right. Let me tell you something, Michael, take it from someone just a few years older than yourself, succeeding here at this company is all about relationships. The little things matter. Friday happy hour. Playing in the fantasy football league. That's where you nourish the relationships that are the foundation of your success."

I imagined myself at the office happy hour interjecting with a comment that implied I didn't fully grasp the mechanics of a fantasy football bracket. Before I could bring up the module again, Lucas sat back down and looked at me with his hands folded on the table.

"Alright then, it looks like I've given you a lot to think about. That's about it, I believe. Do you have any questions for me at this point?"

I had to ask. I couldn't just walk out of there without having asked, I could never forgive myself for that.

"Yes, sir," I began. "I know that since Alan left at the end of last week, the Head of Research position is open."

I waited. Lucas raised an eyebrow. "Yes, and?"

"I just wanted to put my name in the hat for that," I stammered. "I'm not sure if you've had the chance to review the memo I sent you this morning, but what it contains is significant to the eventual resolution of what we identified as a big problem . . . "

Lucas interrupted me with a groan. "Michael, I like you, but you've got to get more serious with me. You've only been out of college for four years and now you want to be Head of Research? You don't even have a graduate degree! This is General Motors, not seed-round Facebook. We have a way of doing things here. Besides, the position has already been filled—Sanjay will be taking over Monday morning."

I opened my mouth to make an objection, but the words didn't come to me.

"You know what," Lucas added, a little more softly. "You should feel free to take the rest of the day off. Get some rest."

4

Later that evening, I waited in the Y Hotel's cocktail lounge for Lawrence, my only friend from Princeton in the city, who was running late. After twenty minutes of sitting alone I started to feel self-conscious, then I noticed the "paintings" on the walls—high-resolution, low-luminosity LED screens that displayed digital oil portraits with subtly animated eyes that blinked and seemed to follow you around the room. Suddenly I remembered reading about this place in one of my interior design magazines. Even though sitting alone in busy social spaces always made me feel conspicuous and anxious, being able to attribute the cause of that feeling to something concrete in the environment somehow made me feel calmer on the inside.

At half past nine o'clock, Lawrence finally showed up. He squeezed my shoulder, recited some apology about a client meeting that ran over, and ordered us Negronis without asking what I wanted. The bartender seemed to know him. Then he started talking, about what exactly I can't quite remember. It hardly mattered. Lawrence was an excellent talker and came from a long line of prominent lawyers in Hong Kong. He had that elusive thing called "polish," a certain social and verbal finesse that made people enjoy conversing with him.

"I hope you don't mind me saying you look a bit glum, Michael. What's the matter?"

I weighed my desire for emotional support against my desire for Lawrence's approval. "It's nothing. Just some shit going on at work," I said.

"I see. Stressful project? An important deadline coming up?"

"No, it's not that. The thing is I feel a little underappreciated."

"Now that I can relate to. Say more."

I told Lawrence what happened at my review with Lucas and he listened with grave concern. When I finished, he ordered me another drink.

"Michael," he said, "during your studies, did you ever learn the history of the transcontinental railroad?"

"Sort of—the one that the Chinese worked on, right?"

"Yes, that one. In the mid-1860s, during the aftermath of the bloody Taiping Rebellion, between ten and fifteen thousand Chinese workers from Guangdong Province set sail to California to work on the transcontinental railroad. The job was treacherous. The Chinese were often lowered down cliffs in man-sized baskets packed with explosives to blow tunnels into the mountain. Many died, but at $28 a month, life was cheap—and plentiful. The Central Pacific Railroad Company sent ships to Guangdong to scoop thousands more desperate young men straight off the dock. In the end, the railroad company saved about one third of the cost of a white laborer for each Chinaman they brought on . . . "

I noticed that Lawrence used the word *Chinaman* without flinching, even though he himself was Korean.

"And then they lampooned us in the newspapers, called us chinks and mongrels and the 'yellow horde,' forbade us from bringing our women into the country with us, eventually banned us from coming at all after we had served our purpose. Would you like to hear the punchline, Michael? The punchline is that we didn't learn our lesson. Only now instead of Central Pacific, it's Intel, Siemens, Microsoft, and Hewlett-Packard. Nothing's changed, only this time what the Chinese who come to California are giving away for pennies on the dollar is the work of their minds, not their limbs. How many Asian guys you know were raised by brilliant, spineless deaf-mutes? Dad comes over with a suitcase and a foreign PhD in hard science. Lands right in an R&D lab and convinces himself that science is his only love, toils for thirty years with no promotions, no raises, keeps his head down, and never, ever asks to eat at the table. Does that sound familiar?"

I nodded discreetly as certain memories of my father that I hadn't revisited in a long time flickered into consciousness.

"I'm an IP lawyer, Michael. I've had the opportunity to observe this phenomenon in the field. I can tell you the patents these humble scientists crank out are often worth tens, sometimes hundreds of millions of dollars. And they know it too, but they'll never say a thing. So tell me, Michael, what kind of a Chinaman would you have been, if you had been born a century and a half earlier? A railroad Chinaman, or a gold field Chinaman?"

I scanned the room to see if anyone was listening, since Lawrence was being pretty loud. "Dude, what the fuck?"

"You heard me. Would you have panned under risk of life and limb for the white man's gold, or quietly poured your sweat over his railroad? Would you have taken what you deserved or what you were given?"

"Of course I'm a fucking gold field Chinaman," I whispered angrily. Instinctively, I looked around again; no one had heard me.

Lawrence gave me this amused yet somewhat approving smirk. "If that's what you say. When's the last time you were with an American woman?"

"I'm not sure, I can't remember exactly—"

"We have our goal for tonight," he said, directing my attention to two girls sitting on the other side of the lounge, a normal-looking brunette and an intimidatingly attractive redhead. They were about our age or younger, looking bored and sipping their espresso martinis. Lawrence led the way over and asked if we could join them. The brunette said yes immediately, while the redhead kept looking at her phone. We switched over to a four-person table and Lawrence ordered a bottle of Gusbourne Blanc de Blancs. Due to global warming, he said, the soil in certain parts of England is projected to become chemically similar to the soil in the Champagne region of France today, and in forty years we'll all be drinking English champagne. For some reason the girls found this delightful and fascinating; even the redhead had stopped looking at her phone. It turns out the girls had been Alpha Phis at Rutgers and came to party at Princeton a few times every month when Lawrence and I were upperclassmen. "Where?" Lawrence asked, giving himself the opening to drop the name of the eating club he'd been a part of, which had its intended effect. When the brunette looked at me expectantly, I had no choice but to defer and felt my perceived relevancy drop. The girls and Lawrence continued to talk excitedly about parties they'd attended at Princeton—Gatsby at Cottage, Black and Yellow at Cap, Casino Night at Ivy—all of which I knew far too much about secondhand from Facebook pictures, which made it impossible for me to insert myself into the stories from a first-person perspective. Lawrence listened sympathetically as the brunette complained about the disrespectful "State night" party Tiger Inn threw in 2012, where they had everyone dress up in state school gear (she'd brought her entire sorority anyway), how mean and catty the Princeton girls had been to her sorority sisters even while they were all dressed in Rutgers hoodies and basketball shorts. I started to get the peculiar sense that although these girls knew that I *went* to Princeton, they didn't consider me to be *of* Princeton in the same way that Lawrence was.

Lawrence was now focusing the entirety of his conversation on the redhead, forcing the brunette to reluctantly shift her attention toward me. When the bottle was finished, the suggestion to continue with a nightcap at Lawrence's apartment in Pac Heights was floated and immediately accepted. He ushered us into an Uber Black that was somehow already right around the corner, me sitting shotgun, him with the two girls in the back. It faintly occurred to me as the unfamiliar intersections went by that this would actually be the first time, for the two years Lawrence and I had been friends in San Francisco together, that he invited me to his apartment.

The driver let us out in front of a wood-and-gold toned high-rise condominium at the end of a quiet street. Lawrence gave the doorman a discreet nod, marched us to the elevator, and pressed the PH button. The two girls were clearly excited that the PH button had been pressed and were now whispering to each other a bit too loudly. There was a ding and the elevators doors opened directly to the inside of Lawrence's living room. We took our shoes off and changed into velvet house slippers, which changed the boisterous energy from the bar into something more subdued. I seethed with jealously at how exquisitely tasteful and Scandinavian his place looked. Nothing I'd never seen in a catalog; each piece of furniture seemed to have a distinct aura and personality. There were hundreds of books on shelves lining every wall as well as an impressive collection of contemporary East Asian paintings. During the tour, the redhead mentioned that she had studied art history in college, which pleased Lawrence immensely and set off a conversation about the John Singer Sargent exhibit at the de Young that apparently everyone except me had seen last week.

We reconvened on the couch in the living room. Lawrence disappeared to the kitchen and returned with four crystal glasses and a green bottle of Korean plum wine that the girls evidently found very exotic and charming. We all sat down on the couch and Lawrence started playing bossa nova, as if that was a normal thing to do. The redhead started talking about studying abroad in Barcelona and Lawrence responded with a well-received anecdote about the construction of the Sagrada Familia. Then, seemingly in the middle of a sentence, he took the redhead's hand and they got up and started to slow dance. A total change had come over her previously lukewarm attitude. For a while I just stared at them; it was only a brief, annoyed look from Lawrence that made me turn back to the brunette, who was now anxiously sipping her drink and tapping furiously on her phone. I knew I had to ask her if she wanted to dance, or the mood would be spoiled for everyone.

"Sure," she said flatly. We rose to our feet and joined our bodies awkwardly via hands on shoulders and waists. I didn't quite know where to look; every time I tried to make eye contact she seemed to look to the side or past me. I noticed she was still chewing gum. We glided like this for a few minutes, before I saw that Lawrence and the redhead were gone.

It turns out that I should not have looked back, because when the brunette caught on she hopped away from me immediately, mumbling something about checking in on her friend. I started to say something about how they probably shouldn't be bothered, but it was too late, she'd already picked up her phone and marched into the bedroom without knocking. I heard some low whispers through the doors, some sharp shushing sounds. After a minute or so, I sank back into the couch and poured myself another drink.

It probably took another ten minutes for me to realize that they were waiting for me to leave. So I finished what was left of my drink and called an Uber back to my apartment.

After I managed to stumble up all three flights of stairs to my loft, I collapsed onto the sofa and started scrolling through my food delivery apps. While I waited for my crispy chicken sandwich with four-piece buttermilk crispy tenders to arrive, I pulled out my laptop, which was still open on Samarkand, and stared at viv798's message. Then, for some reason, I pulled out my phone and called the number. To my horror, it didn't go straight to voicemail, but rang several times. Thankfully, after what seemed like an eternity, I heard the familiar beep and a machine voice that said, "The wireless customer is not available right now. Please leave a message after the beep." I cleared my throat.

"Hello, viv798," I stammered. "This is Michael from, uh . . . from Samarkand. I got your message earlier, and you said you wanted to hear what my voice sounded like, so here it is. By the way, you said you wanted to talk in person?"

Fuck. That would never do. I hit 0 to rerecord.

"Hey, what up? Michael here. Sorry if I sound a little drunk, just got back from a party. Old Princeton buddy's place in Pac Heights . . . "

Beep. Please rerecord your message.

"This is Michael. Who are you anyway? Don't you think it's a little unfair, making me leave a message like this, when you haven't told me anything about yourself? What kind of a weird game is this?"

Beep.

Anyway, I went through probably another five or six of these, the excruciating contents of which I won't subject you to, before I hit on the winner:

"Hey, Vivian. This is Michael. Call me back."

And then I passed out.

5

Returning to consciousness the next morning, I found my sheets and pillowcase soaked with acrid sweat. I dragged myself to the sink and tried to scrub the vile taste from my mouth. Confronted by my shameful reflection in the mirror, I concentrated my sense of intense disgust on my pale, distended belly. I've always been naturally chubby, but in high school three hours of tennis practice a day had helped me maintain a relatively trim physique. Being captain of the team also endowed me with a certain poise and physical confidence that slipped away years ago. Obviously, the only girls who cared that I was captain of the tennis team were Asian girls. Not the hot, whitewashed Asian girls, who invariably preferred guys who played "real sports," but the repressed Asian girls, the female versions of me. Like Jessica, who, when we started dating during our sophomore year, was just another poker-faced, Chinese-school-going, violin-playing grade-grubber who always wore her hair up and never let me go past second base.

When I checked my phone there were already three missed calls from Lawrence, starting from seven in the morning. For some reason I imagined him in a silk bathrobe reading the newspaper while the two girls from last night brought him scrambled eggs and orange juice. Fuck Lawrence.

It wasn't that I was jealous of Lawrence, or sore about how last night turned out. Okay, maybe a little bit of both, but there was also something deeper than that. I had looked up to him during college. How could I not? He cut an impressive figure around campus and embodied the ideal to which I aspired: smooth-talking future diplomat living comfortably between two worlds. Only Lawrence's other world was upper-crust Hong Kong and mine was just make-believe, a fictionalized concept of an entire civilization (called China) to treat my own particular symptoms of double consciousness—a product of a strained imagination and a needy, insecure upbringing. I had, in fact, started out my time at Princeton in the East Asian Studies Department. I modeled myself after everything I thought the Woodrow Wilson School of Public and International Affairs aspired to. It was not so much that I felt called to public service, as much as my subconscious automatically invented a "greater destiny" in order to square all the undignified suffering and hackneyed familial sacrifice that I, un-special Asian nerd, had endured to make it here in the first place. But what I soon discovered was that I had no natural aptitude for the human relations component of my adopted trajectory. This was made apparent to me through a whirlwind of failed socializations, formal and informal, and my then-girlfriend Jessica's matter-of-fact ejection of me from her life. To this day I still have a sneaking suspicion that my decision to switch into computer science after Jessica dumped me at the end of fall term freshman year was an advanced form of psychological self-annihilation, as if to say to myself, *This is who you really are: yellow, mathematical, silent.*

Which is not to say that during the term of my self-imposed exile from all that is recognizably Princeton I did not achieve an approximation of genuine satisfaction. I found solace in the realm of pure intellectual creation I entered when writing code, hemmed in by walls made of silence and uninterrupted hours. I discovered that I had an aptitude and disposition suitable for programming, the most important element of which is the appreciation of craft. For me, reading a beautiful line of code was not *like* poetry—it was better, purer, because poetry ultimately drew on experience and sensation, both of which had been polluted for me. Not that this striving reflected in my grades. I actually did poorly in class because I rarely attended, preferring to guide my own exploration. And so I managed to pass most of my weekend nights during college in blissful isolation, with only the fading of my grand destiny to dampen my spirits.

As these unwelcome thoughts sloshed around my head, I opened up my laptop and saw an unread email, from nine o'clock last night. It was from my new direct supervisor, Sanjay:

Hey, Michael!

What's up my man hope you're having a great week so far (amazing weather around the Bay, am I right?). Anyway just wanted to shoot you a quick email to introduce myself since I will be supervising you from here on out. My name is Sanjay and I am taking over as Head of Research. My first language (not counting Hindi lol) was English and the second one after that was Python haha. I live up in the Marina with three of my bros from UC Berkeley (Go Bears!) and in my free time I enjoy biking, hiking, jogging, windsurfing, corn hole, indoor climbing, and microbreweries.

Can you just flip over to me ASAP (before EOD) a quick self-intro and also update me on what you've been working on? I asked Lucas but he didn't really know, told me to ask you myself.

Looking forward to disrupting the future with you.

Sanjay

Let me first say that until this point I had never spoken more than two sentences in a row to Sanjay. I knew him simply as that one Indian guy who seemed to be really, really in with all the older white guys at the office. In fact, half the time I saw Sanjay around the office he wasn't working at all, just "shooting the shit," as they say, in the break room, or with his feet propped up on some other guy's desk. Also, did he not realize the phrase *disrupt the future* made no sense because the future didn't exist yet? To be honest, even though he was the only other youngish POC guy at the office, I never really considered him my competition because he went to UC Berkeley, which is not in the Ivy League.

My sense of superiority was immediately shattered after I looked him up on LinkedIn to figure out just how much older he was than me and discovered that the answer was one year. My face turned red hot; I was humiliated. How was it possible that someone like Sanjay could be put in charge of someone like me? My eyes focused on the line of the email that said that Lucas had no clue what I was doing. So I was right, this whole time. The reason why I hadn't been promoted was simple: they didn't even know what I had accomplished. I could taste the metallic bile in my mouth. Fuck Lucas. Fuck Sanjay. Fuck the whole lot of them. I would go off the grid, feed them with trivial updates and keep the groundbreaking work I was doing to myself.

I threw a wrinkled button-down over some jeans and headed out of my loft. I looked like shit and was well aware of the fact; I almost *wanted* the other guys at the office to think something was wrong, like, *Woah, we better not mess with this guy, who knows when he might snap* . . . but of course I just sat at my usual desk and no one took notice of me.

I went to the break room and made myself a cup of Nescafé with two sticks of sugar. When I returned to my desk I found another email from Sanjay with the subject line "Action Items for the Day." It was a long list of bullet points detailing some low-level implementation and debugging tasks related to a module I had never seen before. A hot surge of desperate anger swelled up inside of me and I washed it down with more coffee. Suddenly, my phone rang.

I picked it up and basically spat the word *what* into the receiver, assuming it was Lawrence's fourth call of the morning. Instead, there was half a second of silence on the line, then a burst of sharp laughter.

"Is someone a little grumpy from his big night out?" said an unimaginably sweet and British voice.

6

Sorry . . . who is this?" I said, though I already knew the answer and was probably breathing too hard into the microphone.

"Come on, you know who it is," said the voice on the other end of the line. "The girl you left not one, not two, but *five* voicemails for last night . . . "

I bit down hard on my lip and buried my head in my hands. Then I peeked above my cubicle to make sure that no one else was listening in.

"Vivian?" I whispered.

"That's right. I'm at the Powell-Hyde trolley station. It's leaving in fifteen minutes, I think. Can you meet me here?"

"What? Sorry, but I'm at work right now. And I don't think I can just take off either way. Can we meet during my lunch break instead?"

"Well, the train is leaving in fifteen, and I'll be getting on with or without you . . ."

I looked over my cubicle again and saw Sanjay blatantly playing online poker on his desktop with his headphones plugged in.

"Okay, okay, I'll meet you there," I said. "But wait, how will I be able to recognize you? It's so crowded on that stop."

"You'll recognize me," she said flatly, and hung up.

Google Maps said it was a thirteen-minute walk to Powell-Hyde, so if I left now I'd barely make it in time. I zipped up my fleece jacket and started walking toward Sanjay's desk, rehearsing some lame excuse about how I'd forgotten about a dentist's appointment. But just before I got there, I changed my mind and slipped out of the office without telling anyone.

Direct sunlight summoned my hangover from its dark depths. The way to Powell Street was very steep and I gagged as I climbed the hilly sidewalk. By the time I got there, the back of my shirt was damp with sweat. As expected, the station was swarming with tourists. I shouldered my way through a Chinese tour group and scanned the crowd for anyone who could be Vivian.

About 5'9", she wore dark glasses and stood with her arms crossed waiting, not looking, for me. I almost turned back when I realized there was a chance she was slightly taller than me. The sunglasses accentuated her sharp cheekbones and jawline, which contrasted with her soft nose and forehead. She was wearing baggy white pants over chunky sneakers and some kind of lacy black top that she covered with a purple Patagonia shell.

"Glad you made it," she said, taking off her glasses and looking at me disapprovingly. We stepped onto the trolley together and found two seats near the front of the car. Now that I was sitting right next to her, I could make out a faint scar that ran from the left bottom side of her chin to the corner of her lip.

"So, do you do this often?" she asked.

"What do you mean?"

"Meet up in real life with strangers from the internet?" She smiled as she watched me squirm. "I mean, seriously, Michael. There was no profile picture. You could've been in big trouble."

"You're literally the one who reached out to me."

"I know. And I'm only in San Francisco for a short while. I'm really hoping I don't regret this."

I wondered if I still smelled like alcohol. "So, why are you on Samarkand?"

"What do you mean?"

"I'm just saying you don't really look like someone who would spend a bunch of time on a coding forum."

She gave me an incredibly disgusted look. "Wow—sexist much? Haven't you heard of Girls Who Code? I thought Americans were supposed to be sensitive about these things."

Don't panic, but you're completely fucking this up, I thought.

"Okay, fine, fine. But why did you ask me to meet you on a train that was about to leave? Instead of a coffee shop or something?"

Vivian looked bemused. "I just wanted to see if you would make it in time. Plus, I wanted to go see Fisherman's Wharf."

"Why?"

"Because I like seafood?"

Vivian did not care for the seafood at Fisherman's Wharf, which was mostly served in bread bowls. She wrinkled her nose at the gooey cups of crab chowder we got at the Pier 39 Crab House, which we were now trying to enjoy on-the go. It smelled like sourdough everywhere, and the sidewalks were caked with seagull shit.

"Why is there so much corn in this crab soup?" she said, poking around her bread bowl with her plastic spoon without taking a bite.

"People here think it goes well with the crab. You don't like it?"

"Okay. Whatever. By the way, you don't seem to really know your way around here," Vivian said.

"This isn't a place real people go. It's just for tourists."

She sighed and suddenly stopped in the middle of the street. We were next to a merry-go-round, a boxing punch machine, and a creepy museum of twentieth-century penny arcade games. Vivian chucked her bowl of clam chowder in the trash can. “Sorry, this place really isn’t what I thought it was. I’m embarrassed that I suggested it. You can decide where we go next.”

I called us an Uber to Radhaus, an Alpine beer hall in Fort Mason built inside of an old army machine shop. The place was warehouse-sized on the inside and completely whitewashed except for the oak tables, like an Apple store. We sat by the window at an east-facing table with a direct view of the Golden Gate Bridge.

Vivian seemed much happier here. When the waiter came over, she surprised me by ordering in German: trout toast, veal schnitzel, bratwurst with sauerkraut, and two pints of Weihenstephan Hefeweissbier.

“You speak German too?” I said.

“Yeah. I spent a year in Switzerland during uni. Mostly to get away from the insufferable social scene at my four-year-institution in England.”

“Interesting. I heard the skiing there is good. Did you ski a lot?”

“No. I hate the outdoors.” She left it at that.

The food arrived and Vivian went for the bratwurst first, having nibbles of the trout toast on the side and leaving the sauerkraut and schnitzel untouched.

“So what *are* you doing in San Francisco?” I asked finally.

“Work,” she said. “Why else would anyone come here?”

She had a point, I thought. “What kind of work?”

She looked at me while chewing as if that was a ridiculous question. “I’m really big on the internet.”

After lunch we went next door to the Great Meadow Park at Fort Mason. It was chilly here because of the gusts coming in from the ocean and Vivian zipped up her Patagonia shell. We wandered to the far tip of Aquatic Park, a man-made cove. There were a couple of pay-per-view telescopes that looked out at Alcatraz, but neither of us had any quarters so we just squinted at it with our bare eyes.

"What a beautiful island," Vivian said. "I wonder who lives there. Maybe a reclusive billionaire?"

"I doubt a wealthy hermit would want to live in a place where people are spying on him with telescopes all of the time," I said. "Plus, that's Alcatraz. It used to be a maximum-security prison."

"Wow. What kind of crime did you have to commit to end up at a place like that?"

"Oh, it didn't take much. Being late on your taxes, stealing a loaf of bread. Sometimes children were sent there for being disobedient to their parents, but they were usually allowed to come home after a week."

Vivian laughed. "Do you think the prisoners got telescopes too?"

"What?"

"The city must look small from there. Imagine that every cell in Alcatraz had a powerful telescope just like this one that you could look through to observe life in San Francisco up close, as if you were there yourself. Children eating cotton candy on the Wharf, old couples sitting on park benches. Us standing here, watching them. Could you bear the loneliness?"

"That is incredibly grim," I said.

"I would probably spend all day looking through the telescope," Vivian said. "As sad as it'd make me, I think it'd be too painful to live on memories alone." Then she gave me a long, strangely melancholy look—her eyes looked not so much at me but *through* me, like I was standing invisibly in front of a ruined coliseum.

"Probably at least half of the cells just face the Pacific Ocean," I said. "And then you would be staring at nothing. Like D. H. Lawrence said,

'California has turned its back on the world, and looks into the void Pacific.'"

"Smooth," Vivian said, maybe flirtatiously. "Not bad for a computer science guy. But actually, it's looking at China. Always has and will be."

With that, Vivian and I took our leave of the forsaken rock and started walking down toward Bay Street.

"There's some more stuff I can show you," I said.

Vivian shook her head and pulled out her phone. "Actually, I need to get back to my hotel in SoMa for a meeting. Do you want a ride back downtown?" I nodded.

The Uber stopped in front of the Four Seasons on Market.

"Thank you for today," Vivian smiled, this time genuinely. "I really had a lovely time."

"Me too. Wait, when are you leaving again?"

She hesitated. "Saturday," she said finally.

"So I probably won't see you again before you're gone."

Vivian shrugged and took a long look at me before heading into the hotel. "I'm glad we met. Bye, Michael."

For the first time since she interrupted my morning, I thought to check the time and realized I'd been away from my desk for more than three hours now, much longer than what I could explain away with a fictional dentist appointment. I raced back to the office, but when I got there, it was obvious that no one realized I'd been gone. Sanjay was still playing online poker. I sat down and started halfheartedly trudging through some of my to-dos from the morning, but my mind was stuck replaying scenes from the morning. At five o'clock on the dot, Sanjay swaggered into the bullpen and started rallying everyone for dollar beers at Foley's on Stockton. I waited for everyone to leave and headed out on my own.

Back home I had dinner with Daniel in Club Mandarin's kitchen. We squatted on pink plastic stools and ate a staff meal together, some fried rice with egg and *char siu*. I asked him if he ended up buying that motorcycle he had mentioned; he hadn't. Actually, it had been a pretty dramatic week for him. He had just gotten his girlfriend pregnant, so "there would be no need for the motorcycle anymore." Instead, he was saving up to open his own barbecue restaurant with Tony and Jeffrey, one of those tiny places where they hung the roasted duck and chicken carcasses up in front of the window. Daniel described to me with intense enthusiasm the different lots they were considering and the sorts of meats they would serve. I guess that meant they were moving out, which made me feel sad, but now didn't feel like the right time to bring it up.

For some reason, I didn't tell him about my day with Vivian. I'm not sure why; maybe because telling it would make it seem like a real thing, something I should care about, when it seemed pretty unlikely I'd see her again. Instead, I told him about my evening with Lawrence and the two girls from the Y Hotel, which he thought was hilarious. We split a bottle of wine and a few smokes, then I went up to my loft.

At the time of this writing I am sitting in the living room of my apartment and the sun has set over Sydney Harbour. There is no sound other than the whirring of the air conditioner. Through the sea-facing windows I can see the inky dark waters of the bay, feeding into the void Pacific. Vivian was right about one thing: it was too painful to live on memories alone.

7

The rest of the work week unrolled with more disappointments. Sanjay asked to meet with me one-on-one and said he was going to transition my main responsibility at GM to platform-as-a-service, which meant coding tools and services for *other* engineers to use to build self-driving car software, rather than building the self-driving car software myself. "Think about the impact you'll have, bro," he said, "it'll be like everyone is relying on you." On Thursday night, I stayed in and checked Samarkand a bunch of times, but Vivian was offline. I thought about how I needed to get out more—maybe pick up a new hobby. On Friday night, I went to karaoke with Daniel, Tony, and Jeffrey and passed out on my couch before my DoorDash KFC arrived.

But on Saturday morning, Vivian called again.

"Hey. I decided to stay longer. Are you free for dinner tonight?"

I was ecstatic—not just to see her again, but by the faint possibility that she'd decided to stay because of me. I took her to an Italian restaurant called

Sotto Mare in North Beach where we had cioppino, wedge salad with blue cheese dressing, mussel steamers, and seafood risotto. She was wearing a dress and makeup this time, which increased my confidence that I was not mistaking this interaction for a date. During dinner, we talked about Samarkand threads and I learned that she'd studied computer science at UCL and lived in Hong Kong. She answered only the questions she felt like answering and still wouldn't tell me what she did for a living or why she was in San Francisco in the first place. I didn't press her, fearful of breaking the spell that temporarily held her at the table across from me.

After dinner, in an attempt to prolong the evening, I suggested a drink at the Top of the Mark, which Vivian reluctantly agreed to. It was a glass-walled cocktail lounge on the nineteenth floor of the Mark Hopkins Hotel in Nob Hill, some 305 feet above sea level. We stayed there for forty minutes listening to the jazz pianist and looking out the window from our corner, which faced Alcatraz and the Pacific. I told Vivian that story everyone knows about the Top of the Mark, which is that this was where the American soldiers went with their wives during World War II for a last drink and dance before they shipped out to the Pacific Theater; the next morning, the women would gather back at the bar to watch their husbands sail off together on the same ship. Those who returned reunited with their wives in the same place. I couldn't tell whether or not Vivian liked this story. She only finished half of her drink, then suddenly announced that she had to get home. While saying goodbye I couldn't get myself to ask about her itinerary. As I tossed and turned in bed later that night, I realized that I'd let myself get my hopes up.

Luckily, she only made me wait three days before calling again. We met for oysters that evening at Waterbar and a late-night bike ride along the Embarcadero. She wore a thick gray cardigan with sleeves that were too long. I wondered what she had been doing the past three days but didn't ask. At the end of the night, she told me in a cautious tone that she was considering staying in San Francisco for a bit longer than planned. Soon after that, we settled into a rhythm where I saw her about once a week. I'd text her with plans a couple days in advance and steep in anxiety for a day or two to receive an "okay" or a "sounds good." I spent a lot of time between meetings strategizing about places to take her, stories I could tell her—whatever was needed to sustain her interest. There was something Scheherazadian about this situation, except instead of killing me when she got bored, she would just ghost me.

So we dined at Monsieur Benjamin and ate steak tartare, baked brie, and duck confit. I got us lost deep inside Golden Gate Park and she navigated us back to the trailhead without looking at her phone. I took her to climb Twin Peaks, which she said reminded her of the hills in Hong Kong. When we got to the top, I took my phone out to take a picture of her by the Sutro Tower, but she told me not to.

I soon realized that even though we were spending more time together, I was approaching an asymptote in my understanding of Vivian. Past a certain point, everything was closed off. She struck me as someone who had very few close friends. I never saw her text or call anyone. There was a faintly aloof, even antisocial quality about her.

The excursions sapped my attention at work. I was not at all enjoying my new role and started responding more slowly, sometimes not at all, to Sanjay's emails. No one reprimanded me for my negligence or even noticed, which oddly made me worse. I started taking Samarkand jobs during business hours and derived an odd sense of satisfaction from this petty time theft. Meanwhile, during the evenings, I continued to work late into the night on my spurned project, refining certain features, adding others. Some part of me thought there was still hope that the work, if done right, would speak for itself, even if I couldn't speak for it.

The last time Vivian and I went out together in San Francisco was a chilly Saturday morning in July. She wanted to visit the California Academy of Sciences, a science museum in Golden Gate Park. I particularly enjoyed the Neotropical rainforest dome, which featured a transparent observation tunnel that simulated the flooded forest floor; you could look up and see cichlids darting through the roots of a mangrove cluster. Then we hit the aquarium and, after that, the Morrison Planetarium.

Vivian and I stepped inside of the planetarium's vast, chilly auditorium and used the dim orange glow of the walkways to find two seats near the center. The seventy-five-foot digital dome loomed gray and inert over us, triggering a flutter of childhood wonder. Then the lights dimmed and a program called *Searching for Solar Systems* began. Suddenly we were enveloped in darkness; with an orchestral flourish, the image of the earth as a blue and solitary sphere appeared on-screen. A soothing voice-over waxed poetic about the comfort we can find in our cosmic insignificance. The perspective panned out to our solar system, then wheeled through space to neighboring and distant galaxies. I glanced over at Vivian, whose spellbound expression told me that she was as captivated as I was.

After the program ended, the other visitors filed out while Vivian and I stayed behind for a while. The program had triggered a memory, and in the comfortable dark and quiet of the room I found myself telling it to her. I was eleven years old sitting at the kitchen table with my parents, and everyone was in high spirits because I'd brought home a good report card.

"Of course," my dad beamed. "Thank your mother. In China, everybody says the boy gets their intelligence from the mom. Your mom was always top of our class. Number one or number two every time."

"And I still ended up with you!" she laughed.

We were in the middle of our astronomy unit in science class, and that night I couldn't stop regurgitating everything I had learned in class about how there were diamond showers on Jupiter and the fact that eighty-five percent of the universe was made of dark matter. I must have talked for twenty minutes straight, encouraged by my parents' patient, glowing faces. After we were finished, my dad announced he was going out to get some supplies. He knocked on my door later that night with a present. It was a home planetarium the size of a soccer ball. He turned off the lights and plugged it in; with a soft whir, the projector clicked to life and cast constellations on my bedroom wall. We stayed like that until past midnight. He showed me the famous constellations—Orion, Ursa Major, the Big Dipper—and told me the stories, in Chinese, behind each.

When I thought about my dad, I explained to Vivian, I always pictured him hunched over the desk in his study. He was an introverted, maybe even aloof guy who liked working late in his R&D lab at Xerox. Even when he was home, he was usually holed up in his study tinkering with something, so growing up I rarely actually spent time with him. It was nice to remember the planetarium, I said.

I ended my story there and Vivian turned to face me in the dark. I was suddenly aware of how close she was to me; we stayed like that for a second, maybe two, and I thought about kissing her. Then the glowing orange lights of the walkway came back on and we left the auditorium.

We went to the de Young Museum café for a snack and ordered meze and espresso. When the drinks arrived, Vivian asked me to explain to her, this time in more detail, the project I had been so busy with. I took a pen from my pocket and drew a diagram for her on a napkin.

"One of the biggest problems with autonomous driving right now is that cars need to 'see' their surroundings with a great amount of detail and the sheer volume of data is overwhelming," I explained. "And very, very expensive to collect. Which is why you sometimes see those SUVs driving around San Francisco with giant spinning metal boxes on the roof. That box is called a LIDAR and can cost tens of thousands of dollars. So, it's no good for your average consumer."

I drew the LIDAR for her—a spinning metal cylinder mounted on a sturdy base, shooting lasers out onto the road. "Because LIDAR is so expensive, some people have proposed using simple, everyday cameras instead. But the problem here is that cameras are too 'blurry' for fast-changing road situations.

"But what if there was a way around that?" I said, drawing a road filled with cars driving underneath a cartoon cloud. Then I added little dotted lines between the cloud and each car. "For the past two years, I've been creating a protocol that will take data from every car's cameras and *aggregate* them to model a highly accurate 3D map that does better than LIDAR. I call it 'multinodal aggregation.' The cars beam their data up to the cloud over 5G, and the cloud beams it right back. This way cost and latency are both minimized."

"Amazing," Vivian murmured. "A decentralized, real-time data platform for AV vision. When do you think the technology will be ready for the market?"

"Not for a few years, at least," I said, my voice faltering a little. "That's the thing. The problem with my idea is that it'll require an overall unification within the industry. All of the data that the cars collect has to be in the same format, so there are all sorts of regulatory challenges. It's a little utopian. And also 5G isn't good and reliable enough yet to support the required latency and uptime. You don't want there to be a signal outage and for all the self-driving cars to suddenly go blind. So in some sense what I'm describing to you is still highly theoretical.

"But I've been 'testing' this idea independently," I continued, "by posting some of the code, just bits and pieces, over Samarkand, to get some feedback. You've probably seen some of these posts."

"Yes, I have."

"And people love it. The feedback has been great. So, I feel confident that the idea will work. In fact, I'm almost certain that this is the future of the industry. The only problem is I'm a couple years early." I stopped there, because it occurred to me that I was starting to sound a little like my dad, who'd always felt like someone who was stuck in the wrong timeline.

"What did your boss say when you presented this to him?" Vivian asked.

"He didn't say anything at all," I said. "In fact, I didn't even get to present it to him."

"What do you mean?"

"I packaged all of my work together and sent it to him in an email six weeks ago, but when I tried to bring it up he just started talking about something else."

"Well, have you tried scheduling another meeting with him? This is too significant of a breakthrough to get buried."

"Kind of. Not really. Look, I just didn't think it was worth pursuing. These guys at GM, they're not like me at all. They don't really care about technology or changing the way people live. They just want to get home by five o'clock every night and make the same driving machine over and over again."

Vivian leaned in across the table and clutched my hand. "Michael, I'm so sorry to hear that. Don't let this discourage you; your colleagues are just too shallow-minded to appreciate your vision. You need to find your people. I'm just thinking about what you said about 5G and industry-wide unification—this feels like an idea that would get more traction in China. In China, if Beijing wants something to happen, it gets done the next day. You know, unless I'm misremembering, I think my uncle Bo works in this field. I can give him a call—maybe you guys can have a chat or something, just to get another perspective. I think you'd like talking to him."

I looked into her eyes, which told me she meant what she said—that she believed in me—and felt something dormant and hopeful stirring in my chest. "Why not," I said. "Sure. I think I'd like that." We finished our meal, then I got the check and dropped Vivian back off at the Four Seasons. After that, I went back to my apartment and worked furiously on my project until the early hours of the morning.

8

Bo called me at six o'clock sharp the next morning.

"Hello?" I murmured. I probably hadn't been awake that early since junior high.

"Hi, is this Michael?"

"Hello, yes, it's Michael Wang."

"This is Bo. Apologies, I realize I'm calling somewhat early—Asian hours. My niece Vivian told me good things about you. Care to meet for breakfast?"

"Yes, sure," I said. "I know a good bagel place by Nob Hill if that works. . ."

There was a pause on the other end of the line. "I'm here at the Ritz Carlton. You know where that is?"

"I do, yes."

"Good. We can meet here. I'll see you in forty-five minutes," Bo said, then hung up.

After showering and pounding a pre-meeting espresso, I headed to the Ritz Carlton and got there just before Bo. Bo was only about my height but densely built and looked like he was in his mid-fifties. He had the long, broad torso of a swimmer; short, powerful legs; and the long, flowy hair of a much younger man, all of which gave him an aura of intense virility. When he set his hands down on the table, I noticed that his wrists were extremely thick and veiny. I wondered how he got this way; maybe he was one of those old-school mainland guys that were constantly roided out on crushed-up tiger dicks. Bo ordered a big plate of eggs, sausage, bacon, and potatoes while I got a bowl of coconut chia pudding. I asked him what brought him to San Francisco.

"Meetings with my portfolio companies. Some of them are preparing for exits, so I'm here to help negotiate with potential buyers," he said. I guessed that meant he was a venture capitalist. "Xiao Qi tells me you work in the technology industry as well?"

"Xiao Qi?" I said.

"Oh, sorry. I forgot her English name. Vivian." Bo smiled.

"Right. Yes, I am an autonomous vehicle software engineer at General Motors."

"That's very good. We need more capable young men who can build things. And you are from China as well?"

"No. I mean, not really. My parents grew up there, but I was born in New Jersey."

Bo nodded. "I see. And do you go back often?

"Not recently, no. My father used to take me to visit China every summer to see where he grew up. But the visits stopped after middle school."

"And where exactly did your father grow up?"

"Somewhere in the north of Jiangsu Province, I can't really remember," I said, shifting a little in my seat. I remembered very clearly the sweltering humidity inside the crowded apartment, the clicking of the one tiny electric fan in the living room, and the sound of extended family packed in the kitchen: a cast of aunts, uncles, grandparents, and cousins I hadn't seen in over a decade. Then the backseat smell of the cheap cab rides that took me and my father to the rapidly modernizing city center, the office buildings and shopping centers with Western logos that kept popping up year after year. Each time we went back, my father would say, "Look how much this place has changed since last year. Maybe one day there will be a good opportunity for you to come back too."

"China is very different today than the country your parents and I grew up in, even compared to ten or fifteen years ago—you must see it for yourself. Anyway, Vivian told me you have an interesting idea for driverless car computer vision. Maybe you can tell me about it."

Over the next twenty minutes, I explained to Bo step by step what I'd built. I could tell by the way he listened, with his index finger pressed against his chin, that he had also been an engineer at some point. He seemed to get it immediately and asked a lot of smart questions about latency limitations and minimal network density, including some stuff I never thought of. Then at the end, he asked me if I had patented any of this.

"No," I said. "I mean, not yet. I haven't really thought about that. But wouldn't the code technically belong to General Motors because I wrote it for my job?"

"Let me take care of it for you. Send me your source code and I'll have my legal team do the rest. A favor."

I was taken aback. I hardly knew this guy, so why did he want to help me?

"Sorry, that's very kind, but I'm afraid there could be some legal problems and I don't want to cause trouble."

Bo poured another cup of tea. "No problem, I understand you're worried about the red tape. But you should remember—good ideas need the right soil. Especially an idea like this, that can change everything, needs to grow up in a place where everything is changing. I have some friends, former classmates from Tsinghua University who are now on the faculty there. They've organized an academic conference on autonomous driving in Beijing. Perhaps you'd like to attend—meet a few colleagues in the industry, exchange some ideas?"

"Attend an academic conference!" I blurted out. "But I don't even have a master's degree."

Bo waved his hand. "We don't care about stuff like that in China. Beijing is a meritocracy of ideas. Do you know the term *haigui*? It means 'sea turtle'—we use it to describe overseas Chinese, particularly in the United States and Canada, that come back to China, in reference to the sea turtle's migratory habits. It's only natural for outstanding science and technology *haigui* like yourself to visit the motherland, even if only for a short while, to disseminate knowledge from their travels."

But I hadn't migrated anywhere, I thought. *I was born here.*

"Anyway, the conference is next weekend," he said finally. "Vivian will also be in Beijing at that time. Maybe she could show you around."

"Oh, she didn't mention that. I'll go." Why not? It was a free trip. I could use a getaway.

"Great, I'll have my assistant book arrangements for you," he said, rising from his seat. "Very pleased to meet a promising young technologist like you. I have to get to my meeting now, but I look forward to welcoming you to Beijing in one week's time." He took a business card out of his pocket, pressed it into my palm, and left.

BO SONG

FOUNDER AND MANAGING PARTNER,

TERRA COTTA CAPITAL

The card was off-white and cut from thick paper stock. I slid it into my wallet with care and sat in the restaurant for a few minutes by myself while I finished my coffee.

My conversation with Bo had brought back some nearly forgotten memories. I thought back to our first house in New Jersey, a wood-paneled, lilac-colored, one-story building at the end of the block. It was seven o'clock in the evening and my mother, my dad, and I were gathered around the kitchen table. I was still sweaty from tennis practice. Dinner was rice, stir-fried egg and tomato, and sautéed bok choy. My dad was in a giddy mood, eating heartily and already pink in the face from his second beer. Then he announced (I suspect only to me, because it seemed like my mother already knew) that tomorrow he would be leaving for a "business trip" to China.

"Don't call it that," my mother snapped. "They didn't even pay for your ticket."

My father sheepishly shrugged off her comment and took another swig of beer. I asked him what kind of trip it was.

"Son, it's an academic exchange conference for Chinese scientists around the world, sponsored by me and your mom's alma mater," he said. "We'll be discussing some big problems in computer science. Many of our college classmates will be attending.

"You remember them, Min?" he asked, giving my mother's shoulder an awkward squeeze. "I'm sure you remember our old friends Zhengyu and Xiaoming. Ah, the three of you were always the top of our class! I heard Zhengyu is CEO of his own company now—hard to believe he was such a prankster back in the day! And Xiaoming just got tenure at the university. Too bad you can't come with me this time, even though I invited you. Maybe next time you can come."

"What's the point of me coming? There's nothing for me to update Zhengyu and Xiaoming about," she said coldly. My father looked down at his plate.

"But of course, those of us that came to America are considered the real VIPs," he said, turning to me now. "After all, that has always been the dream. Actually, it was your mom's dream to begin with. She was one of only three students at our entire university selected to work for an American company right after graduation. Since she was on a management development track, they flew her to Chicago for training. Such VIP treatment, how jealous we were! She came back with so many stories, convinced me that we needed to build our life together in America and find a way to get there as soon as possible . . . "

I glanced at my mother and was surprised to find her looking uncharacteristically flustered.

"Luckily, at that time the technology industry was booming and everyone needed engineers," my father continued, "so I got a job at Xerox and we moved right away. The plan was for your mom to start looking for jobs once we got settled in New Jersey, but guess what—as soon as we got here, you were born! So, you had your mom with you all this time. You're a lucky boy."

My mother stiffened, then slowly rose from her seat, walked to the sink, and started on the dishes. After a few more stories, my dad abruptly excused himself and darted away from the table. Later that night, as I studied for my biology final, I saw him through the crack in my bedroom door flitting through the hallway between his room and the bathroom trying on different outfits. My dad had never been one to care about keeping up appearances, almost always showing up to work in jeans and a polo shirt. I remember he would wear the same beat-up brown shoes every day. But that night he must have tried on at least eight different outfits, until the light in the hallway finally went out a bit after midnight.

The next morning, my father was gone before breakfast and I found my mom up early surrounded by papers typing away at the PC she had set up in a corner of the living room. She was applying for jobs.

A week later, my father came back at eleven o'clock in the evening. He was in a much less talkative mood. When my mother asked him how Zhengyu and Xiaoming were doing, he just said, "Fine," and left it at that. Then he dropped down to his knees, opened up his suitcase, and beckoned for me to come over. With a wink, he handed me a box of ten Nintendo

DS game cartridges, obviously illegal burns purchased at some electronics store, which delighted me. Then he took out an oversized Louis Vuitton bag and presented it to my mother. Unfortunately, it had been squished flat in his suitcase—my father had never possessed that elusive quality called "showmanship." And neither had my mother, for even as she performed her excitement, something in her expression fell as she looked at the bag more closely.

"Don't worry about the cost, I got a good deal," my father said.

On my way to my room, I glanced back at them. Their two figures, hunched over the suitcase, looked weary.

For the next few years, my father would go on these trips once every couple of months. Each time, he would be in an agitated, excitable state for a week leading up to the trip. Then he would return inexplicably dejected and disappear into his study. During these years an aura of resignation settled over our home. Old mail piled up on the countertop, broken furniture went unreplaced, and Christmas trees lingered until February. As my father withdrew from the world, I felt sympathy for my mother, who had few friends to begin with. All of our family friends were my father's connections from Jiangsu who lived within a ten-mile radius of Tenafly, Bergenfield, and New Milford. Every month was the same potluck where we gathered in some family's tiny kitchen and the women brought out Chinese dishes in aluminum pans while the men played cards, drank Tsingtao beer, and reminisced about their lives back in Jiangsu. I remember my mother looking restless and out of place in these drab settings, which could not have contrasted more starkly to the dazzling America she held in her heart from seeing Chicago as a young woman. She spent many mornings and afternoons taking online English classes and applying for office jobs in Newark and New York City. Though for the most part she kept her head held high, I think even she was surprised by the volume of rejections that came back. Around the summer before eighth grade, she suddenly stopped. None of this ever seemed to register for my father.

At a certain age, maybe the end of middle school, I started to think that maybe my father deserved to feel disappointed for trying to live a double life. But whenever I found myself harboring too much scorn for him, a vague sense of guilt would well up inside me, sprouting from an inkling I'd started to form that he was not entirely himself to blame. As these memories seeped into the foreground of my mind, an acute sense of dread descended upon me. I didn't wish to think of myself as retracing my father's meek footsteps. My anxiety waxed when I remembered that I had not been back to China since middle school; I had, in fact, more or less avoided all of the sponsored trips during college, for fear that a place once so important for my self-mythology would prove disappointing. I'd always thought of China as somewhere my distinctness would be instantly recognized, but some part of me must have known that I would've felt like just another uninvited guest in a foreign country. Well, there was no more putting off the question. With a new sense of purpose, I finished what was left of the now-cold coffee and went back to the office.

I was surprised to find that by the time I got back to my desk in the morning, Bo's assistant had already forwarded me the itinerary for the following weekend. Business class from San Francisco International to Beijing Capital International Airport. Three nights at the Park Hyatt. Filled with anticipation, I didn't get anything else work-related done that day and took off promptly at five o'clock.

9

There's not much for me to say about the week leading up to the trip. The expectation of the conference overshadowed the whole week and made it impossible for me to focus at work. I packed meticulously and got my one good suit dry-cleaned. The morning of, I woke up early and took BART to the airport.

The business class cabin was like another rarefied world, and I did my best to act like it wasn't my first time here. When the flight attendant came over, I ordered a "sparkling white wine" because I was too shy to ask for champagne. I was browsing the bilingual movie selection when I noticed a slim, attractively dressed woman struggling to fit her suitcase into the overhead compartment. I got up to help her and saw that it was Vivian.

"That's a heavy suitcase—how long are you staying in Beijing for?" I asked innocuously.

Vivian chose to ignore the question. "I heard you chatted with Bo. He said he thought you were really impressive."

"He did? Yeah, I'm glad I met him. He probably told you already, but I'm going to this AV tech conference that he's hosting. You said he's your uncle, right?"

"Yes, distant uncle," she said. "Anyway, what should we watch? This is my favorite part about flying."

We scrolled through the movie options together and selected a Chinese fantasy-drama set during the Ming dynasty. The movie was about an anemic young scholar who fails the civil service examination twice and disappoints his family by deciding to dedicate his life to art instead and write an epic poem. One night while composing his masterpiece by moonlight, he is visited by a fox spirit disguised as a beautiful woman and quickly falls in love with her. Aided by his new muse, he progresses quickly on the epic poem but becomes afflicted by a mysterious blood-coughing illness. His concerned parents bring him to the village shaman, who diagnoses him with "possession by a fox demon"—the only cure is to capture the fox and destroy its earthly body. The parents, the doctor, and the rest of the village implore him to reveal the location of the fox spirit, but the scholar refuses and dies with his poem unfinished.

Vivian and I watched with rapt attention. The movie was typical of Chinese period films in its overly dramatic camerawork and stilted, humorless dialogue. Dinner arrived right after the movie ended and we had a lively discussion over a couple glasses of red wine. Vivian proposed that the fox was sincere in her feelings about the human in spite of the disastrous outcome, while for me, the fact that the fox needed to feed on the human's life energy to survive made me call her sincerity into question. In a way, it was like a reverse American vampire movie, where the male vampire proves his love for the female human by subduing his natural desire to feed on her. It was not a very good movie, made worse by a convoluted side plot concerning the backstory of the fox spirit's home world, but even these days I often find myself searching for its title on the tip of my tongue. After dinner, the lights in the cabin were dimmed, and Vivian fell asleep on my shoulder. From where she lay her scar was palely visible under the light blue glow of the flight-tracker screen, which showed our plane inching over the Pacific Ocean.

Several hours later, we landed in Beijing, and Vivian and I sleepily filed out through the Jetway together. A faint trace of morning-after intimacy seemed to hang in the air between us. We stepped into the arrivals terminal and I paused for a moment to take it all in. The cavernous space evoked what the International Space Station might have looked like if China, not America, had planted the first flag on the moon: a ruby-red ceiling 147 feet high veiled by a pale lattice of thin steel sheets, supported by looming, colorless pillars the circumference of California redwoods. A futuristic female voice announced boardings and imminent departures in a sonorous tone over the loudspeaker. In the middle of the common shopping area was a miniature of the Summer Palace, cool water trickling through its many fountains. From the second floor we could see thousands of travelers flowing through the terminals with even coordination, like red blood cells moving through the cardiovascular system.

Vivian and I took the interterminal train from arrivals together and split between the Chinese national and foreigner queues at customs. I was about to suggest meeting up after the checkpoint and sharing a cab into the city when, to my disappointment, she bid me a hasty goodbye and disappeared into the other line.

At the arrivals area, I found a serious-looking man in a black suit and dark sunglasses holding up a sign with my name on it.

"Mr. Michael Wang?" he asked.

"Yes, that's me."

"I am your driver. Please follow me," he said. He took my bags and led me to a black Audi in the parking garage with the license plate JING-A738DH, then wordlessly handed me a manila envelope containing a SIM card and 10,000 RMB in cash. There was no note in the envelope explaining what the money was for. With a sense of unease, I folded the thick stack of bills into my wallet and installed the new Chinese SIM into my phone. After a minute or so, it connected to the network and a few messages popped up.

Jessica: Hey Michael! Just wanted to see if you're available for dinner with me and Nick on the 29th! We know a great bistro in Hayes Valley! I've got a cute friend dying to meet you ;)

Sanjay: Hey, noticed you're not in the office today and feel we haven't checked in in a while. Generally OK to work from home as long as you let me know in advance. Can you update me on the status of the request log?

Lawrence: Hey chap! How about a beer next week?

It was too bad none of the messages were from Vivian.

I hit DELETE on Sanjay's message immediately. That was a problem for me to sort out later; I was in way too deep on this established pattern of truancy to make more empty excuses worthwhile. With Jessica I didn't even bother—not sure why she thought the idea of going on a double date with my ex-girlfriend would be appealing to me. To Lawrence I just typed back "sure."

On our way into the city, I decided to start practicing my Mandarin skills by striking up a conversation with the driver and asking him to explain the layout of Beijing. Occasionally glancing at me through his dark sunglasses in the rearview mirror, he explained that Beijing was organized as a set of concentric rings, each of which corresponded to a ring road that once defined the outer bound of the city, like the growth rings of a tree. Much of the old city was enclosed inside the second ring. Rings three and four demarcated the business and technology districts. As you got further out, the city sprawled into suburbs, and past that, mountains. Listening to his improvised lecture, of which I understood about sixty percent, I thought, in

English, of the translation of Dante's *Inferno* I had read during my freshman year, and what my professor had said in lecture that week about the ringed structure of hell. As we drove deeper into the heart of the metropolis, these two streams of information—physical and literary, Chinese and English, present and past—began to conflate in my mind, and I felt the fog of my jet lag dissipate as I awoke to the significance of entering.

Nearing the city center, we passed a subway stop where the escalator at the throat of the station swallowed a dense throng of identically white-shirted, narrow-shouldered young men. I got the sense that many of these men, like me, had come from somewhere else; from other cities, or remote towns, or the countryside, on planes, trains, and automobiles to fracture their past identities in order to be refitted as widgets in the bustling economic machine.

The driver stopped the car in front of the Park Hyatt and let me out. "I meet you in lobby tomorrow morning, 8:00 A.M.," he said, in English again. I nodded.

An attendant waiting in the hotel's narrow street-level entrance ushered me into the elevator and pressed L: the lift accelerated powerfully and the doors opened again to an airy lobby on the sixty-fourth floor, where the melancholy indigo of the Beijing dusk seeped in through floor-to-ceiling windows. My room was on the fifty-eighth floor, a small suite that looked out directly at the cluster of oddly shaped, Tetris-like skyscrapers in the Central Business District. On the desk I found a glossy purple folder inscribed with a line of golden Chinese characters, and below that, in English, TERRA COTTA PRESENTS: AUTONOMOUS-DRIVING SINOVISION CONFERENCE. I opened it up and found an introductory letter for the conference on Tsinghua University stationery, a glossy itinerary, and multiple wristbands. The itinerary detailed a 9:00 A.M. to 5:00 P.M. schedule of keynote addresses, panel discussions, and individual academic presentations. I moved onto the letter, which included half a page of acknowledgments recognizing a number of professors for their work in bringing together "the foremost global thinkers in interdisciplinary applied sciences united in the human struggle for autonomous driving." The rest of the letter was also written in the same stilted voice, as if machine-translated from some official document in Chinese, except for a handful of conspicuous typos that appeared throughout.

In the back flap of the folder, I found a handwritten note from Bo, which read:

Michael, welcome to Beijing!

We are excited to welcome you for what will surely be stimulating and unforgettable intellectual exchange. I trust that your driver, Xiaowen, has by now provided you with your Chinese SIM card and humble academic honorarium of 10,000 RMB, which you will kindly accept for your travel-related inconvenience. I encourage you to visit the Xiu Bar on the 65th floor, where the firm has opened a tab for you.

I look forward to welcoming you in person tomorrow.

All the best,

Bo

I checked my phone to see if Vivian had tried to get in touch during the last couple hours; she hadn't. To kill some time before bed, I splashed some water on my face and took the elevator back up to the sixty-fifth floor.

I found a seat near the window at Xiu Bar and ordered a Negroni. The lounge was mostly empty and the only sound was coming from a tuxedo-clad pianist playing a soft jazz ballad. By now the sun had set, and the lights from the city far below glowed faintly through the smog like embers in an ashtray. My eyes swept over the city grid and I wondered where Vivian was: which ring of the vast city, which capillary of an alleyway was she passing through right now?

To distract myself, I thought about the conference tomorrow and how I would make a good impression. I pictured myself packed into crowded lecture halls, standing awkwardly in the corner during "mingling" time, and began to sweat. I felt like a fraud for being there and was still confused about what led Bo to invite me in the first place. At what point during the weekend would Vivian decide to return to me? Roughly three quarters of the way through my drink, I started to feel rather self-consciously alone.

My sense of solitude was interrupted when I noticed that a man seated by himself to my ten o'clock, on the other side of the lounge, had been glancing over in my direction for the past half hour. A man about my age with perfectly parted hair, who turned away when I looked at him. A bit alarmed, I left the remainder of my drink unfinished and went back downstairs.

10

The next morning, Xiaowen woke me up with a phone call politely informing me that he had been waiting downstairs for twenty minutes. I apologized profusely, then showered, dressed, and met him outside the hotel, where it was chaotically loud because the Park Hyatt was situated at the intersection of two massive highways.

On the way over to the venue, I rehearsed my self-introduction in both English and Mandarin. Forty-five minutes later, Xiaowen let me know we were entering Tsinghua University, which, to my surprise, looked unnervingly similar to a typical American college campus. I felt like I recognized the buildings made of red brick, the grassy quads where students sat on picnic blankets, the walkways lined with cherry trees. Not at all the gloomy, Soviet-flavored affair I was expecting. There was something just a bit too disarmingly familiar, even midwestern, about it that put me on edge, as if I had been teleported to an alternative timeline where my parents never left China. Xiaowen parked in front of the Department of Electrical

Engineering and Computer Science building, where a team of staffers was checking people in and handing out name tags.

"Hi, I'm Michael Wang," I said to a staffer wearing a Tsinghua T-shirt.

"Let's see," the staffer said, scanning her clipboard. "Oh, Mr. Wang from Princeton University!"

"Well, not quite," I said. "I wasn't *sent* here by Princeton. I'm not a professor or anything. I just went there for college."

But she didn't seem to hear me. Her eyes filled with admiration and she lowered the lanyard around my neck like an Olympic medal. "Such an honor to welcome you, Dr. Wang!" she beamed, handing me a program and pointing me toward the entrance of the building.

Pushing my way through the packed hallways, I headed to Lecture Hall A, where opening remarks would be starting in ten minutes. When I found my seat, I was surprised to find Vivian already sitting there, wearing a simple white cotton top and light-wash jeans.

"How did you get in here? Are you volunteering?" I said.

She rolled her eyes. "Surprise, Michael. Thank you for the invite—very kind of you to squeeze me onto the list last second."

I wanted to ask where she went after the airport yesterday and wondered if she had showed up to the conference just to see me. "No problem. Seriously, though, why are you here?"

Vivian leaned slightly closer to me and made the universal shushing gesture. "Let's not talk about that here. Lots of people listening in this room. Wait until we're alone."

I felt slightly enthralled and decided to hold my questions for later. Then a young man who looked like a graduate student tapped the microphone and started introducing the conference's keynote speaker, one Professor Liu, chair of the Department of Electrical Engineering and Computer Science. The professor sat with emerital gravitas in a folding chair a couple paces away from center stage. When he rose to the podium, many in the audience started applauding, and some graduate students even rose to show their respect. He accepted the microphone from the younger man and began to speak.

"Dear friends and colleagues," he began. "On behalf of Tsinghua University, I welcome you to the inaugural Autonomous Driving Sinovision Conference. Gathered here today are some of the foremost scholars and practitioners in the field of autonomous driving from all over the world. I urge you to maximize your time here, because today is a serious opportunity for China to lead the world one step closer to delivering Level 5 full driving automation by 2028.

"Needless to say, our purpose today is to forge the future. But, as an academic bureaucrat, I would be remiss if I didn't begin with a tedious rehash of the past . . . It may surprise many to learn that Tsinghua began not as a research university, but as a preparatory school. In the aftermath of the bloody Boxer Rebellion, the humiliated Qing government was forced to pay astronomical reparations to the foreign powers that dominated China. In 1909 the American president Theodore Roosevelt took pity on us and agreed to refund a portion of our payment. But there was one condition: that the funds be used to establish a school to prepare China's brightest pupils for study at American universities, so that, having been Westernized, they could return home and 'reform' their own country. Thus, Tsinghua University was originally the Tsinghua School, built on the grounds of a confiscated imperial garden.

"This turned out to be the most humiliating concession of all. While we eagerly awaited the return of our gifted youths, many were transformed by foreign ways and never returned. Even today, how many untold thousands of overseas Chinese who went abroad for study got stuck there, toiling away unrecognized in research labs only to build the strength of a foreign nation?"

The last line seemed to strike a deeply resonant chord with the audience. For some reason, it wasn't difficult for me to imagine that this man somehow knew my father, perhaps even sympathized with him.

"But of course, the tides of history must always revert to their natural rhythm. Our nation's spectacular return to economic dominance has reinvigorated our universities. And so China's wayward sons have returned from all over the world—from Australia, from Canada, and especially from the United States of America. They have come from places such as the University of Wisconsin; the University of Illinois at Urbana-Champaign; the University of California, Berkeley; and Princeton University."

I nearly winced at the mention of my alma mater. I looked around the room, but luckily it seemed that no one knew he was referring to me.

"Let us ask ourselves why they've come home. Apart from the unmatched resources of our national universities, the fact is that our wandering sons have been waiting to return to native soil their entire lives. You see, something that the Chinese have always known is that patriotism, the love of the motherland, runs in the blood."

This note released a ripple of applause that built up into a wave. Professor Liu receded slightly from the podium, smiling benevolently down at the crowd.

"Anyhow, I believe that is enough from me," he said. "Before closing, I would like to thank our financial sponsor, Terra Cotta Capital, for their generous contribution to making this event possible. Please join me in welcoming onstage the Managing Director of Terra Cotta Capital, Bo Song."

Now the professor made room on the podium for Bo, who strode across the stage in a blue checkered suit, suede loafers, and a Terra Cotta Capital jacket. He took the microphone and occupied the center of the stage with commanding physical presence. I glanced over at Vivian, expecting her to be proud of her high-flying uncle. At the time I thought I just imagined it, but in retrospect I am certain of what I saw: a fleeting expression of hate and fear. All the muscles in her face had clenched up, and her lips were trembling, but when she saw me looking at her, her expression transformed back into a sweet and happy smile. She patted me twice on the forearm before turning her head back toward the stage.

Bo only spoke for a few minutes—he thanked Professor Liu for his remarks and dangled the possibility of investment money from his firm to support the development of the best research ideas. After he concluded his remarks, the conference-goers, ushered by the college-aged volunteers, dispersed to the rooms where the various presentations and panel discussions were being held.

For an hour or so, Vivian and I dipped into different classrooms to check out the guest lectures. On the whole, they were rather informal and poorly attended; many of the presenters seemed inexplicably tired, even bored. One Professor Wong from SUNY Purchase, presenting his research on smart city traffic routing, ended his talk after ten minutes and left without even taking questions. Later we discovered that the real energy was in Lecture Hall B, where Bo was holding a pitch competition for student entrepreneurs. There was a QR code at the entrance because the event was being live-streamed. Teams of young start-ups had spilled out on the floor outside of the lecture hall doing last-minute preparation on their laptops and eating muffins from Luckin Coffee. It was so crowded inside that Vivian and I had to stand at the back of the room, next to the student teams that were waiting to present. I overheard them talking about the pitch in a way that made it clear that Bo, his name and his firm, carried some weight.

Bo sat in the middle of a table flanked by an associate from Terra Cotta at each side. The total prize money, I gathered, was one million RMB of seed funding, to be divided among as many teams as deemed worthy. Vivian and I watched a few of these teams present passionately about their AI/self-driving projects. At the end of each presentation, Bo asked engaging questions about technology, team, and commercial potential. There was even an interactive component, where at the end of each presentation audience members could vote on whether or not they thought a start-up deserved to get funding. On my phone, I saw that more than twelve thousand people were tuned into the live stream.

Vivian saw me reaching for a cup of Luckin Coffee and stopped me. "No, that looks terrible. Put it down—let's go get one on campus. Come on, I know a place."

Vivian and I slipped out of the EECS building together and walked into the main quad, which was warm, sunny, and filled with trees. As we put distance between us and the looming auditorium, both my jet lag and vague feeling of worry started to dissipate. With her hair tied up, Vivian looked almost like an ordinary college girl.

"You seem like you really know your way around," I said.

"I'm glad you think so," she smiled back.

"Spend much time in Beijing growing up?"

"Not really. I had a boyfriend who went here, though, so I sort of know the layout of the campus."

I looked around, searching for a believable facsimile of Vivian's ex-boyfriend in the crowd of male students. To my relief, there did not seem to be any suitable candidates—not that I had any real clue what her romantic tastes might be. We continued our long walk and passed a couple of libraries, dormitories, and baseball fields. Then we wandered into an imperial garden overlooking a lake, where we could hear an *erhu* faintly playing. It was one of those pavilions made of stone and red wood, with narrow corridors that stretched across water, the sort of landscaping designed to facilitate ambulatory thoughts. Vivian and I reduced the distance between us as we made our way through the corridors, instinctively following the sound of the *erhu*. So this was the confiscated garden Professor Liu alluded to during his speech, the historical locus from which the rest of the still-expanding university had sprung. During that walk, the other half of that double consciousness I had been dimly aware of my whole life roused itself from oblivion and took over me peacefully.

Whatever was awkward between me and Vivian in San Francisco seemed to melt away.

We sat together on a stone veranda overlooking a part of the lake that was covered with water lilies.

"It feels strange to be here," I said. "Everything is so vivid and familiar. Like a sense of déjà vu, though I'm not sure if that's exactly the right word for it. Maybe what I mean is that I feel like I might've been a student here in a previous life, not that I believe in that sort of thing."

"If you had grown up in China, you definitely would've gotten into Tsinghua," Vivian said. "Smart guy like you."

"It was actually my dad's dream school. I think he was just a couple points off on the national exam, so he went to another college in Beijing. And he loved that place, talked about his college friends constantly and went back a lot, for conferences like this one. Sometimes it felt like he never wanted to leave in the first place."

"Why do you think that was?" Vivian said. I paused.

"I'm not too sure. Maybe it was because he felt like he never found his footing in America." I paused. "To be honest, sometimes I resented that about him," I added, stunned by how easily the confession slipped from my lips. "It was confusing. You know, for me to watch as a young kid. Always one foot back in the motherland, neither here nor there."

"So where is he now?" Vivian asked.

"We don't know, actually," I said, my voice completely flat. "He just disappeared one night. Didn't leave a note and hasn't contacted us since then. But if he's anywhere, I bet it's Beijing." I paused here for a few seconds. A small breeze rippled the surface of the water, making the lilies bump into each other. I took a deep breath and decided to continue.

"I miss him, you know. It seemed like he packed in a hurry, because for weeks after he left, I kept finding the things he left behind or didn't have room for. I started to collect these things in a box in my room, in case he ever came back for them. The brown shoes he wore to work every day, a ceramic mug from his research lab, his trusty TI-89 graphing calculator carefully sheathed in its protective case. I even told myself he'd left these specific items behind for me on purpose, to help me find my way without him. Who knows if I ever believed that. Halfway through high school I finally moved the box of his things to the attic. It's often crossed my mind to come out here and look for him, but something always held me back."

"You're here now, Michael," Vivian said softly, leaning in a little. "That's what matters."

For a few seconds, Vivian and I just sat in silence on the veranda looking down at the water lilies together. With the words I just said hanging in the air between us, I was afraid to look at her, but the air was so still I could feel her breath against my neck. For years, I hadn't come close to being that vulnerable with another person, had considered that story a shameful secret, the defect in the blueprint of my psychological makeup. My eyes were still fixed on the lilies when I felt her hand close over mine. Finally I looked at her, and found in her expression a look that dispelled all my banal and cynical self-condemnations and affirmed everything I ever secretly wished was true of myself. Vivian closed her eyes and tilted her head up. I leaned in and kissed her. When it was over, we lingered for a while and looked at each other. Then she took my hand and we left the garden together.

We made our way back to the main quad at a leisurely pace, floating through pleasant humidity and comfortable silence. The baseball fields, yogurt carts, and bicycles all glowed with the beatitude of the late summer afternoon. My head was still foggy with elation and every now and then I turned to glance at Vivian, trying to commit the moving image to memory: Vivian in her white cotton top walking with both hands on the shoulder straps of her backpack. I felt the powerful pull of nostalgia for a romantic youth I never experienced.

Finally we reached a small doorway on the edge of campus, which led down into a hip basement café. The place was quite crowded and lit up with Christmas lights. *Getz/Gilberto* was playing through hi-fi speakers on low volume. Otherwise, the café was filled with conversation: Mandarin, English, German, and Russian. At the counter, a male barista wearing a black T-shirt and a beaded bracelet dripped hot water into a Chemex filter. Vivian ordered a latte and I had a regular black coffee. I paid while she brought our drinks to an open table in the corner. Then I sat down next to her and we sipped our drinks for several minutes in silence.

"The time I spent in Beijing was the happiest of my life," she said, out of the blue. I looked up at her, but her gaze was fixed on her mug. The barista (or baristo?) had drawn a foam heart in her drink, which Vivian was now absentmindedly stirring into oblivion with her spoon.

"During my senior year of high school, I went for a semester abroad at the American school here. Beijing wasn't a popular destination for the girls I was friends with, who preferred places like London or Paris, but it was as far as my father would let me go. To be honest, I was amazed he even gave his permission in the first place, since for the first seventeen years of my life he never let me out of his sight.

"He set me up in a fully furnished apartment in Wudaokou. The place swept me off my feet. It was like a life-sized doll house that made every girlhood dream I had ever harbored come true. I didn't want to change a thing.

"It was the first time in my life that I had ever been on my own. No guard at the compound gate keeping track of my comings and goings, no chauffeur waiting after school to shuttle me straight home. I was elated. I bought a bicycle and a Nikon camera and rode all over the city taking pictures. I fell in love with art and started spending all of my time hanging out in the cafés and galleries in the 798 Art Zone. There was a lady named Miss Liuwen at this gallery called X Wood and I begged her to give me a job, even though my father's allowance was enough to cover my expenses.

"After Miss Liuwen hired me, I showed up at the gallery right after school at four in the afternoon on the weekdays and ten in the morning on weekends. I helped her set up exhibits, process orders, and give tours. I wasn't very good at the tour part. Since I was so shy, I preferred being backstage. For the first time in my life, I felt completely happy. I started to wonder whether or not it could last forever."

Here Vivian paused for a second and looked down at the mottled puddle of coffee and cream in her mug, from which she still hadn't taken a sip. I waited, impatient for her to continue. I was enjoying this lovely story, imagining her bicycling around the city at seventeen years old.

"One day I was setting up a small new exhibit when Miss Liuwen tapped me on the shoulder to tell me that the artist himself had stopped by," she continued. "I remember being not so impressed with this guy when I first met him, who told me in rather poor English that he was called Vincent. How snobbish of a Chinese painter to call himself that! He seemed extremely confident even though he was not what you would call handsome. He had a round face and long hair that went down to his shoulders. But when he invited me out to tea after work two days later I still accepted, even though I wasn't sure why.

"He brought me to a beautiful park in Beijing called Tuanjiehu. We walked through it for an hour and rented a small paddleboat that we took onto the lake. I learned that he was a student in the Art Department at Beijing University, a couple years older than me, and that his parents ran a small diner in the fourth ring. He was the first in his family to go to college and had disappointed everyone by becoming a painter. After that first time, I kept seeing Vincent, who took me to all the beautiful places in Beijing that didn't cost money. It turned out there were a great many.

"It didn't take long for me to fall in love with him. Through him, the world rearranged itself within the viewfinder of my camera, which always found him at the center. After just two weeks, he brought me home to meet his parents, loving, good-hearted people who cooked delicious food for me. We basked in the privacy of my apartment, often passing entire days there talking, drinking wine, listening to music, and making art. But the whole time there was something in the back of my mind, a terrible thought never left me alone: *this couldn't last forever.*

"We started to run out of time. I was due to return to Hong Kong in a few weeks, and who knows when I would have the chance to come back to Beijing again? Still, Vincent never gave up hope. Until almost the very end, we were inseparable. He wrote me a love letter in the form of an oil portrait, and I cried because it was too large to take with me. He said he would call me every day and save up all the money from his painting to visit me. And I believed every word. That's why I decided to sleep with him, on a warm spring evening only two weeks before my last day in the city.

"After that night, I didn't hear from Vincent for several days. I was confused and anxious—I found myself questioning my memory of the past few weeks, wondering if he had only wanted me for my body this entire time. The blissful freedom inside of me congealed into an insert solitude. At the gallery I became listless and quiet, and only Miss Liuwen took note of the change that had come over me.

"It was Miss Liuwen, finally, who told me that Vincent had been expelled from Beijing University for sexual misconduct, and then asked me, in the most concerned of tones, whether he had ever gotten carried away around me. As soon as she started telling me, the room started to spin. Had there been someone else? I fled the gallery and called Vincent a dozen times. When he didn't pick up, I rode my bicycle to his parents' house, but his sweet mother wouldn't even let me in the door. I sat on the steps outside and waited until dark. When she finally came back outside, it was with a bowl of porridge and to tell me in a shaking voice that Vincent wasn't here and could never see me again.

"The very next day, my father came to help me pack my things, almost an entire week early. The moment he stepped inside, I intuited what he had done from the cold fury in his movements. In my state of grief I had made no attempt to clear the apartment of the evidence of Vincent's presence. I watched as my father swept a few paintbrushes, photographs, even a man's T-shirt into a black plastic bag with complete detachment. I went into my bedroom for a final moment of privacy and collapsed onto the bed. I looked at the clock and registered that it was just past four in the afternoon. Then I saw something so devastatingly obvious it froze the blood in my veins: the lens of a tiny camera, just between the numerals ten and eleven.

"I found more cameras everywhere. Embedded in a painting in the living room. Buried in a fern in the kitchen. There was even one in my bathroom, facing out from the curtain rail. All the memories I had of spending time with Vincent replayed in my head, only this time through the grotesquely inverted perspective of the camera lenses. So he had been watching this whole time. Suddenly it occurred to me that the live footage being captured at that moment would show me discovering the cameras. I listened to my father in the next room. I threw up in the toilet.

"My father brought me back to Hong Kong, where I finished high school, and then I left for college in England. We never talked about what happened, and I never took another lover.

"In spite of all this, the time I spent in Beijing was the happiest of my life. I still remember the quiet joy of afternoons spent setting up exhibits in the gallery, wandering through the alleyway neighborhoods, taking photos of things I might never see again. Since Vincent disappeared, I've often thought of moving back here. I visit from time to time, as much as it brings back painful memories, because I can't help myself. But the prospect of starting another life here by myself feels overwhelming. In the end, though, nothing scares me so much as the thought that this is the only place I can be happy."

With that Vivian finished her story and looked up, her eyes wide with anticipation, and I suddenly realized I was the only man who had ever heard this story. Her knuckles whitened over the handle of the mug and now she sipped the long-cold beverage quickly, glancing up at me. It felt strange seeing her so vulnerable.

But surely it wasn't just sympathy she wanted, I considered, but something more tangible . . . yes, it was unmistakable, what she wanted was a companion to start a new life with, in Beijing. *Maybe*, I thought—and this was a dangerous thought that lodged into my chest like shrapnel—*I could be that companion.*

The last song on the album ended and chatter once again filled the space of silence that the music had left. I squeezed Vivian's hand under the table. Her fingers were cold, which inexplicably made me think of this Vincent and imagine his ghost sitting invisibly, mournfully in the empty third chair next to her, opposite to me. I felt the sting of jealousy and wondered how I could ever warm a hand that longed for another. How could anyone compete with a memory, a ghost? I looked at Vivian, and she returned my gaze with an intensely searching expression. I furiously turned over the verbal possibilities in my mind, trying to gauge the emotional yards between us, find the necessary space for a declaration. I was sure that Vivian could observe this process taking place in my head, as if it were transparent, because all the while she sustained the silence of expectation that finally reached an unbearable boil. In retrospect, this must have been the moment it became clear to her that she had me in her dominion.

"You don't have to start over here alone," I said.

Vivian's eyes, now trembling with hope, emboldened me to continue. "I don't have much in savings, but I can earn enough to support both of us by freelancing. I'm sure I can find a full-time job here as well. We could start a new life in Beijing . . . together, if that's what you want."

Vivian clasped my hands in hers, which were suddenly warm and ready, and pulled herself close enough that I could hear her staggered breathing—it was a quick, springy motion, almost like a pounce. And I her grateful prey.

"Is that what you want, Michael?" she said. "To be here with me?"

"Yes, it is. I'm certain."

"But won't you miss America? Your apartment and your friends?"

I catalogued the things I would leave behind–my loft, the furniture, my job, and Daniel, and Lawrence–and found that they had no weight in my heart.

"I'd make sure you were never lonely," she continued, in an anxious tone that made my heart ache. "I can show you so many beautiful places in this city and we could explore the rest together. We could make our own, private world. And you're so brilliant that I'm sure you'll make your own fortune in no time at all."

My own fortune, in no time at all—was there anything I couldn't accomplish with Vivian by my side? My heart beat with a manic exuberance and I held her hands tighter.

"Yes, I'm certain," I said, this time more boldly. "I'd do anything to make and keep you happy."

A soft, almost tearful smile played on Vivian's face and she blinked slowly, twice. Then a more serious expression settled in and she said: "If you want to be with me, then you have to be with me fully. There would be no going back."

"Ever?" I said, caught a bit off guard.

"No, not ever," she said. "What I mean is that I'd need you to be really be here. No living between two worlds. I couldn't bear it."

Of course, I thought of my nervous father and his black suitcase, always ready to be packed at a second's notice. "No living between two worlds," I said finally. "I'm ready."

Vivian sighed and closed her eyes, looking relieved. We stayed like that for a minute or so, basking in the warmth of our mutual understanding. When she opened her eyes again, there was something sharp and urgent in her voice.

"Two weeks. That's how long I'll need to make some final arrangements at home. It should be enough time for you to quit your job and pack your things. We're running out of time and I think you have to meet Bo soon. In two weeks exactly I'll call you in the morning and we'll meet here, okay?"

"Okay," I said simply, and nodded in amazement, which was all I could do. Vivian got up from her seat and I understood that I shouldn't follow her outside. We exchanged a hurried kiss in the middle of the café, and she whispered "two weeks" into my ear, before looking once more into my eyes and walking away. I counted the steps she took to cover the short distance to the door and disappear onto the street, and felt strangely moved, filled with passionate devotion and the exuberant certainty of our promise.

I checked my phone and saw that I had a message from Bo asking where I was and decided to head back to the conference. On my way there, the words *two weeks* were still floating breathlessly on my tongue. The only thing that slightly bothered me was—how did Vivian know I had to meet Bo soon? Was I only imagining it, or had something hard and determined entered her affect at the last second, just as she slipped away?

11

When I got back to the EECS building, the space had more or less cleared out, and there were just a dozen or so student volunteers left putting away folding chairs. Bo was waiting for me on the far side of the room and asked if I wanted to go for a smoke.

He offered me a cigarette from a pack the color of Phoenician purple with gold-lettered Chinese characters on them. Before I could reach for my lighter, he lit it for me, which obliged me to bend down slightly. The first puff surprised me with smooth, natural tones of plum and barley—it was fragrant in a way that was completely unexpected for a cigarette. I hit a second and third puff in quick succession.

"These are very special cigarettes to commemorate your visit," Bo said. "The tobacco is cultivated from a secret strain that only grows in a particular part of Yunnan Province and manufactured using equipment confiscated from petty capitalists in 1949. There are only 798 cases each year. They are FPMO—For Party Members Only."

FPMO—had he come up with that on the spot? Bo looked smug, as if certain he'd won me over.

"Do you enjoy it?"

"Yes, very much."

"Then you have good taste. I'll have a carton sent to you in San Francisco."

As we smoked, a convoy of black Audi SUVs with Jing A license plates gathered along the street. A few guests from the auditorium were starting to trickle in. Bo explained he'd arranged a small dinner for distinguished guests from the conference and asked me if I wanted to join. "Sure," I said. As we approached our car, the last in the procession, Xiaowen emerged from the driver's seat to open the doors for us. Bo didn't put out his cigarette on the way in, so I followed his lead.

On the way over, Bo said he noticed I stopped into the start-up pitch competition and asked me what I thought of the presentations. I gave him a few of my notes off-the-cuff, focusing my observations around technological promise, and he nodded in approval, saying I had a good sense of intuition.

Dinner was at the Hong Kong Jockey Club, a private social club Bo was a member of. The outside of the club was designed to look like an imperial palace, but the inside conveyed a more Western sensibility, filled with dark wood and lush carpets. Bo led me to one of the ballrooms where they were hosting a cocktail hour. Everyone was still wearing their name tags, which made me realize that of the group that attended the conference, only the American guests were here now. There was a mixture of universities in attendance—SUNY Purchase, North Carolina State University, Georgia Institute of Technology, and corporations—Ford, Chrysler, GMC. Thankfully, no one from General Motors. The average age, I observed, was about forty to fifty-five. I got a few stares on the way in, and a peculiar sense that many of the Americans in attendance knew each other. There was a definite sense of familiarity and camaraderie among the men, who had transitioned from delivering sleepy lectures at the conference to downing glass after glass of Opus One Cab. Many were already in a state of rapidly accelerating inebriation. While we waited at the bar, Bo pulled aside a young bald guy with glasses about my age and introduced him to me as Peng, the CEO of a self-driving car company called Naveon, then left to go mingle with the other guests. Peng was drinking nothing but ice water and sweating profusely. His English was not very fluent and he seemed to be having trouble maintaining eye contact with me. While we were chatting, I overheard the other guests talking about a karaoke session last night that had gone late into the night—could that be why they were so listless this morning? I kept glancing over at Bo. Everywhere he went, the Americans clumped around him, one-upping each other in their flattery. Even those who were noticeably older than him behaved in this way.

There were only two other men my age—Bo's associates from Terra Cotta, who were quietly making the rounds listening in on conversations. Now that we were up close, I suddenly recognized one of them and asked him if he was at Xiu Bar on the sixty-fifth floor of the Park Hyatt last night. He laughed and said no, he was working late, but I was sure it was the same man.

At eight o'clock, a hostess from the club led us upstairs to an ornate private dining room that opened up to an enormous granite terrace. Below us was a Chinese courtyard where a few members in dinner jackets were wandering about the gloam, smoking and tossing breadcrumbs to swans. We found our seats around a circular dining table with thirteen place settings. I was seated to Bo's right, and Peng was a few seats down. The door opened for three waiters to bring in the first wave of dishes: shark fin soup, hot pot of mutton and tripe, steamed chicken with fresh mushrooms, salted flower rolls, and watercress with garlic. The centerpiece was a plump golden brown roast duck that arrived on a cart. The chef used two knives to carve the bird, skillfully separating skin from meat, dark meat from white, and arranging the thin slices on a plate with white sugar and hoisin sauce. Meanwhile, another waiter poured us each thimble-sized shots of a clear, pungent liquor that smelled like soy sauce. I rotated the liquor in my cup, studying its color and viscosity. Bo gave a toast and I downed the glass, grimacing as the harsh liquor burned a raw patch down my throat. My glass was refilled immediately. Now the meal started in earnest, and Bo's guests, already red in the face, ate and smoked voraciously, pausing their consumption only to raise their glasses to Bo individually, each toast more drunken and obsequious than the last.

"We all saw it today—Bo is a role model to the younger generation, and even to us older folks as well. Thank you for funding my research and believing in me when no one else would. I will be accepting a lifetime achievement award at the Michigan faculty next month, and I wish I could give the award to you."

"I'd like to raise a glass to a true leader among us, someone I would follow anywhere. Bo, you are respected and admired by all. Thank you for uniting us all in a common purpose we can all be proud of."

"Bo—I cannot thank you enough for your friendship over the past eight years. You've given me a chance to finally serve my mother country, a dream I had ever since I was a young engineer studying at Zhejiang University."

"Bo, I have no idea how you found me. All I know is that if you hadn't, I would've spent the rest of my life working without purpose or recognition, maybe even lost my marriage. I'll never forget the debt I owe you."

We carried on in this way for nearly two hours. Each plate that came off the table was immediately replaced. Exhausted by the decadent procession of food and drinks, I was having issues inserting myself into the conversation, so near the end of the meal I excused myself to the restroom and sat down in a stall to collect myself. While I was inside, two of Bo's guests walked in to use the urinals.

"We'll be heading back the day after tomorrow—fuck my life."

"Don't complain about your life, Old Wong. I saw pictures of the new house in Scarsdale. You're the richest professor at SUNY."

"They're so fucking stingy at SUNY. Twenty years and they still won't give me tenure. What else am I supposed to do?"

"That's why you're here. You should enjoy this while it lasts."

"The reception was better last year, I thought. I didn't like the seafood lunch yesterday. Maybe the late-night event tonight will be better."

"Old Wong, always full of complaints. Our stipend went up this year by fifteen percent. That's not bad. At least I can bring back some gifts for my wife."

"Shit, you got fifteen percent?! I have to talk to that scoundrel . . . he needs to show more appreciation for those of us who have been with him since the beginning. By the way, where is Dr. Jian this year?"

"Dr. Jian from Georgia Tech? Fuck, I heard he experienced some issues with the university. No one really knows."

"Damn it. This group is getting too big. We need to protect ourselves. Who is that kid, anyway?"

"I don't know. I don't think he's really in this—too young to have anything valuable to contribute. Who cares?"

I waited for thirty seconds after the two men filed out to wash my hands and return to the dining room. By now, most of the party had moved to the terrace, where the hostess was handing out cigars. Bo was being cornered on the garden-facing side of the balcony by Professor Wong, who seemed to be stumbling.

"And I'm so grateful, will always be grateful, for everything you've done, but you know the situation at the university with the budget cuts, it's putting a lot of stress on my family . . . *dage*, could I ask you to consider giving me an advance on next year's spend? I promise I'll pay it all back, with interest, and get you whatever you need."

I couldn't make out what Bo said in response. Spotting me, he pried himself away from Wong and asked me to follow him. We left the dinner party and went up one floor to a different room filled with books. I took a moment to survey the room, dimly lit by a small chandelier. Oil paintings of Royal Ascot hung on golden frames. A spiral staircase in the middle of the room led to a second floor with more shelves and volumes. Equestrian memorabilia was exhibited everywhere: a jockey's leather gloves, silver racing trophies, a few letters from British notables. *This must be quite similar to what I imagined those mansions on Prospect Avenue looked like on the inside*, I thought—the rooms that had persecuted me and swallowed Jessica.

"The others are on their way now to an after-party at a casino, so we finally have some time to catch up. Drink?"

I didn't really need it, but accepted a glass of tawny port anyway. "Thank you. I thought gambling was illegal in China?"

"It is," Bo said. "But you are not like them. Those men back there, they are all well past their prime, were already in decline when I first met them. They're filled with resentment, pride, envy, those kinds of things. I think you can see some of that for yourself. For them, this yearly gathering is a special event, something they look forward to. But they'll never belong to a place like this. They always have to go back to a place where they are not seen.

"You're different, Michael. That much is obvious to me. I'm a venture capitalist, and I hope you don't mind me saying, one of the most successful in this country; my sole expertise is recognizing and elevating talent. I've seen many generations now, and I can tell from a single conversation, usually within a few minutes, whether or not someone is going to be massively successful. You have all the signs of being such a person, Michael. But the truth you must accept is that the kind of future I see for you can only take place in China. If you stay in San Francisco, you'll end up just like those other dinner guests in twenty years. I hope you will join me here in accomplishing serious work."

Bo's words coursed through my chest like a shot of epinephrine. The way that he described the dinner guests' eagerness and irrelevance reminded mc sourly of my father, as if these men were grotesque caricatures of him. "What do you have in mind for me?" I asked.

"Peng, who you met earlier tonight, is the CEO of Naveon, one of my most promising portfolio companies. Peng is a good businessman, but we need real technical talent at the helm. I want to install you as the VP of engineering. You'll start with a team of fifteen engineers, but I want you to hire fifty more. Some of the best and brightest from Tsinghua, like you saw today. You'll be responsible for the entirety of the software stack at Naveon, the brain inside of the car. To be clear, Michael, this is a moonshot company. Success is nowhere close to guaranteed—that's why I want to bring you on board, because I think you can move the needle."

I rotated the glass in my hand. "Thank you for even considering me," I said finally. "It's a huge change and a big risk. I really need to think about it."

Bo set his glass down without drinking from it. "Unfortunately, this isn't an opportunity that you can sit on. Naveon's market is highly competitive and we need someone in the seat as soon as possible—someone who can act with conviction. If it's not you, it'll have to be someone else."

"I'm sorry. Do you think I can talk to Peng first? This is a big decision and I just want to understand the company first."

"Don't worry—I already talked to Peng for you. He's excited for you to join. As for the company itself, you'll have to trust me—and mind you, I always do my due diligence. Let's say things go well. You'll be promoted to CTO within a year or two. In the meantime, you'll make $250,000 in cash every year and receive a significant number of shares in the company. And your signing bonus, paid immediately, will be $200,000."

Suddenly I thought of Vivian and my promise to be with her in Beijing in two weeks. What kind of life did I want to give her? When that thought took hold of me, there remained no possibility of turning back.

"Okay, I accept," I said. "What's next?"

"You'll start in two weeks." Two weeks exactly, I echoed to myself. "Wait for a package in the mail from my people containing further instructions.

I'll open a bank account for you and deposit the $200,000 there—you'll need a bank account anyway, and this way you won't pay taxes on it. As for other preparation—your first task will be to recreate multinodal aggregation at Naveon, so download everything you need from your work at General Motors before you resign, and use the external hard drive I'll send you. That all make sense?"

If only I had walked away then. Here's the thing: for as long as I can remember, I have always been one to avoid trouble. If there's a single thing that can still be redeemed about my character, it's this. I understood beyond a shadow of a doubt that what Bo was asking from me was, in this order, illegal, unethical, and potentially dangerous. The seconds ticked by. But I also thought of the listless half-life that waited for me back in San Francisco. And when I remembered my promise to Vivian, to meet her in two weeks, and the exhilarating blankness of our future together, I opened my eyes and found that I was nodding.

12

I woke up the next morning in a dreadful state and scrambled to cram all of my belongings back into my suitcase and meet Xiaowen in the hotel lobby.

During the hour-long ride to the airport, I carefully played back the events of the previous night in my head and panicked when I realized the full scope of what I promised Bo. I started to recall a training session on intellectual property theft I attended during my first week at General Motors. There were fifty of us packed in this big conference room in Detroit and they'd brought in the Head of Worldwide Security, this portly ex-FBI guy with a crew cut who kept his hands folded behind his back while he talked. The format of this presentation was "scared straight." The security head walked through numerous examples of cons who had stolen from the Company and had their hands proverbially chopped off. Corporate espionage, especially from overseas, was on the rise, he said. As employees of General Motors, it was our duty to remain vigilant against the constant threat of espionage from rival companies, hacker groups, and unregistered foreign agents—he looked right at me when he said this. Remember, intellectual property theft is a federal crime; everything you do here at GM belongs to the Company and if you steal from the Company, I will call my former colleagues at the FBI and you will go to prison.

As I remembered this session, I started to feel increasingly resentful. I knew that if any of this ever came to light, I would be cast as the treacherous, ungrateful thief who tried to walk out the door with his pockets stuffed. But what about the years of unrecognized effort that General Motors had stolen from me? My invention of multinodal aggregation was a completely independent venture; no other engineer at GM had contributed to or was even aware of the project. I'd spearheaded it entirely on my own and devoted my time, energy, and ingenuity to this project; the only GM resource I'd used was a company laptop. All of this for it to be summarily buried without even an explanation. For a breakthrough that could impact the lives of billions of people, wasn't it a greater crime for me to let it go to waste?

In addition to this, I realized only as we neared the airport, that I didn't even know for sure whether or not Naveon was a real company. I frantically googled the word *Naveon*, which pulled up several pages of results, most of which were in Chinese. LinkedIn showed 250 employees, all of whom were based in China. One of the English-language results described Naveon as "one of the most promising autonomous driving start-ups emerging from Asia, led by visionary CEO Peng Liu," then listed a number of venture capital investors that I'd never heard of but seemed to be big in China. Apparently the company had already secured approval from the Beijing municipal government to conduct unmanned road tests in 2022—but that was three years from now. I couldn't find any information online about what Naveon's unique angle was or how their technology was different from their competitors. It all seemed very early stage, very risky. The last thing I looked at was a profile showing Peng on the cover of *Forbes China*. In his portrait, he was wearing glasses and standing under high-contrast lighting that made his round, bald head look significantly more angular and mature than in real life. The profile described Peng's stratospheric trajectory from attending an unknown engineering college in Chengdu to leading the autonomous driving team at Baidu and overseeing a team of five hundred engineers—all before the age of thirty. This made me feel a lot better, though it was difficult to square with the sweaty, skittish man I met this weekend—maybe he was just bad at parties.

Xiaowen dropped me off in front of the United Airlines area at departures, brought my bags out of the trunk, and wished me a safe journey. The hangover hit me right as I pulled up to the gate, manifesting my anxieties into corporeal reality. As we took off, I closed my eyes and brought myself back to those final moments with Vivian in the Tsinghua basement café. In that moment our future together seemed to stretch out before me like a green valley, but now dark clouds were creeping over the mountain range. Why had I summoned them, instead of just starting over with her? The painfully obvious explanation was that I knew I wasn't good enough for Vivian. That's why she could text me and summon me at a moment's notice. If I wanted a chance at keeping her, I'd have to become somebody—and for me, that was worth risking everything.

To put these torturous thoughts to rest, I browsed through the in-flight movie options and selected a documentary called *Enron: The Smartest Guys in the Room*. I usually don't watch documentaries, especially the smirky ones about business and the abysmal state of modern capitalism, etc., but something about this one caught my eye. The story was about a band of nerdy corporate misfits that managed to turn the unsexy Enron corporation into their own frat house/pirate ship before driving the whole operation into bankruptcy. I was fascinated by one character in particular, Lou Pai, who doesn't get much screen time but whose presence looms over the film. Lou Pai, born in Nanjing, who, according to video testimony, no one really knew that much about, other than the fact that he was really quiet; who also regularly blew millions of dollars in shareholder money on catered lunches and strip clubs, fled ship with nearly $280 million, and became the second largest landowner in Colorado. Oh, and I forgot to mention: he emerged as the only one of the bunch who managed to escape prison time or personal tragedy. The way he pulled this off appears to be the fact that his divorce with his then-wife served as a convenient alibi for him to sell his hundreds of thousands of Enron shares early, before the inflated price bloomed to criminal heights. The reason for the divorce: Lou's wife of two decades (and the equivalent number of children) had caught him in bed with a stripper named Melanie Fewell, whom he later married and had a child with.

I considered it criminal that the saga of Lou Pai was relegated to the status of side story, when in fact it should have been the main plot, if not the subject of its own documentary. The profound depths of this Quiet Man's fraudulence was nearly biblical and instantly elevated him in my mind to a kind of postmodern mythical hero of Asian America. There was such a sweet spite to *his* brazen version of the American dream. I relished the fact that he cheated on his own (presumably loyal, unsexy) Chinese wife with a literal stripper. Doesn't get much more American than that. Even his humble and somewhat folksy given name, "Lou," is subterfuge; a Chinese character transliterated, the Yellow Peril hiding in plain sight.

That night I had a strange dream. I was staggering across the barren Colorado desert, dying of thirst, when the shadow of a man on horseback grew long on the distant horizon. It was Lou Pai, wearing a cowboy hat, cowboy boots, and bolo tie with a green jade centerpiece. He invited me to his enormous ranch, "Mount Pai," where his Caucasian stripper-wife, wearing a tight red *qipao* dress, welcomed us inside and served us chrysanthemum tea in blue china cups. Lou and I sat cross-legged on the floor and conversed in a fluent, native-speaker Mandarin, and he told me he was my dad.

13

I made it back to my apartment at around six o'clock in the morning. To my surprise, a package was already sitting on my steps when I got there. It contained a carton of FPMO cigarettes, a printed confirmation for my one-way ticket to Beijing in one week, a confirmation letter for an indefinite stay at an aparthotel in Sanlitun, a check for $40,000, instructions to report to suite 4810 in China World Trade Center II at 9:00 A.M. on Wednesday, and a one terabyte hard drive. There was also a short note on Terra Cotta Capital stationery explaining that the hard drive was for my "convenience, to assist in the transfer of any materials that may be relevant to your new role," while the check was for additional relocation expenses, though I could rest assured the apartment in Beijing was already fully furnished.

On my walk over to the office, I thought about how I would game plan the next few days. Obviously the main thing I needed to do was download the files I promised Bo. I decided it made the most sense to do this at the last possible opportunity to minimize the likelihood of getting caught before I was out of the country. Today was Monday; I'd download the files I needed on Friday and quit on the same day. So the main thing I had to do in the meantime was just to lay low and avoid arousing suspicion.

The problem with avoiding suspicion, of course, was the fact that I'd just been MIA for the past several days. As I got closer to the office I started feeling more and more anxious about how to explain my sudden absence and pulled up to the entrance sweating a weird amount for the cool morning weather. On my way to my cubicle, I found seventy percent of the office gathered in the kitchen munching on breakfast burritos. I accidentally locked eyes with one of the quality assurance managers, a gopher-like man named Jerry I'd only interacted with once or twice in my life.

"Oh, hey, Michael, how was your vacation? Someone from the lobby stopped by on Friday with mail for you, but you weren't at your desk, so we figured you must've gone somewhere for a long weekend."

So until Friday they hadn't even noticed that I was gone.

"Yup. College buddy's wedding in Nashville," I said.

"Oh, terrific. I heard the weather there's amazing this time of year." Then he went back to eating his burrito.

I should have been relieved, but now I was feeling pissed that they never noticed I was gone in the first place.

I sat down at my cubicle and started to kill time by reading the news on my laptop. A *New York Times* headline titled US REPORT WARNS ON CHINA IP THEFT caught my eye, so I clicked into it. The article described a certain report by an influential think tank that had been circulating in Washington, which claimed that the Chinese government was stealing hundreds of billions of dollars' worth of American intellectual property each year, in a brazen and systematic campaign that one prominent American general called "the greatest transfer of wealth in history"—an eyebrow-raising turn of phrase if ever there was one. This astronomical figure accounted for not only software piracy but also acts of corporate espionage—the theft of trade secrets, etc. The language of the report was unquestionably bellicose, calling the problem "an issue of national security."

One term that the report kept alluding to was *Economic Espionage Act*, so I looked it up and learned that it was a 1996 act of Congress that criminalized the act of stealing trade secrets to benefit a foreign government. So far there had only been a handful of cases, mostly involving naturalized Chinese American scientists; one guy got ten years for attempting to steal, of all things, the formula of a chemical whitening agent often used in refrigerator doors and Oreo cookies.

During this research session my mind kept wandering back to the Philosopher-General's thrilling coinage of "the greatest transfer of wealth in history" and wondered whether that appraisal included American slavery, British imperialism, or the rise of Wall Street. Then I thought about the Chinese men that American businessmen imported to work on the railroads, lifted down in baskets, like ritual offerings, to the explosive tunnels, and what Lawrence had said about the real value of the patents their present-day descendants—those meek scientists in R&D labs—churned out year after year. Where did *that* transfer of wealth rank in history? What about the vast fortunes that had been stolen from the Chinese inventors that left their home country for the promise of opportunity in America? I felt a massive reserve of righteous anger welling up inside of myself and took a sharp sip of my Nescafé.

Lacking an immediate outlet for these thoughts, I spun up a VPN on my laptop and started writing a thread on Samarkand linking to the news article: HYPOCRITICAL US ESPIONAGE POLICIES/BAMBOO CEILING. Wired on coffee, I banged out six paragraphs in twenty minutes and hit POST. Then I went next door to grab a sandwich and came back eager to check for comments.

LOL what are you so mad about bro? I'm Asian, work in SWE at Airbnb, two years out of college, total comp is almost $300K and

I get free gourmet food at the office / $5k of Airbnb credit each year. Typical day I work abt 4 hours and spend rest of time hitting gym / raves.

You sound like a boomer tbh lol. Managing other people just takes your freedom away, that's why we're all on Samarkand . . . should just leave America /get a remote job if you're so pressed. Btw, 28, SWE level 3 at DoorDash, $400K total comp.

Random yuppie redpilled by CCP propaganda. Very sad. You need to get off WeChat.

It sounds like you're not happy at your current job. Are you a SWE? PM me, I'm a technical recruiter, just placed another candidate 1 year out of school for +$120k his previous comp, $350k total comp.

I slammed my laptop screen in disgust and went outside to smoke a cigarette. *Just one more week of breathing the same air as these vape-inhaling boba liberals*, I thought. After a few puffs I started to wonder why I was so heated about this topic in the first place and found myself remembering the panel of patent award plaques that hung above my father's desk at home. The Company issued one whenever one of his patents were approved (roughly once every six months), and by the end of our time together, no fewer than sixteen adorned the wall of his study, arrayed in a neat 4x4 grid. My father considered it a great distinction to receive these plaques, and they were his most prized possessions. But while the plaques accumulated, our modest station in life stayed the same. There were many hushed fights about money, which I overhead with guilt and dread. My mother, who was proud, wore the same cheap dresses for a decade until they were threadbare. When our family friends started suggesting more expensive vacation destinations, we stopped going with them. Though he never voiced his frustration out loud, the professional stagnation had a clear impact on my father, who became even more taciturn and reclusive, often excusing himself from dinner before my mother and I were finished eating to hole up in his study—presumably to continue his prolific inventing. He never had any promotions to celebrate, just the aluminum-and-plaster plaques that were mass printed by a trophy manufacturer in Pennsylvania for thirty dollars apiece. And yet those damn plaques were the only items he took with him to China.

At 4:30 P.M. I promptly headed home and tried to put the plaques out of mind. I couldn't shake the irritating suggestion implied by the surface-level parallel that I was somehow following in my father's wayward footsteps. Could that be a subconscious motivator of my actions; was there a part of me that even thought of myself as avenging him? *Of course not*, I thought; my defection was my own invention, a radical act of decisiveness and self-determination. Still, the thought filled me with a deep discomfort and lingered for the rest of the week.

When Friday finally came around, I got to the office at 7:00 A.M. to try and download the files I needed before anyone else got in. Luckily, that morning the office was completely empty. I took the hard drive Bo sent me from my backpack and plugged it into my computer. Then I logged into the secure General Motors cloud, selected the directories I needed, and clicked TRANSFER TO EXTERNAL DRIVE. A blue dialog box popped up with an hourglass icon and a time estimate: fifteen minutes. After the download was complete, I signed out and used the IT manager's log-in credentials to clear my download activity from the cache.

At the end of the day, I printed my resignation letter, dropped it on Lucas's desk after he went home for the day, and left.

I had certainly planned on quitting under more glorious circumstances. For days, actually, I'd been fantasizing about what I'd say to Lucas on the day of. But then I realized that no matter what I said, there was a chance it would come back to bite me, which was a risk I couldn't take. As I left the office that day, there was a bitter taste in my mouth. I couldn't shake the image of Lucas and Sanjay and everyone else laughing hysterically at my nonspecific, boilerplate letter on Monday morning. In all likelihood, they'd never even realize I'd gone on to greater things.

Later that evening, I felt I should celebrate, but I wasn't sure who to call. I was still annoyed at Lawrence from the last time we hung out, plus I had a bad feeling he'd ask too many questions about the new job. I had a few missed calls from Jessica too, but I knew she'd try and drag me out to some Princeton gathering with her smug boyfriend and try to play matchmaker.

Back at my apartment, I went downstairs to smoke one of the Chinese cigarettes and found Daniel, Tony, and Jeffrey hanging out in the alleyway. A sort of somber air hung over their heads, which were bowed and specked with water; I immediately felt that I had intruded on a private conversation. Upon seeing me, Daniel smiled weakly and made a spot for me to lean on the wall. Tony and Jeffrey, seated on plastic stools, gave me polite nods and turned away. Remembering the pack of FPMO cigarettes in my pocket, I took them out and offered some to the group. When he saw them, Jeffrey chuckled and asked me how I came across the extravagant smokes; had I joined the Chinese Communist Party? "More where that came from," I said jokingly.

A couple puffs of the fragrant cigarettes seemed to lighten the mood. I remembered their plan to open a Chinese restaurant together and asked them how it was going. Suddenly all three of them fell quiet. Then Daniel, after locking eyes with Tony and Jeffrey, broke the silence and started telling me about the "money troubles" they had recently gotten into. Apparently, about ten weeks ago, they found a suitable lot on Stockton Street and started pooling together the money they needed for the deposit. They emptied their savings accounts, borrowed all the money they could from their extended families, and took out a loan from a local tong. Jeffrey sold his car. The deal was all set to close until the day they were supposed to pick up the keys, when the landlord called to say that he had never received the deposit. They went to the police station, where a detective explained that they had just been the victim of wire fraud, and there was no possibility of recovering the money. Now they were out $10,000 and owed interest on the money they had borrowed from the tong. On top of that, Daniel was in trouble with his pregnant girlfriend's parents, who had loaned a significant portion of the funds and were furious at him for losing it. They couldn't find a lender for the remaining amount and were thinking about pulling out from the business.

"You're short $10,000?" I asked.

"Yes," said Daniel. I pulled out my checkbook and wrote a check for $10,000.

"Here," I said. "I'm happy to help you."

Daniel shook his head. "*Dage*, we can't take your money. It's not right."

"It's not a gift, it's a loan," I said. "Only I charge zero percent interest and you can pay me back anytime. What's the landlord's name?"

Daniel turned back to Tony and Jeffrey and they started to have a serious discussion in Cantonese. When they finished they all turned toward me, suddenly business-like, and Daniel cleared his throat.

"Okay, how about this. No loan—we give you ten percent share in the business. You can be our partner."

I smiled. "It's done," I said. As I finished writing the check, Tony went back into the restaurant to fetch two bottles of house red. We had a celebratory drink and smoked through the pack of FPMO. I went back upstairs and brought another carton down, and told the guys they could keep the rest of the carton. Suddenly I remembered the sour interaction I had with Jessica and Nick in this very spot many months ago. Would smug, GSB-bound Nick have given Dan, Tony, and Jeff a "micro loan" for their predicament? Was there, perhaps, something a little exaggerated in my sudden show of generosity? Now Jeffrey was putting his arm around me and calling me *dage*—big brother.

14

During my final weekend in San Francisco, the city was hit by an unseasonal Category 3 atmospheric river that was making its way down from the Pacific Northwest. Meteorologists advised San Franciscans to stay indoors and warned of flooded highways and collapsed power lines. I found out about the storm from a viral video on Twitter of a huge oak tree in Napa Valley uprooting during a wine tasting. Napa was only sixty miles north, so I went to the Trader Joe's on Hyde Street to pick up storm supplies. There was something staticky and electric in the droplet-filled air you could almost feel on your tongue. At Trader Joe's, I joined a long line extending out to the parking lot made up mostly of roommate groups and families. They were talking in a weirdly excited tone about the storm, how much property damage it would cause, what would happen to the homeless, which board games they'd play together to pass the time during the stay-at-home order. I just picked up a few frozen meals, a carton of ice cream, and two bottles of wine. After all, I only needed to get through the weekend.

After dropping off my supplies at my apartment, I decided to go for a walk before the storm hit and started trudging up the hill toward North Beach. When I reached the top of the hill, where the road flattened out, the Bay Bridge suddenly loomed into view and you could see down Broadway about three hundred feet straight to the heaving black water. I had an apocalyptic vision of the water swelling up during the storm and swallowing the steep neighborhood block by block—picking up cars, neon store signs, and garbage bins on its way up.

At City Lights Bookstore, I noticed a woman standing by herself in front of the window display. She appeared to be looking at the books in the display, but something about her bearing made it obvious she was waiting for someone. She was about forty-five feet away and facing away from me, but after two or three seconds I got the gut feeling that this woman could be no one other than Vivian.

She started walking again as soon as I got closer. I tried to keep my distance at first, but then she made a sharp left onto a crowded, narrow side street and I had to pick up the pace. Was it just my imagination, or was she moving faster now? I thought about calling out to her, but the fear she might actually turn around held me back. Then, seemingly out of nowhere, I saw a Muni bus leave its stop, and the flicker of a black Chelsea boot lift from the pavement.

It was a harrowing way to start the weekend. Back in my apartment, I looked up Vivian on Samarkand and saw that she had been inactive for three days. I tried picking up a job, but couldn't get myself to focus. I went downstairs to look for Daniel, Tony, and Jeffrey, but realized they had left town hours ago. There were no texts on my phone—not even Lawrence or Jessica checking in about the storm.

I don't remember much about the rest of the weekend besides the rain battering against the windows and the concurrent crescendo of dread that blared deafeningly in my ears. I closely monitored the string of flight cancellations coming out of SFO. Now that my departure date was so soon, it became increasingly obvious to me that the consequences of my actions had spiraled outside of my control. I began to fear—irrationally, I thought at the time—that I was being watched. In response, I holed myself up in my apartment and diminished to an incapacitated state. The nonstop rain seemed to erode the sense of time passing. Drinking served as a way to lubricate the glacial creep of time, and my only consolation was that every so often Vivian would visit me in my feverish dreams.

On Sunday morning, a few hours before my scheduled departure, the storm cleared. I looked out the window and saw the streets filled again with people. Feeling suddenly afflicted with premature nostalgia, I decided to see the city one last time and started walking downtown with no destination in particular. In Lower Nob Hill, the Hugo Gallery caught my eye—Vivian and I had stopped in here after our Sunday afternoon at SFMOMA a few weeks ago. I made some small talk with the middle-aged curator, an Israeli man with an immaculately groomed beard. He asked me where I lived and I told him I was moving to Beijing today, which piqued his interest. When he found out I was an executive at a Chinese tech company, he rose from his desk and offered me a tour. The paintings were abstract, stimulating, and above all else, gave the aura of priceless objects—all were large format, clearly designed to lavish impressive rooms. I wasn't paying much attention to the specifics the curator mentioned, only picking up that the broad genre on display was contemporary American abstract, which he repeatedly emphasized the global appeal of, particularly for audiences overseas.

When we reached the end of the exhibit, he told me he had even more inventory to show me on the second floor, so we took the stairs up. I wandered around the floor for a bit and started gravitating toward an unusual oil painting in a poorly lit corner of the room. It depicted a slim, teenage Chinese girl sitting with her legs crossed on an ottoman in front of a sunny balcony. She was wearing a thin, strapless olive-green dress that revealed her brittle, bird-like shoulders and rode up a hand's length from her hip. Most of her face was obscured by an old-school film camera, and the blackness of the camera lens sucked in the viewer's attention. Indeed, the zoom lens of the camera seemed to break through the cracked surface of the painting and bore into your eyes. As I studied the painting, an unsettling feeling of recognition started to build up inside me, like coming across something in real life you saw first in a dream. The shape of the girl's face, her hands and shoulders—was I losing my mind, seeing her everywhere I looked? Then I read the artist's signature in the corner of the frame: Vincent Lim.

"Excuse me—who is this artist, Vincent Lim?" I asked, my voice shaking.

"Ah, I see you are admiring *Girl and Camera*. It's a very special piece, though I don't know too much about the artist. This one in particular I'm afraid has already been spoken for."

"How did this get here? And how long has it been here?" I said, suddenly alarmed by how loud my voice was. The curator looked confused.

"We received a special request from a long-standing client overseas to acquire this particular piece on his behalf. I was not personally involved. I really can't tell you much more. The painting's collector insisted on the utmost privacy, which is why the piece is on our second floor. I'm very sorry, I should have covered it."

I looked at the impossible painting once more and felt the terror of discovering an anomaly in the universe. "I'm sorry, but I feel sick. I have to go."

Now the curator was following me on my way to the stairwell with a concerned look on his face. "I'm very sorry, sir. Would you like a glass of water?"

"No, thank you," I said. "But I have to go now."

I rushed out of the gallery and back to my apartment, where I grabbed my bags and immediately called an Uber. On the way to the airport, I found myself turning over the two unexplained events from the weekend in my head over and over again, convinced they must be connected. Surely there must have been some stray detail, a telltale clue that I overlooked. There was something surreptitious about flying by night, and as I traveled over the Pacific Ocean I felt myself steeped in dread, as if past, present, and future were collapsing in on me and I was hurtling toward a fate I'd somehow already been forewarned of.

15

My flight landed in the early afternoon, and to my relief, Xiaowen was already waiting for me in the international arrivals area, holding a sign with my name on it. He helped me load my baggage into the trunk of the black Audi and we departed for Beijing.

My apartment complex was in the Sanlitun District, where most of Beijing's expats lived. Seeing us approaching from the other side of the street, the guard nodded to Xiaowen and raised the gate for us. The sprawling compound had five or six high-rise apartment buildings, tennis courts, a gym, even its own grocery store and restaurant. Xiaowen brought me to the welcome center, where the cheery young receptionist explained the amenities of the complex and how to use them. There were group exercise classes in the quad every morning as well as wine/coffee classes in the restaurant and book clubs in the clubhouse. I was in Building C on the fourteenth floor, apartment 1415. I could access my unit and all the shared facilities using my key card, which reminded me of college. The receptionist had me look into a webcam that was sitting on her counter to take an ID picture for their database. All entrances and common areas, she explained, were continuously monitored by security cameras that used facial-recognition technology to identify nonresidents.

Xiaowen drove me to Building C and we took the elevator up to the fourteenth floor. I tapped my key card against the digital lock and pushed open the door. The place was a bit smaller than my loft in SF, a tight 600, maybe 650 square feet, but had high ceilings and large windows that let in a lot of light. It was a park-facing unit, which meant you couldn't see the city through the windows, just the self-contained common areas of the complex. In the bathroom, body lotion, shampoo, and conditioner were all prefilled in the shower bottles. I did a walk-through and took stock of the furniture, which was nice enough, though obviously mass-produced and had that generic, faux-Scandinavian look that made me think of a WeWork. I felt a sharp pang in my chest remembering the antique redwood table I had left behind in San Francisco, which was now just gathering dust in Chinatown; it had taken me forever to find, why hadn't I arranged to have it sent over? Or my La Marzocco espresso machine, or the collection of Bearbrick figurines I had spent months collecting? There was a letter written on Terra Cotta Capital stationery on the desk in my bedroom explaining that the firm was pleased to offer me the use of this unit indefinitely and gratis as long as I was employed with them.

I circled back to the living room, sunk into the couch, and noticed that Xiaowen had left. Gradually, a small sense of relief and even excitement began to stretch inside me. Though the aparthotel was not at all my design sensibility, there was enough empty space to imagine it as a canvas for a fresh start. I imagined filling the space with the life that Vivian and I would build together, the slow accumulation of small things: toothbrushes on the sink, magazines on the coffee table, flowers in vases, jars in the pantry. I was filled with the sudden imperative to prepare this place for her, for our reunion later today. I put on a clean shirt and headed out toward Sanlitun Road.

Taikoo Li Sanlitun was filled with attractive, carefree people wandering the shops who had no work to accomplish during the day. My first order of business was to make myself presentable for Vivian, so I dropped into a salon and got a haircut. Next I spent a few hours at the mall buying new clothes, picking up several new shirts, sneakers, and a few pairs of chinos.

Afterward, I went to a Western supermarket in the subterranean level of Taikoo Li Sanlitun and bought some things that I thought we might need: toothbrushes, wine, towels, candles, coffee beans, cooking oil, fresh vegetables, pastries, pasta, filet mignon. I looked forward to preparing our first meal together that evening, the two of us working in the kitchen together each with a glass of wine in hand. My last stop was at a florist just off the main Sanlitun Road. I bought a bouquet of hyacinths, poppies, chrysanthemums, and daffodils, as well as a vase to put them in.

Over the next two hours, I leisurely put everything in its right place. I showered, put on my new clothes, sunk the flowers in the vase, and lit the candle. I'm not sure why, in the end, I was surprised that her call never came.

16

My first thought was that maybe something awful had happened to Vivian. Perhaps she had been abducted by an Uyghur resistance group or a gang of organ traffickers. A lot could go wrong in two weeks. Maybe that mysterious, omnipotent father of hers had caught wind of her plan to meet me and sent his henchmen to take her back to Hong Kong. None of these were as horrifying to me as the possibility that she had simply changed her mind. There were, of course, any number of explanations as to why she didn't call me that day, but for the sake of my sanity, I preferred to focus on the ones where I could rescue her.

In any case, it was too early to start worrying. There was probably a benign explanation for her radio silence, something as simple as her phone breaking or an unfortunate travel delay—in which case, I was convinced, she would reach out soon through other channels. No matter what, I had my first day at the new job to prepare for, and I couldn't let any unfounded anxieties derail my first impression.

The next morning, I steeled my nerves with a double-shot espresso and set out to my first meeting with Bo. The day was bright without being oppressively warm. I was wearing a black suit, brown loafers, and a white shirt with no tie. In my backpack was the hard drive containing my files from General Motors.

I descended into the subway and it was a quick three-stop ride to Guomao, or Central Business District. A tunnel took me from the subway doors through a subterranean mall directly to Terra Cotta's lobby. I showed my photo ID at the front desk and took the elevator up to the fiftieth floor. The receptionist told me I was a few minutes early and asked me to take a seat.

To my surprise, I ended up waiting in the lobby for nearly an hour. Every now and then, someone would pass through and give me an odd look; I must have looked like I was here for an interview. Finally, Bo stepped out of the hallway wearing a thick gray cardigan and greeted me.

"Sorry I kept you waiting, Michael," he said, gripping my hand tightly. "I'm glad you made the journey safely. Come, follow me, we'll talk in my office."

Bo's corner office was sparsely decorated, save for a few framed pictures of Bo doing impressive-looking activities: giving a keynote, cutting a ribbon to commemorate the opening of a factory, sitting at a banquet with political leaders. He kept a lot of books conspicuously lying around, a mix of Chinese and English titles, though some of the English-language books were embarrassingly elementary, like *The Great Gatsby* or *1984*. Bo gestured for me to take a seat on the L-shaped sectional, and his assistant brought in some tea and steamed buns.

"Please, eat," he said. "You must be hungry. How's the apartment?"

"The apartment is incredible," I said. "Thank you so much for arranging it."

Bo waved his hand. "It's nothing, Michael! We just wanted to make sure you're comfortable. Sanlitun is a trendy place for young people. If you need anything, just let me know. Now, I must ask . . . was there any problem with your departure from the US?"

"No problems. Everything went smoothly."

"I'm happy to hear that. Then you have the materials we discussed?"

I took the hard drive out of my backpack and handed it to him. Bo nodded. "Very good, Michael. I knew we could count on you."

A pleasant lull came in the conversation. Bo took a bite out of a steamed bun and I poured some tea for us.

"So, Michael, now that you've settled in, it's like a new start for you. I wanted to ask you—what is your mission in life?"

The question caught me off guard. I had not contemplated my "mission in life"—or even entertained the seriousness of such a concept—since writing my common app essay my senior year of high school.

"I want to make the most out of the opportunity you've given me. I hope we have the chance to work together for a very long time."

"Of course, Michael. I have the highest confidence in you, that's why I brought you in. You're going to do great things in China and make a lot of money. But every man must live for more than himself alone."

I didn't know what to say. "Sorry, what do you mean?"

"Every man is born in a particular place in a particular time. Every time and place has its unique challenges, so our birthright is to inherit these challenges. It is a great honor. Do you understand this?"

"Yes."

"Let me give you an example. I was born in 1965. My father was a cook in the People's Liberation Army. Our home was in Heilongjiang, a very cold and impoverished place. Everyone was poor. But, I was born during an important time in history. When I became a young man, Deng Xiaoping declared 'To get rich is glorious.' China would open itself to the world and develop socialism with Chinese characteristics, starting with the development of the manufacturing industry."

I nodded, recalling the rough outline of Bo's subject from a modern China class I had taken many years ago. Deng Xiaoping was Mao Zedong's successor in the Chinese Communist Party; he led the economic reforms of the 1990s that made China the "factory of the world."

"After I graduated from college, I went back to support my family in Heilongjiang, working as a civil engineer for the provincial government. There were three generations, ten people in total, living under one roof. At the time, my father was too sick to work, and it was a very difficult time for my family. But I left them to answer Deng Xiaoping's call for young men to perform revolutionary works, and moved to Shenzhen. They cried out and said they'd never forgive me, but I knew I had no choice; it was my place in history. In Shenzhen, I opened a factory to manufacture trucking parts. I failed many times, but knew I could never give up; I had a responsibility to my workers, to their families. Finally, we were successful. I opened many more factories and made powerful friends. In Shenzhen, I met my wife, and many years later, I moved to Beijing and started a family."

Bo's voice softened as he continued. "I have many regrets too. When I left Heilongjiang, my big sister stayed behind. Growing up, we were best friends—inseparable. I had such a big appetite, and whenever we ate together she always saved her last bite of meat for me. But after I left, she never spoke to me again, and she passed away three years ago."

Bo picked up a picture of his family that was sitting within reach and showed it to me.

"I have my own family now too. Terra Cotta was formed ten years ago. I already made a lot of money before that, and my wife has been asking me to retire for many years. This is my only son, Kevin. Because of how much I work, I rarely get to see him. But I continue to do what I must do, because now we are in different times with new challenges."

Here Bo paused again, and when he did, I noticed that I was hanging on his every word.

"Michael, you came to Beijing during an important time in history. We're reaching an inflection point. After Deng's economic reforms, China became the fastest growing economy in the world. Millions rose from poverty. But this progress is not sustainable. Now that ordinary people have money, they don't want to work in factories anymore.

Everyone is moving to the city. Global companies have started relocating their factories to cheaper places: Vietnam, Thailand, Laos. That's why Li Keqiang announced a new national initiative: Made in China 2025. China will become the world leader in the most important technologies for the future. By 2025, we will make the best smartphones, semiconductors, and smart vehicles in the world—we'll unlock creative energy and bring lasting prosperity to people who have waited several lifetimes. We must do this, because if we don't, China will remain a second-world country forever.

"That's why my partners and I started Terra Cotta. Our mandate is to invest in the strategic industries Li Keqiang identified for Made in China 2025. We will make the world champions in these industries. Artificial intelligence, 5G, clean energy, advanced robotics. So you see, Michael, you were born in the United States, but now fate brings you to Beijing. I think you came just in time."

After Bo finished his remarks, I sat back in awe. Now the room was completely silent and something stirred inside me. I recognized it as inspiration but also something more—perhaps the feeling of being ensconced in history.

"It's an honor to be part of this mission," I said. "When do I get started at Naveon? Any advice for my first few weeks?"

Bo shook his head. "You will need to be patient, Michael. It's not the right time to bring you into the organization yet. Things are disorganized at Naveon right now; Peng tells me there are some issues with the core technology, specifically with the 5G chip and the internal combustion engine. We need to wait for a more stable time to introduce you as the new VP of R&D."

"Oh, okay. That makes sense. Do you have any idea how long that will be? Or what I can do in the meantime?"

Bo shook his head. "Hard to say—could be a month, maybe several months. In the meantime, it would be best if you can try and get in touch with some former colleagues or classmates to see if they can share anything that can help the team. While we wait for the right moment to bring you into the organization."

I blinked. "You mean see if I can get any of my connections to send me IP?"

"Yes, correct."

"Got it. Is there anything specific I should be looking for?"

"For now, it will be good to cast a wide net. Feel free to send whatever you find directly to me."

I nodded. Bo smiled and excused himself, saying he had to catch a flight to Tokyo. Just as he disappeared into the corridor, I thought, for a moment, about whether to ask him about Vivian's whereabouts, but something held me back.

17

Several days passed with complete radio silence from both Bo and Vivian.

Something about the offhanded way that Bo had asked me to recruit others to steal IP deeply unsettled me. I'd uprooted myself and come to Beijing partially because Bo had seen great potential in me. If he really thought I was so capable, wouldn't he want me in the trenches helping fix the roadblocks, not waiting on the sidelines? After agonizing for several days, I decided to pitch the idea of letting me join the company early, so I called Bo's cell phone several times, but he never answered. Every time, it went straight to voicemail. Finally, I resorted to calling his office and spoke to his assistant, who didn't know who I was and told me she couldn't put me through because Bo was stuck in important meetings. I found that confusing—if Bo's assistant didn't know I was joining Naveon, then who did?

Three days after our meeting, I went back through my Samarkand DMs to Vivian's original message from January and discovered that her account had been deactivated one day ago. This new information greatly alarmed me. Samarkand accounts didn't automatically delete themselves, no matter the period of inactivity. Further, the platform is obscure enough that even if Vivian had been abducted, it's very unlikely her captors would have known about it. I had to confront the overwhelming likelihood that she herself, for one reason or another, had chosen to deactivate her account without notifying me.

By day three, the flowers I'd fetched were starting to wilt in their vase. I'd shut myself in the apartment so completely I could almost watch it happen in real time. Flies were starting to multiply, attracted by the growing pile of takeout boxes from the delivery meals I'd ordered on Meituan.

Paranoia set in. I knew Bo and Vivian were connected—could her sudden disappearance have something to do with the situation at Naveon? Maybe Bo was hiding her from me and the key to her release was me delivering something valuable to the project. What if, on the other hand, they were somehow conspiring together against me?

On day five, I had an idea: what if Vivian had left a clue for me somewhere? I combed through my memory of places she'd mentioned. And then it came to me: X Wood, the name of the gallery in 798 Art Zone she'd worked during the summer she turned seventeen. I typed the name into Google and found the place immediately.

X Wood—798 Art Zone D-06

No. 4 Jiuxianqiao Road, Chaoyang, Beijing

Founded in 1996 by visionary curator Miss Liuwen, X Wood has been a fixture of Beijing's modern establishment for nearly three decades. The gallery is known for exhibiting works of utopian avant-garde as well as cynical realism. Appointments required.

I slammed my laptop shut and called a car immediately.

After twenty minutes, I reached the border of the 798 Art Zone. The Zone was constituted by an array of decommissioned military structures from the Soviet Union–People's Republic of China industrial cooperation in the 1950s. The vast structures, gray and austere, made you think of cathedrals and bomb shelters at the same time.

The car stopped in front of X Wood, a diminutive, cerulean building tucked away on one of the side streets. It was a Tuesday afternoon and the place was almost empty. There was one attendant there, and I asked her where I could find Miss Liuwen. She asked me if I had an appointment.

"I'm very sorry. Unfortunately, it's really urgent; this has to do with a missing person case involving someone who worked for Miss Liuwen several years ago. I'll be happy to wait as long as necessary."

"Oh," she said, a look of unwelcome surprise falling across her soft features. "In that case . . . I suppose you can take a seat."

I waited on a small plastic stool in front of the gallery's entrance for an hour and a half. Finally, a door on the other side of the gallery opened and the attendant gestured for me to enter. When I walked in, I found Miss Liuwen sitting at her desk writing something down in her notebook. She was an elegant woman in her late fifties who wore thick, black-rimmed glasses. She glanced up at me and gestured for me to take a seat in the armchair across from her desk.

"Michael, please. Have a seat. Jingyi tells me you have a problem you think I can help with. She says it's quite urgent."

"Yes, sorry to bother you. I'm looking for my friend Vivian, who has gone missing. She's an art collector and worked as your assistant for a summer eight or nine years ago. I wonder if she's been in touch with you lately or if you have any other information that might help me find her."

"My assistant? Vivian, Vivian . . . that doesn't ring a bell. Did she go by any other name?"

"No," I said, even though I didn't even know that Vivian was her real name.

"Okay. Why don't you show me a picture of her?"

"Actually, I don't have a picture."

Miss Liuwen looked at me skeptically. "You don't have a photo of the missing friend you're looking for?"

"That's correct," I said. Then I described Vivian in as much detail as possible, emphasizing the scar on her chin. Miss Liuwen shook her head.

"I'm sorry, Michael. Except for the scar, the woman you described resembles a lot of young girls in Beijing. But I don't remember anyone with that name or that scar. Seven or eight years ago, let's see . . . ah yes, back then I had an assistant named Jennifer who was with me for several years." She showed me a picture from her phone of a girl who looked nothing like Vivian. "I don't suppose this is the person you're looking for?"

"No, that's not her . . ." I said, my voice trailing off. An awkward pause entered our conversation. Then I had another idea. "Actually, this would have been the summer you were exhibiting a Chinese painter named Vincent Lim, who was studying at Beijing University. Does that ring a bell?"

Miss Liuwen blinked slowly and gave me a strange look. "It's very odd you say that. We did exhibit a painter named Vincent Lim many years ago. He's quite obscure, and to be honest I'm very surprised you've heard his name. But Vincent Lim was definitely not enrolled in Beijing University that summer. My exhibition was a retrospective—Vincent worked in the 1950s and died young of Creutzfeldt-Jakob disease in 1959."

The vertigo I first felt at the Hugo Gallery came lurching back. I started sweating profusely. "I—I see. Thank you for your time," I said.

"Best of luck," she said with a slightly pitying expression on her face.

Within a few hours, the longing and restlessness I'd endured since my arrival in Beijing metastasized into anger. This was irrefutable evidence that Vivian had lied to me. If the story she'd told me about her summer in Beijing was made up, what else had she been lying about? Shaken with grief, I threw away the extra toothbrush, towels, and house slippers that I had prepared for her. For the next few days, I shut myself in the apartment, unable to sleep and completely paralyzed with dread. I called Bo's office five separate times, but each time his assistant said that he was unreachable due to work travel. I started experiencing panic attacks and felt I was losing my grip over reality.

Who knows how much longer I would have stayed in this purgatory. But on the eighth day, I got an email from my mother that pulled me out.

My Michael,

Where are you? I tried calling you so many times but it goes straight to voicemail.

You know I don't like to bother you. This time I have no choice. My hands started to shake just like your grandfather's. Now I can feel my leg getting limp too. I always knew this would happen one day, but I thought I had more time. Maybe it's punishment for leaving your grandfather alone back home.

I'm not sure what I should do. What do you think I should do?

Love,

Mom

18

I thought about my mom during the entire flight. I was afraid of seeing the toll that the disease and the years I'd let pass by had taken on her. I'd visited her just once since moving to California nearly five years ago, right after I graduated from college. The reason I saw her so rarely was Gary, the American guy she started seeing after my father disappeared. To me, Gary's relationship with my mother felt unnatural and I didn't like how soon after my father's disappearance I first started seeing him around.

We never celebrated a traditional American Thanksgiving, and I'd actually come at the insistence of Gary, who reminded me that my mom's birthday was the day after. I flew to Newark and took the 166 bus from Port Authority to the Hillside Avenue stop in Tenafly. From there it was a twenty-minute walk to my childhood home. On the way, I passed by the low red-brick façade of my middle school, the Stop & Shop where my mom and I went every Saturday to buy groceries, and the Vietnamese café I'd taken Jessica to on our first date. I felt warmed and recentered by the familiar sites, which seemed to dissolve the anomie that had been building up inside me like asbestos since I moved to San Francisco.

There was a new car in the driveway. My mother answered the door wearing more makeup than usual and a stiff, boxy dress that looked unnatural on her. In the living room, I found Gary reclined on the couch watching football on a new Walmart-sized flat-screen TV. I reluctantly sat down next to him while my mom went back to the kitchen to continue working on the turkey. I noticed Gary was wearing my father's old wooden house sandals—the sides of his wide, flat feet spilled over the edges. When he finished his beer, my mom took the bottle away and brought him another one. I stiffened when he squeezed her shoulder.

"Add some more scallions into the stuffing, okay? I love that stuff now," he said.

Gary asked me if I watched football and I said no. These were the sorts of questions we were still on. Since they didn't live together, it was easy to avoid him during most of high school and all of college. There'd been some tension between us since last spring when I'd explicitly not invited him to my college graduation. I'd made the argument that since they weren't married, he wasn't technically my stepdad or any recognized part of the family; in reality, I just didn't want him in the pictures, didn't like how he made my mother look cheap standing next to him.

Later in the afternoon, the doorbell rang and six members of Gary's extended family poured in. There was Gary's brother Tony and Tony's two daughters as well as two cousins of ambiguous affiliation. Between all six of them they'd brought a cherry pie and a dish of mashed potatoes. While the greetings went around the foyer, my mother tensed up and looked lost in her own home. The relatives crowded into the kitchen and ate the appetizers my mom made, then piled onto the couch to watch football. My mom brought more beer and chips to the living room before retreating back to the kitchen where I went to join her. I found her squinting at a recipe for green bean casserole she'd printed out while awkwardly mixing cream of mushroom soup, milk, and black pepper together in a dish. I was certain she didn't know what a "casserole" was. Growing up, I never saw her follow a recipe; she cooked based on memory and intuition alone, had a natural way with Chinese ingredients. My father especially loved her food, in particular the handmade pork dumplings she made for us every Friday night—he said the same thing at the end of each meal, which was that no one in the world could make dumplings that tasted like my mom's. Seeing her now looking so confused, crowded in by cans of cranberry sauce and green beans, I felt at first infuriated by the burden that this Thanksgiving dinner had placed on her, then resentful toward her for submitting to it. Why was she in the back of her own home cooking a feast for these strangers? And why was I back here with her?

We stirred, chopped, and whisked in silence; half an hour passed where we couldn't find words to say to each other. Had it always been this way, or was I making myself forget about the good times?

"I'm glad you're home, my son," she said weakly. It didn't feel much like home to me; I told her I was going on a walk and left her alone in the kitchen. I took the keys to my dad's old car and drove around town. It was dusk now, and this time around the place looked drab and alien to me. As I circled by Roosevelt Common on Jefferson Avenue, I saw the two cousins sitting on a park bench smoking pot. In a moment of desperation, I texted Jessica to see if she was around.

Hey! Nah not around ☹ With Nick's family in Connecticut!

When I returned my mother was anxiously laying out her spread on the kitchen counter. Gary's entourage lined up buffet-style to fill their plates while I looked for more chairs around the house to fit everyone. After everyone else was seated, my mother fixed her own plate and sat down with us.

"Please, let's eat," she said, raising a glass. "If anyone needs something—"

"Hold on now, we still have to say grace," Tony interrupted. "Gary, you want to lead us?"

Gary awkwardly clasped his hands together and we bowed our heads. I saw my mother peeking at Tony's daughters, trying to copy their hand position.

" . . . and may we always remember to be grateful for the gifts we have been given. Amen."

There was a clattering of silverware, then Gary asked one of Tony's daughters, a college-aged puffy-faced brunette to tell us about the study abroad in Ireland she'd just come back from. During the story, the other daughter, who was slightly younger, kept glancing at me and making a face at her sister like there was something funny about my presence here. Tony heaped praise on the mashed potatoes that one of the cousins brought even though they were over-buttered and congealed. My mother didn't say a word the entire dinner, just looked around anxiously to see how her food was being received and occasionally excusing herself to fetch another bottle of wine. Gary's relatives left at around ten o'clock in the evening, thanking us profusely, and when their cars finally pulled out of the driveway, my mother looked relieved and almost happy. She got started on the dishes while Gary helped store the leftovers in Tupperware. Something about the way they moved in sync around the tight kitchen made me feel like an intruder, so I excused myself.

I slipped through the hallway and opened the door of my childhood bedroom. I was surprised to see that my mother had made the bed for me, something she never did when I visited from college. It wasn't until I laid down on the bed that I noticed the home planetarium still sitting on my nightstand, its dark lens speckled with dust. As I stared at the planetarium, its projector lens started to look like a camera, and I turned away. The room looked exactly the same as it had during high school. My old tennis trophies were still lined up on the bookshelf, from the tournaments across the state my mother always drove me to on Saturday mornings. We'd spoken very little during high school; the issue of my father's disappearance loomed like a black hole that hopelessly sucked every other possible topic into its dark gravity, so I kept her at arm's length and poured myself into academics. I looked at the laundry basket at the foot of my bed and the stainless steel thermos on my desk. It wasn't uncommon for three or four days to pass during which our only interaction was her picking up the laundry hamper or refilling my thermos with tea when I studied late into the night. I suppose, in her own way, that she had done her best for me. I laid back but was too restless to sleep. I watched the light from the hallway seep in under my door and felt an urge to go see my father's study.

I knew before I even turned the lights on—everything had been cleared out. The broken computer chair my father had occupied for ten years, the old picture of him and my mother with their arms wrapped around each other in Pebble Beach, the gold medal I'd won in sixth grade Science Olympiad. In the place of all these things was a monstrous, Gary-sized massage chair in the middle of the room that smelled like fake leather and a mini fridge stocked with Budweiser. A crooked nine-foot indoor putting mat had been unrolled on one side of the tiny room. As I surveyed the desecrated room, an unbearable sense of anger and humiliation took shape inside of me and directed itself toward my mother. She'd allowed this to happen, I realized; she held some responsibility. Even though she was the only person who could've helped him, she'd driven my father away by ignoring the disease that was consuming him, and now she'd erased his memory entirely. Whatever fragile peace I'd achieved since he left seemed to collapse and I resolved to never forgive her for this.

At breakfast the next morning, Gary sang my mother's praises for hosting last night and talked excitedly about the hike he wanted to take us on before her birthday lunch at an Italian restaurant downtown. My mother was scooping bowls of congee and asked me if I wanted a soft-boiled egg in mine. As soon as she sat down, I told her that I needed to go back to San Francisco today to work on something urgent for my job and that I was sorry to miss her birthday.

She fell silent, and for a moment her expression crumpled, which she hid with two hard blinks. When she opened her eyes again, they were wide and brimming with tears, but there was also a tinge of resignation in her expression that caught me off guard.

"Wait," she said finally, her voice quivering. Then she went to the fridge and came back with a large bag of her frozen dumplings. "Take this with you. I put in ice packs so it'll survive the flight back. You can eat it in San Francisco just like at—if you have no food."

"Thank you, Mom, but I really can't fit that in my suitcase. Besides, I can buy my own food."

"Okay then," she said, still holding onto the corners of the bag with both hands. I got up and gathered the bags I had packed the night before. I caught a glimpse of her on my way out the door. She was still standing in the hallway looking at me; her shoulders were hunched over and she appeared to be shaking.

Even in all this time, I'd never been able to put that image out of mind. I couldn't let that be my last memory of her.

The captain's cabin announcement to secure our seatbelts and prepare for landing alerted me to the fact that we had breached American airspace. Thirty minutes later, the plane connected on the runway with a shuddering throttle that gave me the unsettling sensation of being re-aborted onto native soil. Moving through the Jetway, I tried to reshelve the memories that had been dislodged during the flight and focus on the task at hand. But when I reached the gate, something looked wrong. Two large men in blue jackets were leaning against the far wall.

There was a Chinese American man and a brown man. As soon as they spotted me, their broad bodies sprang into action and homed in on me. The Chinese American man wrung my hands behind my back and handcuffed me while the brown man read my Miranda rights. As they marched me through the crowded terminal, I kept staggering as the force of the agent's hand at my back constantly threatened to push me over. Somewhere a side door opened and the men ushered me through it to a gray room where they photographed and fingerprinted me. Then, they brought me to a different, smaller room down the hallway with no windows and left me alone there for about five minutes.

It's important for you to understand that prior to this, I had never really gotten in trouble. The last time I had been so nakedly at the mercy of the authorities was in Mrs. Greenberg's classroom in the sixth grade. I'd let Tiffany Chen, a girl I was too afraid to approach even in Club Penguin, copy my earth science homework, which Mrs. Greenberg explained was as bad as doing the copying myself. Now if Tiffany had copied my homework *without* my permission, Mrs. Greenberg said, now was the time to tell the truth, before adding that Tiffany herself was waiting in the classroom next door. I remember saying loudly with my lunchbox-sized chest that not only had I *let* Tiffany copy my homework, I had *offered* it to her in the first place. Mrs. Greenberg shook her head and wrote something down with exaggerated slowness, as if inscribing it onto my permanent record. Then she called my mother in. My mother's voice was shaking as she pleaded for Mrs. Greenberg to give me another chance, to count on her to punish me, if only to spare my future at the school. Even then, sitting in the interrogation room, I wondered if my mother was looking in through a two-way mirror, begging the agents for forgiveness on my behalf.

The men came back into the room and took their seats across from me. They introduced themselves as Agent Lim and Agent Reddy from the FBI. Agent Lim spoke first.

"On April 1, an individual named Bo Song reached out to you and you met him for breakfast at the Ritz Carlton in San Francisco. He invited you to an academic conference in Beijing the following week, where you negotiated a deal to transfer software belonging to the General Motors Company in exchange for a cash payment of $250,000, a package of stock options from a Chinese start-up called Naveon, and a promotion. On April 30, you used an external hard drive to steal all of the files, then quit on the spot and left for China the next morning."

The agent paused abruptly, scanning my face and body for involuntary movements. I felt every twitch and spasm in my face magnified by the overhead lighting in the room and focused on steadying my breathing.

"Now let me tell you something you don't know," he continued. "The software that you traded was worthless. I had our technology experts at the bureau look into it—they said your 'multinodal aggregation' had been independently achieved—and then abandoned—by at least six companies in the US and China as far back as 2015."

"That can't be right," I blurted out. My voice sounded shaky but came out louder than I expected. "The technological building blocks of multinodal aggregation were only formulated a year ago. You don't know what you're talking about."

Agent Lim leaned back in his chair with a smirk on his face and let the bubble of my outburst hang in the air for a moment. "You sure about that, Michael? Even Newton and Leibniz invented calculus at the same time. Really, ask yourself how it could possibly be the case—that of the dozens of teams around the world, each with hundreds of engineers focused solely on these seemingly unsolvable problems, that *only you*, working by yourself no more than thirty hours each week, managed to crack the code in one year? I've seen this story play out before, Michael. Probably about a dozen times now. He made you feel special, didn't he? Saw something in you everybody else couldn't, or wouldn't, see?"

When I realized Agent Lim was right, I found myself suddenly unable to meet his gaze.

"Obviously, the Chinese knew this when they recruited you. Are you beginning to understand now? The hard drive you inserted into your laptop on April 30 uploaded a Trojan horse into the General Motors cloud that gave the Chinese access to the entire company's file directory. That would make it the most significant US–China industrial breach in the past decade. It's over, Michael. You left evidence on every possible surface—we have emails, flight itineraries, illegal download activity. You'll face charges of economic espionage and theft of trade secrets that carry a sentence of up to fifteen years. The best thing you can do now is cooperate with the investigation and get your affairs in order."

Just as Agent Lim finished, the door behind him opened and another man motioned for him to step into the hallway. I was left alone with Agent Reddy, who told me not to worry about my mother and apologized for the email, which Agent Lim had written himself. The funereal suggestion of getting my affairs in order hung in the air—I felt I had been charged, tried, convicted, and buried in the space of thirty seconds. A few minutes later, Agent Lim was back, this time accompanied by a jowly man in a pinstripe suit, who took the seat directly facing me while the two agents flanked him. With a finger on his chin, he studied me for several seconds. Then he introduced himself as Richard Scully, the US attorney for the Northern District of California. He was going to be the federal prosecutor handling my case, he said; why didn't I start by explaining my relationship with Bo and what I knew about him?

With the three-headed dog of the justice system staring me down, I took a moment to collect myself and began by addressing the thinking head. "Bo was the one who recruited me. I've only met him three times—the first time in San Francisco, the other two times in Beijing. I know he runs a China VC fund called Terra Cotta Capital, which invested in a self-driving start-up called Naveon. Bo was supposed to make me a VP of engineering at Naveon when I moved to China. But in the two-ish weeks I've been there, he kept stalling by saying the company's tech wasn't ready, and that I should go see if I can bring some expertise from outside of the company in."

"As in recruit American scientists?" Agent Lim interjected.

Scully made a quieting gesture with his hand. "I think it's fairly clear what that instruction meant. Okay. And did you carry out that order, so to speak?"

"No, I haven't. I swear," I said.

"Okay. That makes things a little easier. To continue this conversation, I need to tell you a couple things about the man you know as Bo. He's gone by many different names over the years. His real name is Yuanhong Wang. He's never been an entrepreneur or investor. 'Bo' is a high-ranking operative within the Ministry of State Security, which is loosely China's version of the CIA. He was born to a prominent family in Shanghai and graduated from Fudan University in Shanghai in 1987, which would make him about fifty-two years old. Bo first came to America in 1986 on an exchange program between Fudan and Fordham University. The MSS recruited him straight out of Fudan and he's never worked anywhere else. We know Bo has been visiting the US professionally since the early 2000s and built a considerable network of spies in America that we've only just started to untangle.

"Your case is unusual in two respects. The first is that all of the espionage cases we've been able to tie back to Bo have involved Chinese aliens. You are the first Chinese American—born on our soil, no less—to have been successfully converted. The second is that since my office has started to ramp up prosecution of Chinese economic espionage cases, Bo has been careful about leaving the country. According to our records, the April 1 San Francisco visit was his only domestic appearance in two years. We don't yet know why he would risk that for you."

"I'm sorry, why are you telling me this?" I said.

Scully looked at Agents Lim and Reddy before taking a deep breath and turning back to me. "It's a long shot, but we'd like to at least explore the possibility of working with you. This is called affirmative cooperation. With the evidence we uncovered during our investigation of you, we now have sufficient basis to arrest Bo. But first we need to lure him back to the US, and this is something we think you might be able to help us with."

"Wait, you want *my* help?" I blurted out. "What am I going to use to lure him out?"

"Not sure. You'll have to ask Agent Lim and Agent Reddy. That's their area of expertise."

I glanced over at the agents, but neither of them said a word or offered any sign of assent. "You said he is one of the most skilled operatives in the MSS," I said. "Why would you believe I can do this?"

Scully looked around the room wearily and rotated his empty coffee mug. "To be honest, I don't. As far as I can tell from this investigation, covering your tracks doesn't seem to come naturally to you. We'd have Agent Lim and Agent Reddy train you on tactics, of course. But considering the size of the prize, and the risk involved to you personally, I can give you my word that my office will set your case aside—if, and only if, you are successful."

I didn't really see another play here. How bad could affirmative cooperation get, compared to fifteen years in prison? "Okay," I said. "I'll do it." I waited for Scully to extend his hand, but all I got was a nod. Meanwhile, Agent Lim was clenching his jaw so hard I could almost hear it.

"I'm going to warn you, Michael," Scully said. "Bo is dangerous. Everything somehow gets back to him. China has successfully dismantled the CIA's intelligence network in the country over the past three years and all of our assets have gone offline. They can imprison you or worse without cause. We will of course do everything in our power to help you succeed. But if you choose this path, I'm afraid we won't be able to protect you in China."

Over the next two weeks, I met with Agent Lim and Agent Reddy every morning for six hours. Since I was now technically a government witness, the FBI put me up in a cheap motel off the New Jersey Turnpike. The purpose of these meetings was to go over the FBI's plan for luring Bo back into the United States. The mousetrap was going to be a list of veteran Chinese and Chinese American engineers and professors working in sensitive areas that the FBI had been monitoring. The plan was for me to pass along fabricated email exchanges between myself and these "assets" that alluded to meetings I had supposedly had with them about potential knowledge transfers. Over time, we'd use these conversations to feed Bo bits and pieces of IP—small wins but no landslide victories. Bo would start to see me as a valuable and trusted asset. When the right opportunity presented itself, we would dangle a large enough prize to convince him to risk leaving the country.

To carry out the job, I had to become fluent in the key technologies prized by the MSS as well as the biographies of each of the assets with whom I was supposedly corresponding. On the technology side, the main resource was the Chinese Communist Party's Made in China 2025 strategic planning document, which listed what China thought of as the key industries in its next phase of industrialization.

On the personnel side, the source material was a database of dossiers maintained by the China Initiative on persons that had come under suspicion. For example: [X—Z—], thirty-eight years old, expert in industrial IoT and data observability; born in Shaanxi Province, current resident of San Francisco; emigrated to the United States for graduate school at University of Illinois Urbana-Champaign in 2014; software engineer level 4 at Samsara; married with two sons, six and eight years old. Each file also contained more intimate details: XZ sent regular wire transfers to his brother in Xi'an who suffered from ALS; XZ's wife had attended

AA meetings in Outer Richmond. The most critical part of each profile was the "reason for suspicion." A few individuals had ended up on the list because of a dual appointment at a Chinese university, the fact that they had received Chinese government grant money, or made paid appearances at Chinese conferences. Other reasons struck me as less convincing. One profile cited "frequent trips back to China"; another simply said "disaffected at work." Most of the individuals felt just like my parents' circle of friends from New Jersey—normal Americans living their lives, unaware they lived under surveillance. Each morning, Agent Lim quizzed me on the contents of the files. For each person, I could recite birth date and location, hometown, names of immediate family members, career highlights and disappointments, and the top two or three areas of concern in their lives, all of which made me feel a personal connection with them. The only fictional aspect of it was how I knew them. I familiarized myself with two dozen or so dossiers in total. I wondered what the true magnitude of the government monitoring was but was too afraid to ask.

Another objective of the training was imparting some basic principles of espionage to reduce the likelihood that I'd get caught and spend the rest of my years in a Chinese prison. This section was thinner than I would have liked. The basic rules were: assume every room was bugged; convince yourself that you really are working on Bo's behalf; if you are discovered, do whatever you have to do to get to the US embassy before the authorities capture you. The rule they repeated most often was to *never* accidentally let slip Bo's real name. The agents repeated that what I had agreed to do broke Chinese law, and since the United States didn't have an extradition treaty with China, they wouldn't be able to get me out if I got caught. To my disappointment (though not surprise), no special gadgets were made available to me—no poison-tipped umbrellas, wristwatch cameras, or molar-embedded suicide pills, the latter being the only thing that crossed my mind to request.

Given what was in it for myself, I couldn't say that I expected any heartfelt appreciation for what I was helping the US government with. Agent

Lim, however, seemed to go out of his way to be cold to me, especially when Agent Reddy was around. Once when he and Agent Reddy were stepping out of the conference room at the same time for a break, Lim joked to Reddy that he shouldn't leave his laptop in the room alone with me or he'd have to buy it back on Taobao later. Reddy stiffened at the joke and for a second looked almost embarrassed.

It actually wasn't until the last meeting that I thought to ask how I'd get in contact with them while I was undercover. The question seemed to make Agent Reddy uneasy. His exact words: "We don't have a lot of good men in China anymore." He explained that they were setting me up with a handler named Ferris Guo, who was undercover as a language teacher. Reddy assured me I was in good hands—"one of our best"—before begging me again to be careful.

Later that night, I did some research on the internet and learned that at least a dozen CIA sources had been killed or imprisoned in China since 2010. The source of the leak was an ex-CIA agent born in Hong Kong named Jerry Chun Shing Lee, who had sold a list of CIA names to the MSS for hundreds of thousands of dollars. The mugshot from his arrest showed powerful, sloping shoulders; a broad, flat face; and the yellow eyes of a caged tiger. There was something almost admirable about the defiant way he stared into the camera.

19

Bo had ignored the first few emails. The hook was an adjunct professor at MIT named Dao Lin who was working on novel chemical processes applicable to electric vehicle battery design. I wrote in my email to Bo that Dao had joined MIT just a few months ago from a secret Ford research lab and therefore was likely to have had recent exposure to cutting-edge fabrication techniques. After a few days, Bo responded, asking about when he could speak with Dao on the phone. I introduced them over email and set up a dial-in for them to connect in two days. Apparently the call, which was fielded by another FBI agent posing as Dao, went well. After that, Bo invited me to lunch. The agents seemed pleased with this progress and arranged for me to fly back to Beijing the following evening.

Our lunch was set at a Peking duck restaurant in the busy Chaoyang District. I couldn't sleep the night before and was now running five minutes late. It was more than jet lag—Bo had been frightening enough as a ruthless businessman, but as an MSS operative? Maybe he already knew I was onto him; I pictured a waiter lurking in the corner with a chloroform-soaked towel tucked neatly into his waistcoat. When I finally arrived at the restaurant, I was surprised to find Bo sitting by himself at a table in the open, rather than in a private room, dressed in a polo shirt and khakis.

"Michael, it is good to see you!" he said, waving me over. "Thank you for being so understanding with the situation at Naveon. For an appointment of your stature, it is important to wait for the right moment—not a time when the organization is so distracted."

As soon as I sat down, the waiter set down a platter of roast duck carvings with spring onion, black bean sauce, and thin pancakes on the side. Bo beckoned for me to start. Remembering my manners, I poured tea for both of us, but got a little spatter on the tablecloth because my hands were shaky. "No, of course I understand," I said. "For now I'm just focused on doing everything I can to get Naveon on steady footing technology-wise."

"It's a good start," Bo said, and we clinked our teacups together. "So, how did you get to know this man you introduced me to, Dao?"

I recited the backstory that the FBI gave me: Dao did some graduate work at Princeton, I'm friendly with his former advisor, and asked him to put us in touch.

Bo rested his chopsticks on the table. "But earlier you told me you weren't in touch with anyone from Princeton?"

Was it a genuine question or did he suspect I was lying to him? Why had he stopped chewing?

"I just meant people I used to see socially, like in my graduating class," I said. "For professional contacts like this, I've made an effort to stay in touch over the years. Luckily I had a good relationship with Dao's advisor while I was a student, so he was quick to respond."

"I see. Fair enough. Relationships must be nurtured, you'll learn this soon enough. Will Dr. Lin come to China? For these things it is often good to meet face-to-face."

"I've asked him—he's too afraid to visit China, given the high-profile cases against other Chinese scientists in the past two years. I'm happy to act as a conduit for anything he shares with us. Maybe we can offer him an honorarium to show our appreciation for his time."

"Yes, an honorarium is a good idea. Though I should add that in these delicate situations, money really is just a way for us to show our appreciation, nothing more, certainly not a bribe. In my correspondences with many talented *haigui* over the years, Michael, I've noticed a few commonalities. Money is almost never the main motive. It's usually a patriotism of sorts that is difficult for those who grew up in the West to comprehend—a desire to help the motherland, as natural as a son returning home to take care of his elderly mother, even though he has a family of his own. Those who pursue science feel this noble instinct even more strongly than the average person because their entire existence is dedicated to improving the human condition. For them, it is an honor to lend help, not a service they provide for compensation. It is quite a shame that the government in America has criminalized this noble instinct."

To my surprise, his tone struck me as sincere. "You're right," I said carefully. "As you said to me once, good ideas need the right soil."

"That's right!" Bo said. Once again, we clinked our teacups together. "One more thing. Have you seen my niece lately?" His eyes were still smiling but seemed unusually watchful.

"Vivian?" I asked.

"Yes, Vivian. Her mother—my sister—called me the other day, hasn't been able to get ahold of her. This is not uncommon, as her interests seem to take her to far-flung places on short notice. The two of you seemed close, so I thought to ask."

"No, I haven't been able to get in touch with her. Will you let me know if you hear from her?"

"Of course. Anyway, how have the first two weeks in Beijing been for you? Anything interesting to report?"

Did he know that I went back to the US this weekend? Surely someone of his stature could pull my flight records.

"So far it's been good," I said. "Maybe a bit lonely. I haven't gotten around to making any friends yet."

"Oh, don't worry about that. I'll have my assistant Fanfan show you around. She's around your age. Free tomorrow, I'm guessing?"

"Sounds great," I said.

20

The next morning, I used my apartment complex's gym. The basic training Agent Lim and Agent Reddy provided made me realize how obvious it was that I was being watched. The staff in the apartment—and there were so many—would openly write down my comings and goings in a notebook.

At half past noon, my doorbell rang. A girl with short hair waited in my hallway, attractive but not intimidatingly so. As promised, about my age.

"Hi, Michael," she said. "I'm Fanfan, but you can call me Christine. Bo sent me here to give you this and take you out to lunch."

She handed me an envelope. "Thanks," I said. It was a platinum Amex with a sheet of paper instructing me to use the card for any of my expenses while traveling abroad. "You don't have to take me out for lunch though. You can just tell Bo we had lunch."

"No, Bo always knows when I'm lying. Plus, I feel bad for you. Look how nice it is outside, basically everyone is out and about right now. Just you all alone here."

I blinked, having not expected this level of directness. "Okay," I said finally, and we set off. Fanfan asked me if I ate spicy foods. I nodded. She brought me to a dry hot pot restaurant on the sixth floor of a large shopping center where all of the menus were tablets. I let her order everything, contributing absolutely nothing to the selection of our meal except a Diet Coke for myself.

"Are you trying to lose weight?" she asked.

"Oh, no," I said. Since I saw my extended family so rarely, I had forgotten how blunt the Chinese were about weight. "I just don't really believe in drinking calories."

Christine seemed to not know what to say to that and looked at me as if I had said something incredibly lame. She asked me a few softball questions about my life back in the United States, which I answered with varying degrees of vagueness. Then the food came, which to my irritation was too spicy for me to eat.

"So, how long have you been Bo's assistant?" I asked, trying to make conversation.

Unfortunately, this question did not land. "I'm not Bo's assistant, I'm his *chief of staff*," she said. "I hate it when he calls me that. He was the one who promoted me! In so many ways, Chinese society is still so backwards and misogynistic. I am sure this kind of thing doesn't happen in America, does it?"

I wasn't sure how to convey to Christine that I was in no way equipped to answer her question. My own thoughts on the issue were so biased as to be worthless. Most of the smart women I'd been acquainted with at Princeton (like Jessica) became investment bankers or consultants, which at the time I took to mean I'd end up working at least one or two levels below them in five years. Those who expressed any interest in software engineering were funneled into diversity hiring programs at Facebook, Google, etc. I first noticed this during my freshman year, when Jessica (whom I had always considered to have sprung from the same sexless mold as myself in Bergen County) somehow came out ahead of me in every supposedly gender-blind selection process on campus. Somehow, in college and in life more broadly, (Asian x female) seemed to unlock a hidden fast track while (Asian x male) redirected you to the spam box. It was like some twisted karmic retribution in the West of the One Child Policy in China, which had created such a strong preference for boys that the gender ratio had been irreversibly skewed in macabre ways I won't get into.

Christine didn't seem to notice that I hadn't answered her question. "If you're a pretty girl in China, you can get whatever you want. But you're constantly dealing with perverts," she said.

I thought about Gary, who was certainly some type of pervert. Or the anonymous men on SamarChat whose obsessive commentary struck me as at least pervert-adjacent, but that wasn't quite it either, since those internet men in general seemed impotent and unable to dispense whatever it was that the pretty girls wanted. They were not the power perverts.

We finished our lunch and Christine insisted on taking me on a walk around the neighborhood. She helpfully pointed out the local grocery store, café, gym. Again, she lobbed lightly probing questions at me and I fed her bullshit, more or less. That she was obviously a spy did not diminish the impression of her sincerity. When she asked me what I was doing later in the evening, I told her I was meeting my Chinese teacher for drinks and had to go get ready. She let me go, but not before putting her number into my phone by using it to call her own.

21

I took the subway to Ferris's office, a simple one-story building in a suburban part of the city's west side with a sign that read HAIGUI LANGUAGE EDUCATION CENTER. The lobby was plastered with images of cartoon sea turtles and framed photos of students that had achieved perfect TOEFL scores holding acceptance letters to obscure American universities. The receptionist was excited to tell me that I had signed up for the VIP package, a year's worth of weekly one-on-one lessons. The news made my head reel. I had never asked the agents back home about the timeline, but clearly there was no escape jet standing by offshore.

After five minutes or so, Ferris walked into the lobby. He was about my height and had a round, forgettable face. "Nice to meet you, Michael! Thanks for choosing our center! Since it's your first lesson, why don't I take you for a coffee?"

I got up and followed him out the door. The receptionist, clearly a fan of Ferris's, waved us an enthusiastic goodbye.

Ferris took me to a Luckin Coffee on a busy street and we ordered two coffees with cream and sugar. On the way over, he explained that the language center specialized in TOEFL exam preparation for Chinese students applying to programs at American universities. A smaller part of their business was Chinese lessons for expats on business. The center employed five tutors and there were hundreds of establishments exactly like it in Beijing.

"So, are you actually giving me Chinese lessons?" I asked. "My Chinese is okay. Listen, what I really need is some intensive spy training. I got a little bit from the FBI agents before this, but I didn't really come away with any, you know, hard skills."

"I'm not surprised. The FBI is good at catching spies. But they're not running agents themselves. It's a little bit different. Don't worry, Michael. No special training needed, we won't be asking you to do anything that would put you in the way of grievous bodily harm. There'll be no safe-cracking or high-speed chases in your future. Leave that part to me."

He punctuated the last bit with an unbearably corny wink that made me want to groan. It was difficult to imagine someone like Ferris, whose physical resemblance to the cartoon sea turtle mascot in his lobby I was now recognizing as uncanny, doing secret agent activities. The front of his shirt was unbuttoned and you could see his round belly pushing against the white tank top. He looked exactly like the thousands of other men in Beijing you passed by in the street every morning on your way to work.

"Here's how it'll work. Once a week, I'll meet you at a different location for our 'lesson.' You'll update me on everything that happened during the week, especially your interactions with Bo. Train yourself to remember the most insignificant details. The more you tell me, the more likely I'll be able to help you and get you home faster. If there's an emergency, drop an orange peel near the trash can on the northwest corner of this intersection. Then I'll meet you at the café bar across the street. Periodically, I'll give you new profiles to present to Bo or specific instructions to carry out. How's your memory? We're going to use as little paper as possible."

"I have an excellent memory," I said, and told him about my lunch with Bo, re-creating our conversation nearly word for word.

"It sounds promising," he said. "In addition to pushing the prospects, try to get Bo more involved in small but subtle ways—for example, ask his advice. You want him to feel invested in what you're doing, and for Bo to view himself as a mentor for you. Remember, this is HUMINT: if you're going to be successful, you'll need to use every ounce of resourcefulness you have to understand Bo as a person. What keeps him up at night? What is he willing to put himself at risk for? That's the key to luring him out."

"Sorry to ask, but how long have you been doing this?"

"I've been living in China for eleven years now," he said. "And running the tutoring center for ten of those years."

If Ferris had arrived in China in 2007, that meant he had survived the purge that took place in 2010. He could tell what I was thinking.

"Michael, I always put my students first," he said. "In my decade of teaching, I've never lost a student."

"How many others are there?"

"The less you know the better."

"I guess I'll have to accept that. Why teaching as a cover?"

"The best covers are what we gravitate to naturally. Peter Matthiessen was a writer, and when he worked for the CIA in Paris his cover was starting the *Paris Review*, which, of course, became an important part of his real life, even after he left the service. My father was a teacher of sorts, and I studied education in college. I think if I had stayed in the United States, I would've ended up as a teacher anyway."

"Oh. I had thought it was to catch spies on their way into the country."

"That's hardly the case. I've seen about eight hundred students over the past ten years and have only suspected one or two. One of the best things about the Chinese people is that they always want the best for the next generation. The *haigui* phenomenon is different now. Just fifteen years ago, it was all rich families sending their sons and daughters abroad. There's still a lot of that. But increasingly it's upper-middle-class families, and the numbers are only going up. When the upper-middle class sends their kids to the United States, they bring Western values back home with them. What the Chinese haven't understood about change yet is that it doesn't all have to be radical, smashing the olds and violent rebellion. In the long run, change is all about hearts and minds. When my students come back, they are changed people. When this generation comes to power one day, things will be different. So I came to the conclusion long ago that even if nothing else comes of my life, at least I'll have this."

So Ferris's job as an English teacher wasn't just a cover, but a parallel life of sorts that had its own meaning, and, to some extent, the same overarching goal; two lives headed toward the same destination. Now our drinks were done and we were preparing to leave. Our conversation left me feeling surprisingly reassured, maybe because Ferris, unlike Lim and Reddy, seemed like a real person.

"A couple of important don'ts," Ferris continued. "Never discuss your work over the phone. And don't speak of the stress you're under. Believe me, I understand the toll that this job takes. If you need someone to talk to, talk to me. And if you get captured, don't try to protect me. You don't have the training to withstand interrogation, and more importantly, you didn't sign up for this life. That's the risk and the path that I chose."

I didn't quite know what to say. I'd gotten so used to being treated like a dubious impersonal "asset" that I was touched by the fact that someone appeared to feel a genuine sense of responsibility for me. There was a sense of being allies in enemy territory that made me feel closer to him; from the way he described things, Ferris was counting on me as well.

22

Over the next few weeks, I worked hard to find an inroad with Bo. To my disappointment, this involved a lot of waiting, and it became clear I wasn't the only source competing for Bo's attention. I lobbied Ferris to get the FBI to send me more leads, but he kept reminding me of the perils of moving too quickly. This left me with nothing to do but wait for the correspondences ghostwritten on my behalf to appear in my inbox.

Two successful transfers I had facilitated (one in lithium-ion batteries, the other in LIDAR) had been enough to secure me a standing thirty-minute weekly meeting with Bo at his office in Guomao, where he plied his craft of impersonating a venture capitalist. By the second or third meeting it became clear that Bo had a keen interest in semiconductor manufacturing, a field that had nothing to do with the technical challenges at Naveon (indeed, the general topic of Naveon seemed to disappear from our discussions entirely). Bo often encouraged me to visit the States to meet my prospects who had semiconductor-related knowledge in person, but gave no indication of being willing to leave the country himself.

During these meetings, I worked hard to understand Bo on a fundamental level. On the morality and values front, I came to the unfortunate conclusion that Bo was a "true believer." Consistent with his elite upbringing, he didn't seem primarily motivated by the pursuit of money or status in the way Chinese civil servants stereotypically are. Rather, with his vast knowledge of Chinese history, Bo struck me as a highly intellectual person, someone who might have even plausibly been a professor in another life. He spoke convincingly of the moral case for economic espionage, which for him was an activity as natural and necessary as war. As far back as the eighteenth century, he told me, Jesuit priests were sent to China from Europe to steal porcelain techniques. During the Industrial Revolution, Alexander Hamilton openly paid bounties to anyone who could deliver British manufacturing secrets to the United States. China's technological progress had been stunted by the domination of Western powers during the nineteenth century, and now it was justified to use any means necessary to catch up. When we discussed these subjects at length in his office, I often felt an uncomfortable consonance between his ideas and views I'd mulled over in San Francisco long before I met him.

Meanwhile, I continued to meet with Ferris in secret once a week. The geographic coordinates of our meetings were encoded in the assigned page numbers on my syllabus. I opened each of these meetings with an update on the week's progress—which profiles seemed to spark Bo's interest, what I had learned about him as a person. Ferris would interrupt with questions and give me feedback and coaching. We'd play back interactions beat by beat and he'd tell me—the next time Bo presses you on X, respond with Y. Fairly soon we settled into a comfortable mentor-mentee dynamic; I found myself eager to show progress and get his approval, perhaps because he was the only one who could see the work I was doing.

One of the great and terrible things about my relationship with Ferris was that it was explicitly one-directional. I could confide in him about the anxiety and loneliness I experienced during the mission, but the professional boundaries of our relationship meant he'd never share anything back; he was almost like a shrink in that way. Over the next few weeks, I opened up about the chronic insecurities and disappointments that have plagued me over the years as well as the regrettable decisions that landed me in the present situation. He listened to me in the way I always imagined a true friend would, patiently and without judgment; I often found myself thinking I was lucky, in spite of everything else, to have met someone like this. When I finally told him about Vivian, he said he felt so sorry for me he had to buy me a drink immediately. He took me to a bar in Dongjiaomin Hutong that was loosely pirate-themed and smelled like fried anchovies.

"Don't be too hard on yourself, my friend, the way you described her I would have fallen for her too," he said. "Try to see the humor in it. Plus, you have to realize there are a lot of clever women like this in China. That's why you have to be careful."

We had talked through the Vivian saga for the duration of two beers now, and it might have been the end of the conversation. I figured with everything now out in the open I may as well ask Ferris what was really on my mind. "Let me ask you something," I said. "Do you think Vivian is working for Bo?"

Ferris crossed his elbows on the bar and furrowed his brow for some time, appearing to give the question careful consideration, though I got an odd sense he'd seen it coming. "It's too hard to say without a careful review of the facts. There are many possibilities, and I don't want to speculate. But from what you've told me, circumstantially it seems like her working for Bo is a plausible explanation."

"Is there any way we can find out for sure? Maybe we can trace the encrypted number she used to call me? I just want to know, so that I can have closure."

"That's a dangerous path to go down, Michael. To look for people who don't want to be found. My advice is, the best thing you can do is forget about her."

I showed my assent with a sustained slug of beer. As I neared the bottom of my glass, I tried imagining a world in which Vivian had never entered my life, and found myself craving a cigarette. "By the way, Ferris, I never told the FBI agents anything about Vivian. Because I thought she might be in danger. They think I'm just working for Bo to make money. Can we keep this just between us?"

"Of course, Michael. You have my word."

So now we had a secret.

During one of our talks Ferris mentioned that he hadn't been back to America for eleven years, and he didn't know when, if ever, he would be cleared to return. He spoke tenderly of the country that he missed, an America stuck in the year 2007. He reminded me of one of those men who worked on freezing oil rigs in the middle of the ocean to support a family at home that he never got to see.

At the same time, it was obvious that Ferris relished his life in Beijing. He had a rotating social group of former students, expats who'd stuck around the city, who were always begging him to join their outings. There was Hans, a German who worked in the Beijing office of BMW; Lisa, an Australian who owned her own yoga studio; and Christian, a Dane who worked as a promoter for electronic music festivals. Ferris had a way with people, a special ability to make them feel important and seen. Whenever we went to a bar or restaurant, people would pause their conversations to come up and greet him. I found this fascinating because I always considered that level of respect and popularity to be the exclusive privilege of the extremely wealthy or good-looking, and in the latter departments I felt Ferris and I were starting from the same modest building blocks. I took copious amounts of mental notes. I noticed that the more I observed Ferris succeeding in these environments, the more I tended to view myself as fundamentally similar to him. Ferris's charm extended to the realm of women as well, and inevitably over the course of a night out one or two women would try to pin down his attention and get him to take her out, but he always politely let them down easy. I always thought this was strange and asked him once why he was so disinterested; was it because he already had a girlfriend, or maybe someone at home? But he always just said he didn't want more complications in his life and left it at that.

One Saturday, Ferris and I went for a nightcap of cumin lamb skewers at a dive bar in Nanluoguxiang at the end of a long night. I asked him how he ended up getting recruited by the CIA.

"Why do you ask? Are you thinking about joining us full-time?"

"Probably not with how this internship has been going so far. But I've been curious to hear the story for a while."

Ferris did a quick scan around the bar, which was basically empty except for a few drunken college kids.

"I was recruited out of college, actually. I still have no idea how they found me. I was just standing in front of the student lounge vending machine one day when a man wearing a suit approached me and said, 'You're Ferris Guo; do you mind if I speak to you?' followed by, 'Have you considered a career in the CIA?'

"At first I thought he was a scammer. Of course I hadn't considered a career in the CIA. I was actually set to move back to Ann Arbor after graduation to teach public school. So when he invited me to interview, I said yes mostly out of curiosity.

"The interview took place in a hotel conference room a few miles away from campus. The first thing the interviewer wanted to understand was family background, which I assumed he already knew everything about. I told him that my father had been a pro-democracy activist in China who'd fled the country before I was born. Back home, he'd been somewhat well-known for running an underground political magazine that published the country's leading pro-democracy thinkers, an activity that made it unsafe for him to continue living in China. He thought of his forced migration as a sort of pilgrimage. He figured since no one hated Communists more than the Americans, he was certain to find his people here.

"My father had the misfortune of arriving in America in 1972 during the week of the historic and highly televised Nixon visit to Beijing. Millions of Americans watched their president shake hands with Mao Zedong and eat Peking duck on television. Suddenly, sentiment toward the threatening Communist power was never warmer. My father the journalist failed to connect with his audience, but he never gave up the fight. I distinctly remember when I was seven years old, he started a fund to support radical democracy activists in Hong Kong and tried to collect donations at our local church after Sunday service. When that didn't work, he printed out pamphlets about the human rights abuses of the Communist Party and made me stand on the street corner with him handing them out. Imagine that! We became social outcasts. At school, other kids would bully me and say my dad was a spy for China.

"I think some part of him missed the standing and notoriety he enjoyed back home. Here he was a nobody, he'd had a whole string of jobs he was no good at: office manager, insurance salesman, assistant to a veterinarian. At the dinner table he'd brag about correspondences he had with famous Chinese dissidents that also lived in the States, but none of them ever showed their faces. He saw the jobs he had as somehow beneath him, taking away from his true purpose of changing the course of history in a country I'd never even seen. But what about his responsibility to our family? Since he was so delinquent, my mother had to be the breadwinner. She'd been someone in China as well, a doctor, but gave it up without hesitation and got a job at a laundromat. The stability she created restored some sense of normalcy to my childhood. At first we were ostracized for my father's strange political activities, then when that was forgotten we became invisible, just another struggling immigrant family whose names no one bothered to remember. At first I used to resent this. But seeing my father struggle made me fearful of grandiose dreams at a young age. I came to think of myself as someone who would be grounded and realistic about what the future could hold."

While Ferris spoke, I was thinking of my own father and the meek, self-effacing way he'd carried out his family duties every day for ten years, until the day he suddenly stopped. We'd spent the summer of his disappearance elbows pressed together in the garage working on a remote-controlled battery-powered car for the county science fair. We didn't use a kit—designed the whole thing from scratch and shipped the component parts from China. It was a complex, six-week build engineered by my father, who even hung a Gantt chart on an easel pad to track our progress. When we started falling behind schedule, the daily time commitment and intensity increased; toward the end, at my father's insistence, we worked for eight hours a day, not even taking a break for lunch, which my mother would bring into the garage for us. We finished on a glorious August afternoon and took the car, which we called the Tenafly Swift, for its maiden voyage in Roosevelt Common, where we set up an obstacle course to test the car's maneuverability. My dad handed me the remote control and watched with pride as Tenafly Swift completed a perfect loop. Then we went for a celebratory father-son dinner at the Vietnamese restaurant on Sunset Lane and stayed until close. He disappeared the next day.

"I figured I'd write off the first interview as free therapy, but to my surprise I got a call to come in for an all-day aptitude test, which consisted of eight hours of logic and verbal questions. Apparently I passed that too. Then they flew me to Langley, where I met with another man who would only tell me his first name. I ended up working for him for eight years. I was struck by how little they tried to sell the job during the interview process. The pay was low. No flashy perks. I might get to travel the world, or I might not. I'd have to tell all my friends I was working at the State Department with an unimpressive low-level job title.

"It was a grueling interview process that dragged on for six months. The whole time, I was pretty sure I wouldn't take the job, but something kept pushing me to the next step. When the offer finally came from the Clandestine Service, the division of the CIA that runs undercover missions to recruit foreign agents, I thought there had been a mistake. 'No mistake,' they said, and on top of that, they told me I was likely to get deployed in China. Pretty ironic, considering I'd been avoiding the country my entire life. I was ready to just laugh it off when my father finally passed away three weeks before graduation. Before that, we'd been in a fight about my plan to go back to Ann Arbor and teach public school. I was his only son, he wanted me to go to law school and become someone 'significant.' My father spent his entire life in America sitting on the sidelines and clamoring for attention, and in the end, only five people came to his funeral. He never could accept what fate had in store for him. But I could; I could transcend the alienation and invisibility I felt for my entire life by devoting myself to serving a country that had never embraced me. I could give my life away knowing no one outside of the Agency would ever know my name, and prove to myself I didn't need the recognition my father chased for so much of his life."

As Ferris wrapped up his story, I reflected on the remarkable similarities between our lives. Like me, he'd also grown up as an only child, an outsider raised by a father who'd never found his footing in America, whose life had changed by getting recruited out of the blue by a mysterious agent. Unlike me, however, Ferris had answered a calling, not a phishing message. Ferris measured his life by the extent to which he lived in accordance with his values, while all I ever craved was the feeling of being seen. Ferris didn't feel tortured by his invisibility; he wielded it. It struck me that at the end of it all, this must be the irreducible difference between us. It was what made him the perfect spy, and myself someone who could be easily manipulated, never sure of himself and always captive to the judgments of others.

Was there a possibility I could learn to be more like him? We were, after all, of the same mold.

"Something changed in me when my father left too," I said. I figured no context was necessary since everything I would've told him was surely in my file already. "He didn't leave a note, so I spent much of middle school trying to piece together why he left. At first I blamed my mother. She never understood what he was going through, and he could never understand how she was somehow able to never look back. As I got older, I started to think more about the struggle and humiliation he'd suffered outside of the home—the stuff I never saw directly. Similar to yours, my father never found what he was looking for in America, always had this defeated look in his eyes. I pitied him. But over time, that pity turned into resentment. I decided I wouldn't end up like him; in fact, I'd forget about him. That's why I made sure I was always the best at school, tennis, got into Princeton. But in a strange way, ever since I turned eighteen and started living by myself, I've felt myself inexplicably following in his footsteps. Even my being here today; it feels like his disappearance is still overshadowing my life, as if in all this time all I've done is look for him."

It suddenly occurred to me that I was speaking with one of the only people in the world with the power to find my dad. Now something unspeakable and heavy seemed to shift beneath the surface of our conversation.

"The worst part is, for all the time he was in my life, he was a good dad," I said. "That made it hurt even more when he left, because it felt like he was robbing me of all the good memories he'd given me."

"I'm sorry, Michael. It's never fair to those who are left behind."

"What about your mom? Were you able to explain everything to her at least?" I asked. Now it was just the two of us left in the bar. The staff had started mopping and I wondered if we were going to miss the last train back.

"I called her a week before graduation to tell her that instead of coming back home to Ann Arbor, I would go become an English teacher in China, the one place she could never hope to visit me. That's what she believes to this day. She is still alone in Michigan, with no family to lean on, spending every holiday alone. I know she wonders why I never visit. To be honest, given how singularly she devoted herself to making America a home for me, I wonder if my decision made her feel like her life was spent in vain. Over the years I've searched deep within myself for a justification that could put my guilt to rest, but nothing makes it go away. I've come to accept that in life, and especially in this line of work, a certain degree of betrayal is unavoidable."

A fleeting darkness eclipsed his face that was so surprising, for a moment he became unrecognizable. The terrible notion that "a certain degree of betrayal is unavoidable" struck me as alarmingly incompatible with the idealistic Ferris I had come to know, though perhaps what was really idealistic was the heroic image I'd formed of him, am forming in your mind even now, because the notion of a perfectly good spy was a paradox. A certain degree of betrayal, I've learned as well, *was* inevitable—and looking back, I wonder if I had listened to him closely enough in that moment.

23

Bo never called first, so when his name appeared on caller ID, I picked up immediately. He wanted to have dinner together on Friday evening and didn't explain why. The reservation was for four at an Italian restaurant in Chaoyang District. His wife would be joining—perhaps I could see if Christine was available?

Despite her apparent surprise when I called her, it was clear that Christine had already been briefed. We agreed to meet at her place the evening of and take a cab together. She lived in an old five-story walk-up apartment building on an uphill side street of Shuangjing. She opened the door really quickly when I got there and immediately ushered me to the couch, then paced around for several seconds before putting a glass of water in my hand and retreating to the bathroom to finish getting ready. From the couch, I took a look around Christine's tiny, cramped studio and found it difficult to believe a spy lived here. Her coffee table was piled with months-old magazines. The fridge was covered with souvenir magnets, and brown-tipped houseplants crowded every shelf and counter. On her narrow writing desk, an English textbook with rows of highlights glowed under the white light of an LED lamp. Finally, Christine stepped out of the bathroom in an attractive black cocktail dress and said she was ready to go.

The place was called Il Ristorante and sprawled across the first floor of the Bulgari Hotel in palatial blocks of marble, wood, and leather. The hostess brought us to a private room where we found Bo and his wife, Michelle, already seated. Michelle was wearing an elegant black cashmere cardigan over a silk shirt. She had the same pixie cut as Christine, but it worked better with her lapidary bone structure and pale complexion. To my relief, Christine led the greetings and we took our seats. A waiter came in and poured us glasses of Château Lafite.

We ordered carpaccio, arancini, clams, gnocchi, tagliata steak, and lobster ravioli. Bo mentioned that his wife was a professor of architecture at Beijing Normal University. The conversation started with how I was settling into Beijing, what I had been up to. I reported the couple of excursions I'd had with Christine and mentioned I was also taking Chinese lessons. Bo nodded with approval. When the food arrived, Christine took a picture with her phone, which made Bo's wife frown. We carried on in this way for a pleasant forty-five minutes. Then Michelle excused herself to use the restroom and Christine said she would join her. When they left the table, I asked Bo how things were going at Naveon. He shook his head.

"Between you and me, Michael, Naveon is in chaos. I am not sure that Peng is the right man for the job. It could be a while before things stabilize there. But don't worry, you've proven yourself to be smart and resourceful; indeed, we have bigger things in store for you inside of Terra Cotta."

"Your venture firm? I'm not sure I really have the skills for that."

"Perhaps I ought to tell you a little more about Terra Cotta. Terra Cotta Capital isn't a normal venture capital firm, Michael. It shares some similarities with In-Q-Tel in the United States, but operates within a different governance structure and at a much larger scale," he said.

I remembered learning about In-Q-Tel during my freshman year in the Woodrow Wilson School. It was the CIA's independent venture capital arm, tasked with funding cutting-edge technologies that might become interesting to the Agency in the future. My application to spend the summer there had been rejected.

"For Terra Cotta, the significance to the nation's interests is even greater. Remember what I told you about Made in China 2025. The past four decades have lifted millions of Chinese out of poverty, but we can't be the world's sweatshop forever. MIC25 is the national strategy plan to ensure China becomes the global leader in the high-technology industries of the twenty-first century: AI, self-driving and electric vehicles, advanced robotics, quantum computing, and the like. That's where Terra Cotta comes in. Our mandate is to use capital—both financial and human capital—to accelerate the domestic development of the most strategic technologies. We're doing this with the direct support of the Premier and the State Council.

"You may have no experience with investing, but from what I've seen so far, you have a talent for the human dimension. Would you like to know why we named the firm Terra Cotta? Tell me, Michael, have you ever visited the Terra Cotta Army just outside of Xi'an?"

"No—I remember learning about them in Chinese school back in New Jersey though," I said. "The clay soldiers of the first emperor of China, right?"

"Correct. In total, more than 8,000 soldiers, each with a unique face, 130 chariots, and 520 horses buried with the Qin emperor to protect him in the afterlife. It must be considered the eighth wonder of the world. Historians say over seven hundred thousand workers labored on the project, compared to only one hundred thousand for the Egyptian pyramids. Remarkably, their existence was unknown for more than two thousand years. We did not discover this massive reserve force until 1974, two years before Mao Zedong's death and five years before Deng Xiaoping's economic reforms brought China into modernity. The delay was fortunate. Had the Terra Cotta Army been discovered just a few decades earlier, during China's 'century of humiliation,' I am certain they would be displayed in the British Museum or the Louvre today, alongside the Egyptian sphinxes and the trophies of other subjugated empires.

"The Qin emperor conquered China with his military. That's why he buried the Terra Cotta Warriors with him, to aid him in the next life. In the next century, hopefully a peaceful one, it's technology, not militaries, that will determine the next world power. China's warriors will be our scientists. Today our scientists are buried all over the world; we need to wake them up and return them to their rightful place. That is the only way to protect China for the next millennium. Your father is such a soldier, Michael."

I was frozen by the sudden realization that this was the first time anybody had spoken of him in the present tense for several years. "You knew him?"

"Yes, I've known Ruoqi Wang since you were six years old. I first met him at a technical conference in Beijing, where he gave a presentation on his pioneering work in cryptography that was at least five years ahead of its time. I invited him to give a keynote at one of my conferences the following year. Over the next five years, we shared many long talks. I understood he had a burning desire in his heart to help the motherland, and we found a way to make this dream a reality. Since he came back to China, he has had a remarkable career."

"Excuse me," I said, wringing my hands beneath the table. "I'm not sure I understand what you're saying. Where is he now?"

"He is based in a secret research facility in the mountains forty kilometers outside of Beijing, where he leads a staff of two hundred. Because of the highly sensitive nature of his work, strict security protocols limit his visits to the city. If you'd like, we can arrange for a visit when the time is right."

At first, my heart seized with cold anger. I didn't—I couldn't—believe him. Even though by now I'd gotten used to Bo's lies, I was still shaken by the realization that no deception was off limits for him. But then I felt the wound beneath the dull scar in my heart opening up again, pulled apart by the malignant hope that Bo was somehow telling the truth. Now an unfamiliar pride bloomed inside me, followed by a whirl of questions: What was he working on? Why hasn't he tried to contact us? Did he have another family? "Yes, I'd like to see him," I found myself saying. Before I had the opportunity to ask any more questions, Michelle and Christine returned from the bathroom.

"Anyway. As I was saying, Michael, if you're interested, I do have a job I could use your help with. A way for you to test out the new role."

I nodded and took a long sip of wine.

"I've been in contact with a senior engineer at Intel named Zhang Jianwei. He's the leading expert in a specialized clean manufacturing process critical to semiconductor production. He's interested in working with us, but won't come to China to meet me. So I need you to go to Fremont and close him for me."

"Okay, I can do it. What's our angle?"

"Zhang was born in China and only came to the United States late in life," he said. "Doesn't sound like he really fits in there. He's always wanted to help the motherland but couldn't find any opportunities in the semiconductor industry here because it didn't exist at the time. If I were you, I would talk about how he could be a founding father of Chinese semiconductor fabrication. Don't worry, I don't think it'll be too difficult. He's just a little nervous and wants to see a human face."

I knew who Zhang was, could even recall the outline of his driver's license photo. He was file number 1393 in the FBI's China Initiative database. He'd been working at Intel for eleven years and made $180,000 last year. His address was 2875 San Carlos Way, a one-story home on the outskirts of Fremont purchased in 2009 for $320,000. He had a wife and son at home. The son, I remembered, had an advanced neurodegenerative condition.

"Don't worry, I'll handle it," I said, though the idea of meeting someone from the China Initiative list face-to-face made me feel faint. To my horror, Bo ordered another bottle of Château Lafite, even though it was already half past ten in the evening. I couldn't really talk; I was thinking about my dad, somewhere in the mountains outside of Beijing. Could that really have been the glory he chose? I tried to picture what he would look like today, sixteen years removed from my last memory of him. What would I say to him? *I've always known where to find you. I'm sorry it took me so long.* For sixteen years I'd clung to the illogical certainty that my father was in Beijing; the fact that I now knew I was right this entire time made our reunion feel preordained. Christine seemed to sense my state of preoccupation and took over the talking for the both of us, raising her glass frequently to speed us through the bottle. After dessert, Bo overpowered me for the bill and we parted ways. Christine and I stepped outside the restaurant to look for a cab. I lit a cigarette and she had one with me, even though she didn't smoke. On the cab ride back, I thanked her for being there tonight and turned to the window. When I dropped her off at her apartment, she lingered at the door. I bid her goodnight and went to the nearest convenience store.

I took the subway to Ferris's stop, deposited the orange peel, and waited at the cafe-bar we'd designated as our urgent rendezvous point. Ferris showed up thirty minutes later and I told him about the assignment I had just received.

"That's a breakthrough," he said.

"How am I going to pull this off on my own? What if Zhang doesn't cooperate?"

"Don't worry, you won't be on your own. The FBI will have Zhang Jianwei in custody before you land in SFO. Just follow Agent Lim's lead."

The idea of folding in under Lim's command gave me pause.

"There is one other risk though," Ferris continued. "Given it involves semiconductors, our government may decide that the IP he's holding is too strategic to risk falling into the wrong hands. If they decide to make his arrest public, Bo will know that you talked."

"But that's Scully's call, right? Can't we just ask him to keep the arrest under wraps while I work on Bo?"

"I'm afraid not. When semiconductors get involved, it goes all the way up the chain. It could take a few days to get everyone aligned. If that happens, you'll need to find a way to stall with Bo."

I didn't tell Ferris what Bo had told me about my dad. Even though I trusted him, I knew he would be compelled to report it to Agent Lim and Agent Reddy, which would make them view me as a compromised source and potentially jeopardize my cooperation deal. That was the first time I betrayed him.

When I arrived at the gate, Agent Lim and Agent Reddy were waiting for me again. This time they didn't handcuff me, just gave me a microphone to wear while I was with Zhang. We walked to the parking garage together and drove to the San Francisco County Jail where Zhang was being held.

The three of us waited in a small questioning room. The warden brought Zhang in and shoved him hard into the seat. He was a rotund, meek-looking man in his sixties who squinted and sniffled as he looked around the room. For some reason, they had him in handcuffs, which looked tight around his fleshy wrists.

"Please," Zhang said. "Can I have my glasses? They got lost on the way here. I can't see—"

Agent Lim interrupted him by slamming the table with his open palm.

"Man up, traitor. What if your family saw you blubbering like this? You betrayed the country that took a chance on you three decades ago. Don't even bother telling us it's the first time you've done this."

Zhang was heaving so hard it was difficult to make out what he was saying. I averted my eyes, embarrassed to watch a man my father's age cry. He kept begging us to spare his family and saying that he was going to commit suicide.

"Enough! Quiet! This man here," Lim said, pointing at me, "is who you were supposed to meet at your home for dinner this evening. I'm guessing your wife already cooked. So you're going to go do that, but don't worry, we won't be far behind. You're going to act normally, like nothing happened, do you understand? Afterward, you tell no one about what happened today."

Now Zhang was just rocking back and forth, seemingly in a catatonic state.

"Do you understand?"

"Yes, I understand," he said.

Zhang and I didn't speak a word to each other during the forty-five-minute drive to his house in Fremont, a modest one-story home with peeling lemon-colored paint. Zhang's wife was waiting nervously on the lawn outside and straightened her posture like a flight attendant when she saw us approaching the driveway. Lim texted me that he and Reddy were in position behind the house.

Zhang's wife received us warmly, introducing herself as Luoling, and invited me in. The house had been meticulously cleaned, but there were signs of thrift everywhere you looked: worn matting to increase the lifespan of cheap furniture, used cereal boxes that implausibly doubled as filing cabinets, plants sitting in glass water bottles instead of vases. It smelled wonderful everywhere. For dinner she'd prepared red-braised pork belly, a seafood stir-fry, dan dan noodles, and Chinese broccoli with oyster sauce. Luoling ushered me to my seat at the head of the table.

"Muchen!" she said, turning to the living room. "*Chi fan*!"

Half a minute later, their son entered the dining room on an electric wheelchair. Cerebral palsy, I guessed. He was wearing a freshly ironed blue dress shirt that sagged around his crumpled chest and shoulders. Luoling smiled. "This is our son, Muchen," she said, putting a hand on his shoulder. "Believe it or not, he's around your age. Please, let's eat."

She served me first, then Muchen. For the first half hour, she asked me inviting questions about my life that I tried to answer as enthusiastically as possible. Every minute or two, she would feed Muchen with her chopsticks, using her other hand to cover his mouth while he took in the food. Muchen drank from a straw in a green plastic cup connected to his wheelchair and didn't say a word. Periodically, I noticed Luoling glancing over at Zhang, as if nudging him to participate in the conversation.

"You're smart for going back to China at such a young age. In China, it is all about the talented young men now," she said. "Will you look out for old Jianwei when he goes home?"

I swallowed. "Of course I will."

"Our Jianwei is so brilliant. Even though his title is modest, he has made many important contributions. He would have a higher position if we stayed in China like our classmates, but we come here to make a better life for Muchen, and what we have is enough. Thank you for taking a chance on him," she said.

I was puzzled: if they had enough, why was Zhang leaving his family to go to China? "Oh, please don't thank me," I said, suddenly conscious of how hollow my voice sounded. "I'm just a representative. I had nothing to do with this."

Luoling leaned over the table and scooped some more pork belly onto my plate, an anxious look in her eyes. "What do you mean, Mr. Wang?

You're being too modest," she said. "Your boss Bo told my Jianwei about the new clinical trials for cerebral palsy that are starting next year at Shenzhen Southern University. He said you were the one who found a spot for our Muchen. Our Jianwei is so grateful he wanted to pay you back any way he can, that's why he agreed to go work in China, isn't that right?"

Zhang stood up abruptly from his seat and the chair made an awful grating noise as it slid across the floor. "I'm going to have a cigarette," he said in Chinese to no one in particular. Luoling glared at him as he walked out the front door.

"Yes, of course, the clinical trial," I said quickly, my voice cracking as I suddenly understood the sickening consequences of the lies that Bo had set into motion. I could not bring myself to meet Luoling's hopeful eyes. "You never know how these things will pan out, but hopefully we'll have some luck. Don't mention it."

Luoling thanked me again profusely and started clearing the table, apologizing for her husband and saying he must have gotten too excited; it was strange because he quit smoking years ago. I thanked her for the meal and told her I would catch a Lyft. Then I disappeared around the corner and got into the van with Agent Lim and Agent Reddy.

The arrest of Zhang Jianwei set off a shitstorm in the intelligence and defense communities. According to Agent Lim, Zhang's recruitment had been considered a "near miss," as Zhang had had access to extremely proprietary trade secrets that would have accelerated the Chinese semiconductor effort by several years. Semiconductor production, Agent Lim explained, was a top-level strategic priority for the Chinese government, as they were required in nearly all technological applications of commercial and military significance, and three countries—the United States, Taiwan, and Korea—essentially controlled the global supply. Various government agencies rushed to take credit for the interception, which thankfully the US attorney general decided to make secret until they decided how to proceed with Bo's IP.

While we waited for the government to make up its mind, I had to stall with Bo. I sent him an email, explaining that things were taking a bit longer than expected, as Zhang had invited me to stay with the family for a few more days. Bo responded with: *Good. Do what you need to do. Send pictures.*

I told Agent Lim, who promptly carted me back to the Zhang household, posing as a colleague from the China office. He entered the living room without taking his shoes off and lined the four of us up in front of the fireplace: me and Muchen in the center, the parents on each side. I could feel Zhang's hand on my shoulder shaking as Lim lowered the scope over his eyes. He made us redo the shot four or five times, chiding Zhang for looking so serious. Then he announced that we had to get to another meeting and bid the family goodbye.

When we got back to the FBI office that afternoon, we were informed that the order had come down from DOD that the IP was acceptable to share with some redactions that would render it unusable, but which would only be discovered several months into the fabrication process. The bureau's IT experts downloaded all of it onto an encrypted SD drive for me to take back to China. I emailed Bo, saying I had Zhang's code, was on my way back to Beijing, and included the picture we had taken at his home. It didn't hit me until I was halfway back across the Pacific that a man as guileless and desperate as Zhang would never have insisted on a face-to-face meeting.

In the final picture, Zhang stands on the right of the fireplace—his face is ashen and his eyes shell-shocked, staring into something far beyond the camera's lens. On the left side, his blissfully unaware wife poses elegantly while resting both her hands on her son's shoulders. There I am in the middle—the interloper with the wooden smile. Because Zhang used an old digital camera, the photo has the date and time stamp in glowing red numbers on the bottom right, which gives it the look of something from an old family photo album. It's a picture I can describe in exact detail, because I had a physical copy printed and framed when I moved to Sydney, where it now sits in direct view on my writing desk. Next to it is a printed clipping from the *San Francisco Reporter* from six months ago: "Veteran Intel engineer found dead in his prison cell. Described as a quiet man by his colleagues, Zhang Jianwei is survived by his ex-wife, Luoling, and their son, Muchen."

24

Back in Beijing, I shut myself away in my apartment for two days straight, forgetting to eat and avoiding my reflection in the mirror. Christine had texted and called several times but I couldn't bring myself to get back to her. It felt like a chasm had sprung open inside me and I was being pulled into it.

When Tuesday finally came around, it was time for my Chinese lesson, an excuse to get out of the apartment. I took the subway to Tsinghua University and navigated to the coordinates encoded in my syllabus, which brought me to a small café not far from the main quad. I was about fifteen minutes early, so I pulled up two stools and lit a cigarette. It was a cool evening and the air smelled of flowers and fresh rain; the road beside me flowed with slow-moving cyclists, mostly young students, and the soft ringing of bicycle bells. All of these pleasant impressions passed through me and fell into the chasm.

Would I look out for old Jianwei when he went back home?

I'd knowingly made a promise I couldn't keep, which made me feel shameful and broken. I thought about the way his wife had stood waiting for me in front of their home, how anxiously and gratefully she had served me at dinner. I imagined the indignation she would feel when the truth about my involvement came out. Without my intervention, Zhang might never have been discovered. I'd *condemned* her husband, a man better than myself—better because he had stolen for love.

But hadn't I stolen for love as well?

I searched the river of faces for the reflection of a dull scar. It'd been six weeks now since our abandoned reunion. We weren't more than six blocks away from where I'd last seen Vivian; for a moment, I allowed myself to remember the walk we had taken together that afternoon and the kiss we'd shared on the bridge. My mind took me back further, to the time we'd spent together in San Francisco, which now felt like a distant memory; how different and damned the cityscape had seemed on this last visit. I missed our long talks, the feeling of being understood. Now I felt like there was an invisible membrane separating me from others, through which words could pass but understanding could not. Because when I met Vivian I had nothing to hide, had only hope brimming in my heart and a deep desire for someone to take the time to really understand me. How sick it was that even though she'd (probably) used this knowledge against me, she'd at least understood me in the first place; to her, I was not invisible.

But I knew it wasn't love alone that brought me to this point. There was the part of Bo that drew me here as well: my dormant high school dreams of greatness, the indignation of being treated like less than what I was, and the possibility of becoming something greater. Now self-actualization was the least of my worries.

"Everything okay?" It was Ferris. He'd turned up at 8:00 P.M. on the dot, wearing a short-sleeve shirt and a baseball cap. I told him about the mission and showed him the pictures Agent Lim had taken.

Ferris grimaced. “I’m so sorry, Michael. Give yourself some time. That kind of experience, it leaves a scar in your soul. I’ve been through it before.”

“I shouldn’t have gone,” I said.

Ferris shook his head. “No. Your involvement here was merely circumstantial; Zhang’s fate had nothing to do with you. If it wasn’t you, Bo would’ve found someone else to do the job. You did what needed to be done; if Bo had doubted you for a moment, it would’ve been all over.”

“It’s just his poor wife—I can’t stop thinking about her.”

“Everything you’re experiencing right now is normal, Michael—but you must be careful not to let these feelings consume you. In the world that I come from, this is called collateral damage. I’ll tell you a story from early on in my career. At this point I’d been undercover in China for two years. I’d recruited an asset, let’s call him XP, from deep within the MSS bureaucracy. Someone who was behind the front lines but knew the intricacies in and out. He was an incredibly brave man with a family. Because of him, for ten months, we had the best intel we’d ever had on the inner workings of the MSS. Then I made a terrible mistake. I used the same drop point one too many times and the Beijing surveillance machine discovered the pattern. I watched him get taken away by military police from the safety of my second-floor balcony. And I’ll tell you one more thing, even while he was being taken away, not once did he glance in my direction. He was brave to the end.”

A chill ran through the back of my head. Could a similar fate be waiting for me?

“Did you ever find out what happened to XP?” I asked.

“We never heard from him or his family again. That’s a weight I’ll carry for the rest of my life. For months after XP disappeared, I spent every waking hour chasing every lead I could get my hands on, long after the trail went cold. It drove me to previously unknown depths. But Michael, and you must listen closely, the way I finally got myself out of that spiral was by asking myself a simple question: Would I let that man’s death go to waste? Once I saw that I had a responsibility to him to see the mission through to its end, clarity came back to me. You saw how Zhang suffered, and you know that for his wife and son, the suffering is only beginning. Whatever role you may or may not have had, I think you owe it to them to not let their sacrifice go in vain, to do everything in your power to save future lives from ruin."

I took a moment to carefully consider what Ferris was saying. It seemed plausible that I had a broader responsibility to fulfill here—if I succeeded in bringing down Bo, perhaps others would be saved. But was that enough to dignify my mission into something nobler than sordid self-preservation? At the same time, was the moral validity of any course of action determined by its initial intent alone? I was troubled by the undeniable fact that Bo was, by every measure, more committed to his principles and broader responsibilities than I was, which seemed to diminish the sense of rightness that Ferris was trying to cultivate in me. Either way, I had no right to wallow, because it was Zhang and his family who had paid the price.

"Now that you've completed the mission, it's safe to assume that you've won some trust with Bo," Ferris continued. "What's critical for you right now is to keep building that momentum. So here's what I suggest, Michael: let's get back to work. I'll be with you every step of the way."

At this, I found myself nodding—however murky things were, there was no way to go but forward. We rose and parted ways at the Tsinghua subway stop.

25

The next morning, Bo called me at half past seven to ask me if I wanted to play golf. The idea of golf was triggering for me. Even though I'd grown up in New Jersey, I'd never touched a golf club, the very institution of golf seemed inexplicably connected to the threatening idea of an unwelcoming, colorless East Coast establishment. The convoluted rules and etiquette appeared designed to trip up outsiders and those who didn't grow up with the sport. The Asian American kids I grew up with tended to gravitate toward tennis, with its clean, mathematical lines and video game–like cadence; a tennis racket was basically a stringed instrument.

I told Bo that I'd never played before and didn't want to slow him down. Unsurprisingly, he dismissed that thought immediately.

"Don't worry, Michael! We'll start with the simulator, my honor to be your instructor. Meet me at the Hong Kong Jockey Club around 9:00 A.M."

It was disorienting to see the Jockey Club in broad daylight, and I shuddered walking past the rooms I recognized from the last time I was here.

Sporting a hat that read SHANQIN BAY GOLF CLUB, Bo brought me up to the third floor, where the golf simulator was set up in a high-ceilinged, oak-paneled room.

Bo flipped a switch that dimmed the lights. The projector whirred to life. An immaculate green vista materialized before us on the slightly concave screen, which seemed to draw us inside of it. From the surround-sound system came the sound of birds and somewhere, inexplicably, a scent of fresh pine. Using his remote, Bo glided us in bodiless ghostlike perspective over the eighteen holes of the course. Something about the terrain struck me as aggravatingly familiar, and before I could ask Bo told me it was Pine Valley in New Jersey.

Of course—Pine Valley, one of the most exclusive golf clubs in the world, where the wait list was ten years long. The Pine Valley hat was a staple accessory in Princeton's dining halls.

"First, we just try to hit the ball," Bo said. He showed me the proper way to form a grip, demonstrated the basic principles of a swing, and invited me to step up to the tee. I thought it didn't seem so hard. I squared up in front of the tee, wound back, and sent my club slicing through the air. I swung again twice, missing the ball both times, and felt my face turn red.

"Not as easy as it looks, huh! That's just a beginner's mistake, easy to correct. Watch."

Bo grabbed the remote and showed me a slow-motion replay of my last swing. The problem, he explained, was that I was pushing up with my legs slightly before the point of impact and straightening out my torso, which raised the bottom of the swing arc above the ball. He stepped up to the tee and demonstrated how to keep the body position stable throughout the swing, then invited me to try again.

I swung again more than a dozen times, trying to imagine my lower body as being planted to the ground. Finally, the club connected and the ball made a satisfying thwack as it collided into the screen. The impact sent a fleeting ripple across the surface of the simulation; now the ball was flying, and us with it, until it reached a stopping point on a hill 219 yards from the hole. The platform beneath my feet tilted slightly to reflect the gradient of the hill I was now hitting off of. Bo had me swap out the driver for the two hybrid and started gesturing excitedly about how to stage the next swing. Unfortunately, the next shot that connected sent us face-down into a pond. No matter—we simply rewound the simulation and transmitted ourselves back to the exact same point. Bo replayed my swing in slow motion again and showed me how I had loosened my grip and changed the angle of the clubface at point of contact. I tried again about fifteen times; the tilt of the platform was challenging and messed with my mental model of how the swing should complete. Finally, I got the ball onto a flat surface thirty-three yards from the hole. We played around with the putters for a few minutes then called it a day.

After we finished at the simulator, Bo and I headed down to the restaurant for a late breakfast.

"Not bad at all for your first day, Michael, I think you have some talent. Now you must be persistent. I recommend practicing three or four times a week; come back to the Jockey Club anytime and give them my name to use the simulator. After a few weeks, you should be ready for the real thing. If you'd like, I can even have them set you up with an instructor."

"This was fun. I'll definitely come back," I said. Why not? It was something to do.

"Golf is still the language of international business. Meeting on the golf course means friendship and mutual respect. One day you will play with important people, so you must start learning now. Here in China, we are behind. Mao banned the game in 1949, calling it a 'sport for millionaires.' Golf didn't become legal again until 1984, when I was in college. Of course, back then I had no money and the game was only for Party elites. I didn't get to play my first round until I was thirty-four, the year that I sold my manufacturing business in Shenzhen and moved my family to Beijing to look for the next challenge. I remember one day watching the

2003 Presidents Cup on TV and seeing George Bush Senior shake hands with a Korean golfer named K. J. Choi. I said to myself, one day I will also shake hands with the US president on the golf course. I quickly became addicted. I only wish I had the opportunity to learn sooner, that's why I started my son as early as possible."

For some reason, it wasn't a stretch for me to imagine Bo at Pine Valley shaking hands with the president.

"I see. Is your son an avid golfer as well?"

"Yes, he loves the game. And very talented. He is captain of his school team at Beijing No. 4 High School and probably a top ten student golfer in the country. In my opinion, it would be a waste not to send him to the US to play for a college team. The problem is that the coaches in the US don't take him seriously. They won't talk to us, even when we send official results from national youth tournaments in China, they say they don't know what this is."

"The college sports recruiting process makes no sense anyways," I said. Then I told him about the thirteenth graders.

At Princeton, a not insignificant portion of the student-athletes each year came in with not four, but five years of high school. The "PG year," as it was called, was common practice for wealthy families to get their kids into Ivy League colleges by sending them off for a year at one of the elite New England boarding schools that have deep connections with college coaches and recruiters. Of course, the true star athletes had no need for this system, could get admitted with abysmal transcripts and test scores. But for those whose athletic talents were more borderline, it helped the coaches save face with admissions by rebranding the potential recruits with a prestigious and ostensibly rigorous academic experience. Bo listened with fascination and shook his head. "That doesn't make any sense at all," he said, somewhat crestfallen.

After breakfast, Bo and I walked out of the Jockey Club together. On my walk back to my apartment, I thought some more about the thirteenth graders. My freshman year roommate, Chip, had been a lacrosse thirteenth grader at St. Paul's School in New Hampshire, and when he explained the system to me, I too reacted with disbelief. Until that point in my life I had believed in very little besides the absolute supremacy of meritocracy as a mental model for explaining the world, an illusion that Chip ruptured with the lacrosse stick he kept in our shared bedroom. Chip often spoke about his fifth year of high school like it was some sort of traumatic penal experience, stuck with heaps of homework and no beer in a dorm with thirteen-year-olds in freezing New Hampshire while his lax buddies from back home in Westchester County were already "rawdogging life" at Bucknell, Trinity, or wherever else they had gone. Only Chip had the strength of character to suffer for delayed gratification, which was now paying off richly. To my shock, Chip's supplementary high school experience was seen by our classmates not as a mark of shame, but a sort of social distinction. Apparently the really embarrassing way of earning a place at Princeton was just by being a regular nerd. Chip ascended quickly, and was often gone on weekend trips I only found out about after the fact on Facebook. The worst part is, he also had shockingly good grades and was nice to everybody.

After I got back to my apartment, I found myself watching YouTube swing tutorials and reading articles on *Golf Digest*, trying to familiarize myself with the sport while also attempting to distance myself from the notion that on some subconscious level I craved Bo's validation and wanted to impress him. Somewhat pathetic, I thought, given the very premise of our relationship was Bo tricking me into working for him by pretending to believe in me. Nonetheless, the fact that Bo was a serious golfer and wanted me to become one too showed he saw a trajectory for me, and if I'm being honest, this felt good. The problem, of course, was that the potential he saw in me had been based off trade secrets spoon-fed to me by the FBI. Which meant that when the time came for me to drop the cage over him, I would have to face his disappointment.

26

A week later, I got an email reminding me to RSVP for Princeton Reunions, which were coming up at the end of the month.

I'd never actually attended, at least not as an alumnus. But I remember the ritual well from my days as a student. Princeton Reunions were a big deal. People like to say it's the single largest alcohol-consumption event that happens in the United States every year, but that's technically not true—it's the single largest *private* beer order in the country (350 kegs). It's also, in my cynical and perhaps unfair view, the single largest dick-measuring and ass-kissing event in the United States. The alums who return are desperate to convince their former classmates that the course of their lives have fulfilled the promise of Princeton. Nothing, of course, is as impressive in WASP world as generosity, which creates opportunities for current students. One friend who stayed after classes ended to work as a driver for the septuagenarian classes told me he made $1,400 in tips over the course of four days and landed a last-minute internship for the summer.

Funnily enough, the email came from my ex-girlfriend Jessica, who had been elected class marshal or class president, whatever it's called, the fall after we all graduated. She was an obvious choice—upbeat, supremely organized, cool but didn't make you feel uncool. For months I'd been ignoring her mass messages soliciting donations, feedback on class events, the design of the five-year "beer jacket," etc. This time, though, there was a personalized reply to the mass email list, addressed just to me.

Hi Michael,

Have you been getting these messages? I don't see your name on the RSVP list, but I'm still holding out hope that you'll finally join us this year! People really miss you, probably more than you think!

Anyway—Lawrence is organizing a Princeton in Asia panel at Jones Hall on the Saturday of reunions at 10:00 a.m. He said he hasn't been able to get in touch with you and wanted me to reach out and ask if you'd maybe be interested in being one of the panelists? Apparently a few people in our class and the class above have been asking about you since you started that new job at Naveon.

Also—you just moved to China without even saying goodbye? Obviously I'm happy for you . . . but come on! Find a way to make it up to me!

Your friend,
Jessica

The notion that others had been not just talking but *inquiring* about me filled me with exquisite delight, because it suggested they cared enough to potentially feel jealous. How refreshing it felt to be the object, rather than the subject, of jealousy at Princeton for once! I was convinced instantly. I replied to Jessica, saying I had to check my travel calendar and would let her know. Then I set off to see Ferris.

"I don't think it's a bad idea for you to go back to Princeton Reunions," Ferris said. "It'll build credibility with Bo, by showing that you're proactive and highly networked in the university community. He'd also most likely take a harder look at the leads coming out of your trip because they will seem more proprietary."

We were at a shitty American restaurant in Sanlitun District called Blue Frog. We'd met here because I wanted a burger, probably a symptom of early onset nostalgia for America in anticipation of reunions.

"I think I can definitely pitch it to him. Do you think Agent Lim and Agent Reddy will bite?"

Ferris nodded. "I think so. Should be pretty straightforward for them to set up shadow meetings for you with researchers at Princeton and Rutgers. They may even want to identify some high-value 'targets' for you to preview with Bo to build interest."

The burgers arrived, oversized and pinkish gray. To my disappointment, there were not enough fries. Suddenly I wanted a milkshake, but a vision of the suit I wanted to wear at Reunions prevented me from ordering one. Ferris had a milkshake.

At our next meeting, Ferris briefed me on a new batch of profiles that had just come in from the FBI. The clear standout was Yang Xujun, a forty-six-year-old Princeton faculty member who was a leader in the field of microchip design and fabrication. I knew instantly that Yang was the perfect bait. He held a dual appointment with National Taiwan University and had worked as an independent contractor for the national champion Taiwan Semiconductor Manufacturing Company, which meant it was virtually certain he had inside knowledge on secretive semifab techniques that Bo's stakeholders were trying to replicate. In Bo's office, I explained how the circuit timing/control and thermal management techniques Yang developed could improve the power density of modern microchips by an order of magnitude and showed him evidence from interviews in trade publications about Yang's work at TSMSC. Bo pressed his fingertips together and interrupted with lots of questions, which I've learned shows that he's excited.

"I agree, Michael, it sounds quite promising. Will you have an opportunity to meet with Dr. Yang?"

"Yes, I'll be meeting him during Princeton Reunions. We're scheduled to have dinner together on the Friday evening of that weekend."

"A man like Dr. Yang must receive many solicitations from headhunters and answer almost none of them. How did you get him to agree to have dinner?"

"My freshman year floormate is a PhD candidate in his lab," I lied. "I found out from her that outside of his academic work, Dr. Yang chairs a nonprofit dedicated to poverty alleviation in the Chinese countryside. Apparently, fundraising's been difficult. I asked her for an introduction positioning Naveon as a potential sponsor of his organization."

"I see. Good work. Make sure you leave a good impression. I think this man can make a significant impact for us; opportunities of this size don't appear very often. Don't talk to him too much about money, but make it clear we can make this very much worth his time. If your meeting with him goes well and he's willing to work with us, I'll want to meet with him face-to-face as well."

"Understood. Thank you." I couldn't believe it—this was the first time Bo expressed any degree of interest in an in-person meeting. Sensing an opening, I continued. "By the way, Bo, there was one more thing."

"Tell me."

"What you mentioned last time. Finding a time to see my dad. When can we do that?"

"Soon, Michael. I spoke to him right after our dinner. He knows you're here and wants to see you as soon as possible. But as I mentioned last time, certain state security policies restrict his visits to the city. He and his staff are in lockdown until the final delivery of the multiyear project they are very close to completing—what your father came to Beijing to do. The exact timeline, whether that is weeks or months, is unclear. But perhaps I could use some of my connections to get a security clearance for you to visit the facility. Give me some time. Maybe after you return from your trip to the United States."

I looked hard into his black, depthless eyes. Was he bullshitting me? If the work my father was doing was so top secret he couldn't even visit Beijing, how could the authorities consider granting a security clearance to a random American? There was also something disingenuous and contingent about the way he'd proposed the timing of the visit, as if he was holding my father hostage until I gave him what he wanted. I felt an adrenaline-streaked tingling around my eyes and temples that threatened to explode. I had to remind myself how dangerous this man was in order to calm down. There was something dark about Bo, the way he invisibly shaped events.

"By the way, do you have everything you need for the Reunions weekend?" he said. "Christine gave you the company card, right? Please spare no expense in making this visit a success. Anything you need, you have my direct approval."

"Yes. I appreciate that, Bo," I said.

The following day, I finally returned Christine's call. She picked up on the first ring, but there was a touch of annoyance in her voice.

"Well, Michael? I assume this call means you made it back to China in one piece. I worried about you, in case that wasn't obvious."

There were six missed calls from her in my call history starting from when I got back, which was five days ago. "I'm really sorry it took so long to return your call. Things have been very strange lately."

"You don't have to apologize. But the next time you need to talk to someone, I hope you just call me."

I wasn't quite sure what to say. I suppose a small part of me was touched.

"I'm free for a bit this afternoon," I said. "Would you like to get a coffee?"

There was a brief silence on the other end of the line. "I don't drink coffee," she said. "But sure."

I met Christine at Bracket Coffee in Sanlitun and bought her a latte, which she drank with both hands cupped under the mug. I could tell she was trying to be cold and standoffish but in reality was happy to see me. I told her about my plan to attend Princeton Reunions and find a way to introduce Bo to Yang Xujun. I also mentioned that I would be co-hosting a panel for Princeton in Asia. She laughed.

"So you are . . . a guest of honor?"

"I guess you could say that."

"Not bad, *dage*! They definitely wouldn't let just anybody do that. You must be such a big shot."

She gave me two thumbs-up, which made me feel slightly irritated. I told her I needed to do some shopping for Reunions and she agreed to help me, so we went to Taikoo Li, the outdoor mall. We looked at the Reunions itinerary on my phone together and Christine picked out three outfits for me. She really knew what she was doing, and by the end of the afternoon I was surprised to find myself looking somewhat presentable. It was almost dinnertime, so to thank her for helping me I took her to a Spanish tapas restaurant and ordered ham croquettes, seafood paella, and a pitcher of white sangria.

The shopping and the sangria had put me in an excited and chatty mood. I started to feel warmly toward Christine, even thought that my dad could have used a woman like her in his life, someone to polish the rough edges. Christine only picked at the food, often cupping her right cheek in her palm. When we reached the last quarter of the paella, I started to wonder if all my excitement about Reunions was coming across as lame. Plus, we still hadn't talked about what happened in San Francisco.

"So it's a five-year reunion—that means most of your classmates still won't have had kids right? But probably a few that are married or engaged?"

"Yeah, that's right," I said absentmindedly. Princeton Reunions were notoriously a great place to meet someone new or reconnect with an old flame. But this was far from my mind.

"Are you allowed to bring a plus-one?"

"Some do, but most don't," I said. An image of Vivian's arm pressed against mine in the garden at Tsinghua University came vaunting back from memory, which instantly soured my mood. I took another gulp of sangria. Vivian would have been, of course, the ultimate finishing touch for my triumphant return to Princeton. Stewing over this, I retreated into myself for a few moments, and when I looked up again, I noticed a slightly downcast expression on Christine's face.

"I see," she said.

I didn't realize until we got the check that I hadn't asked her a single question about herself.

27

According to Ferris, there had been a bit of trouble brewing on the American side.

A recent increase in tariffs on US corn had crippled the competitiveness of that export in the China market, driving down revenues for farmers in the Midwest who were seeing lower bids in their futures contracts. This supported the hawkish administration's long-standing argument that China unfairly disadvantaged foreign competition in its own market while exporting freely to the rest of the world. On top of this, the American agriculture lobby argued, China's entire fertilizer industry was based on industrial techniques stolen from American companies during the last decade.

"Hold on a second. Is that last part even true?" I asked Ferris.

"It's not entirely off the mark. In 2016 a DuPont agricultural engineer driving home late from work caught a Chinese agent digging up seeds from one of DuPont's corn fields in the middle of the night while another agent waited in a car nearby. After they were arrested, federal authorities found hundreds of ears of stolen corn stashed away in a hidden storage facility in Des Moines. The agents had been secretly shipping seeds back to China in boxes of Pop Weaver brand microwave popcorn."

"Wow," I said. "That is impressively hardcore."

Ferris shrugged. "Gotta respect the enemy, I guess. Probably not how I would have gone about it, but you can't argue with results. The agents that got caught are in federal prison now, but on the scale of China's population, the tech they stole, just by shaving off five percent of corn production costs, changed food accessibility on the scale of millions. Agent Lim was actually the agent in charge for the case."

I was surprised by the dispassion in Ferris's account. For him, it was a game of chess, and the only moral certainty was which side of the board he played on. I had a vision of him in another life deployed as the Chinese agent in Iowa under deep cover—Ferris among the alien corn.

"So how does all of this impact us?" I asked.

He gave me a stern look and I braced myself for what he was about to say next. "The AG has put pressure on the DOJ to deliver near-term prosecutorial victories against the China Initiative and show the agriculture lobby that the US will fight hard without dragging the country into a wider trade war. Right now, the most pressure is on Scully because his colleagues at the DOJ think of him as the person who's primarily responsible for the China Initiative. What this means is that our timeline for luring Bo to the states has been compressed. We probably have no more than thirty days before the clock runs out."

So the room for error had essentially been reduced to zero. I felt my shoulders clench up immediately and fought to maintain my composure in front of Ferris. "And then what happens?"

"If we can't get Bo out within thirty days, Scully will order for you to be recalled back to the US."

I was overcome with a sense of vertigo. Just as we neared the target, the floor was shifting under my feet, like the golf simulator at the Jockey Club.

There was something revolting about the naked savagery of this setup: the Iowans demanded oriental scalps, and so it would have to be either Bo's or my own.

"So that basically leaves us with the three weeks leading up to Reunions and only one week after. I'm guessing that my meeting with Yang is still our best bait. What's our plan B if Bo doesn't bite?"

"That's correct. Yang is still plan A. As for plan B, let's cross that bridge when we get there. We've still got one really good card left to play, so let's make sure that we play it right."

I waited for him to say more, but he didn't. I tried not to fault him for it—surely it was part of Ferris's specialized skill set to recognize when the odds on a mission turned long. Suddenly I wondered how many others before me he'd had similar conversations with. If Ferris couldn't help me with a plan B, I thought, maybe I'd have to come up with one myself.

28

The first piece of corroborating evidence that something had shifted in the macro environment came from Christine, a few days after Ferris told me about our new deadline. We had started to have dinner together every week or so, and were eating at a hot pot restaurant in Guomao.

"By the way, Michael, have you noticed anything different about Bo recently?"

"What do you mean?"

"He seems a little on edge recently. Canceling a lot of his meetings last minute. He and his wife are usually very social, but they haven't asked for my help entertaining in quite some time."

"Maybe it's a busy period at work," I said.

"No, I don't think it's that," she said, lowering her voice to almost a whisper. "Three days ago two men with government IDs came into Bo's office without an appointment and spoke to him with the door shut for two hours. That *never* happens."

I paused. "Are you sure you should be telling me this?"

"I know. I shouldn't be telling you. But I'm scared and I don't know who else I can talk to about this."

"Listen, Christine. The next time something like this happens, can you let me know?"

She nodded.

The next time I saw Bo, the changes that Christine described were immediately obvious. He seemed gaunter and yellower, like he hadn't been sleeping, and his eyes, usually jovial, had taken on a much blacker tone. During our weekly meetings, I felt his mind was occupied elsewhere. Every time I brought up the possibility of meeting Yang in person, he seemed to deflect onto another subject.

The color from Ferris was that there appeared to be a general freezing out within the Chinese intelligence community. We didn't know whether or not it was connected to the hawkish US response to the corn tariffs. Many of Ferris's assets had stopped delivering meaningful information and one had cut communication entirely. It was becoming dangerous for us to make a move.

Despite his warnings, I pressed Ferris to send as many high-value profiles to me as possible in the little time we left. Each time, he cautioned me about the dangers of pushing Bo too hard. Powerful people behaved unpredictably when threatened, he said. Being discovered by Bo would result in much more serious consequences than standing trial in the United States.

Still, with time running out, I continued to lobby hard with Bo. Once, I think I pushed him too far. I was in the middle of telling him about an MIT AI researcher who wanted to meet him in Brussels when he suddenly lifted his hand and cut me off.

"Michael," he said softly. I noticed his hand was shaking. "This is all good progress. But I have a question for you. Why do so many of these scientists suddenly want to meet me outside of the country?"

I froze. Bo's black eyes bored into mine. This was the first time he seemed to be really listening during the entire meeting. Perhaps he'd already figured everything out; would it be better to just tell him everything now and expose the FBI conspiracy against him? Maybe if I promised to be his fall man with the DOJ, he'd show some leniency.

"I was confused too at first," I said. "It's definitely been happening more lately. I think it's due to more extensive media coverage of unfair DOJ prosecution of Chinese-born scientists under the China Initiative. There are now many examples of academics at Harvard, MIT, being put on watch lists simply for visiting China. And speaking to many academics myself, I'm keenly aware of how quickly these rumors are running through the whisper networks. While I'm always happy to establish and work the relationships, I don't have the stature myself to secure a commitment on my own. You should understand that at some point, we may need you to get involved personally."

As I finished speaking, Bo shifted his gaze off of me, giving no indication as to whether or not he believed my explanation.

"Perhaps you are right about the changing climate in the US. Nonetheless, it's not a good time for me to be leaving China right now."

In this way, three weeks passed with very little progress. As time ran out, I started to feel mired in hopelessness. There was something quite absurd, maybe even funny, about the situation I now found myself in. I, Michael Wang, who was not politically savvy enough to even procure an eating club guest pass for ninety percent of my weekends at Princeton, was now expected to lure a seasoned Chinese intelligence operative out of hiding. *Expected*, perhaps, was probably not the right word, though, since it seemed no one really believed I had a chance of succeeding. After debriefing the last meeting with Ferris, the stream of profiles started to slow. So now I was left with nothing but time and the obligation to spend it. I began to reflect more on my short life and the series of small disappointments and large overcorrections that had led me to this point.

During this interim period, the artifice of my life in Beijing started to become more noticeable. When I first came to China I thought, perhaps naïvely, that it would be a place where I could lead a life that would be closer to my "true self," unencumbered by whatever it ultimately was that kept me at a distance from others in America. By contrast, everything here felt staged. I had everything I needed inside the benevolent ecosystem of my apartment compound—gym, green space, even some restaurants and grocery stores. Whenever I used the facilities, the attendants would give me the same smile, greet me by my name like in a country club, and record my comings and goings. Everything felt designed for me to stay within Bo's carefully calibrated boundary conditions. When I did venture outside the compound to bars and restaurants, it seemed like the staff at restaurants and bars were already half expecting me; they knew my name and my connection to Bo, and somehow always had a table open for me. It was quite the opposite of being invisible, yet in a way somehow more alienating. Was it really possible Bo didn't already know of my plan? I was certain that my apartment had been bugged. I turned my place inside out looking for hidden cameras and microphones; my failure to find any only made me more convinced they'd been cleverly hidden. I started to think of myself as instance number 798 of a large-scale simulation programmed by Bo. Random coincidences appeared mysteriously connected, imbued with deeply encrypted meaning. I discovered that the Economic Espionage Act of 1996 was enacted on October 11—my birthday. One day I saw the Club Mandarin in the background of a TV news story about fires in San Francisco. I kept thinking of the *Girl and Camera* painting I'd spotted at the Hugo Gallery on my day in the country.

The money that automatically appeared every other week in my Bank of China account also seemed virtual, since there was no way I could move it out of the country or expect to hold onto it after the simulation came to an end. Since it was not realistic for me to assume that I, instance number 798, would be the one to break the boundary conditions, it fell upon me to simply enjoy my remaining runtime as much as possible. Every night I booked VIP tables at nightclubs and lounges in Sanlitun and invited Hans and Christian to join me. The hostesses would come with bottles of potentially counterfeit foreign vodka that tasted like numbing agent and plates with sliced-up pineapples and watermelon with mini plastic umbrellas sticking out of them. Who wanted to eat watermelon at a club? I started smoking again, this time a copious amount, and always had the Yunnan tobacco aftertaste in my mouth.

Christine and I kept up our weekly dinner date, but each seemed to go worse than the last. To me, she was part of the simulation as well. This was because her entrance and continued presence in my life was completely contrived. Bo had plucked her out of MSS Central Casting and cast her in a boilerplate role, bait and switched her for Vivian without explanation. As we got closer to Scully's deadline, I started to realize that I was and had been deeply angry about this. She was so ordinary and we had no special chemistry; I wouldn't have risked everything and cut myself off from my life for a woman like Christine. Every time she did something thoughtful for me, like dropping home-cooked food by my apartment, it felt programmed and impersonal, like an email drip campaign. My anger was directed not just at Bo but also toward myself, for simply accepting it without complaint. Still, some of it inevitably found its way to Christine. One evening we were having dinner on the candlelit terrace of Malaparte, an Italian restaurant in Dongzhimen. I didn't care much for the spaghetti, which was too sweet and getting cold. Neither of us had said anything for five minutes before she finally broke the silence.

"What's going on, Michael?"

"Excuse me?"

"You've been acting so distant lately. Did something happen?"

"Of course not. Everything is great," I said. I spooled a few strings of spaghetti with my fork and gestured at the terrace. "Look at this beautiful food on such a beautiful evening. What could possibly be better?"

"It's just me, Michael. You can talk to me." She looked at me imploringly and rested her hands on the table. I leaned back in my seat and rotated my wine glass.

"I'm not sure what you want," I said curtly. "Bo sent you to me to be my companion, maybe even keep a bit of an eye on me, though we never talk about that, and that's what we're doing, isn't it? So if you don't mind, let's just keep going through the motions."

Christine exhaled sharply and refolded her napkin across her lap. For a second I thought she would leave. "When we first met, Bo told me to text you once a month and see if you needed anything," she said flatly. "Everything else was me."

Throughout all of this I continued with Bo's suggested practice regiment of three times per week at the golf simulator. It was a good way for me to pass the hours I'd otherwise have spent dwelling on how little time I had left. In the end, I was glad I practiced, because one day Bo called out of the blue and asked if I was ready for the real thing. He took me to a private course in one of the outer rings of the city. Even though we were thirty-seven miles from the city center, the smog was still thick, and I found myself huffing and puffing between holes. I focused on playing fast over playing well to avoid slowing down Bo, who seemed pleased by the progress I had made. I noticed an overall uplift in his spirits. The bags around his eyes had softened, and his movements were less stiff. We finished our eighteen holes at around the four-hour mark and Bo patted me on the back.

"Very good performance today, Michael, especially for your first time on a real course. I can tell you've been practicing."

"Thank you—that means a lot to me. The real thing is way more enjoyable."

“It’s good to have a love for the game, especially a game like this that you can still play even when you’re well past your prime like I am. To be honest, the courses we have in Beijing are not world-class. One day, I’ll take you to my favorite course in Scotland.”

I allowed myself the momentary satisfaction of imagining Agent Lim slapping handcuffs around Bo’s wrists right at the arrivals gate in Heathrow. As we made our way to the parking lot, I pulled out my phone to call a cab home.

“Hold on, Michael. Would you like to join me for dinner with my family? Our house is not far from here.”

29

The black Audi sedan picked us up from the golf club and made a course northwest through winding mountain roads. I recognized Xiaowen, the driver who had first picked me up in Beijing, but he didn't acknowledge the connection. As we ascended the mountain, a thick fog rolled in from the forest and clouded the car windows. Xiaowen turned on the low beams and slowed us down to a crawl.

By the time we arrived at the gate, it was raining. Xiaowen rolled down the window to have his face scanned by the security camera; there was a blueish flash, then the gate clicked open and we started climbing up the steep driveway to Bo's home. As we rounded the bend, the granite facade of the massive villa loomed into view. Xiaowen dropped us in front of the oaken front doors and disappeared to park the vehicle.

We descended a graceful set of steps from the foyer into Bo's minimalist living room. The room was awash in the blue-gray light of early evening, which seeped in from the garden through a window wall. Bo's garden was bounded by impressive laurel privacy hedges ten feet high, the type commonly seen in wealthy suburbs on the US East and West Coast. I could make out a koi pond, a limestone scholars' rock, and a Blackstone grill.

Bo excused himself and left me alone in the living room. I checked my phone and saw I had no signal. We'd driven at least an hour from the course and must be far outside of the city. Something about the rain and the fog this high up in the mountains was disquieting; it felt like a place I could easily disappear. Some orchestral music started to play on the surround sound system. Then, Bo reappeared with his wife, Michelle. They opened a bottle of red wine and sat down together on the couch across from me.

"This is a beautiful home," I said.

"My wife will only be too happy to hear that," Bo said, beaming. "Michelle is an architect, you remember. She designed the entire place herself. We used to live in the city when our son was in grade school, but I bought this plot of land in the mountains a decade ago as an anniversary gift for her; I told her it was a canvas."

Hearing that kind of sentimentality from Bo caught me off guard. "What a lovely story," I said. "And it's so quiet up here. Do you have neighbors?"

"None. And that's of the utmost importance for us. Privacy is the highest luxury in Beijing, where there are CCTVs everywhere on every street corner. Because of my work, I have many guests here from foreign countries—often people in highly sensitive positions. They love to stay here because it is so quiet, and they feel they can speak freely. I hope you feel similarly."

I searched Bo's face for signs of suspicion. Was I imagining the malicious subtext in his last sentence?

"You must stay with us tonight too," Michelle said. "When Bo told me you were coming, I set up the guest bedroom in the south wing for you. You'll be comfortable there, and Xiaowen will drive you back to the city tomorrow morning."

"Ah, I'd love to. That's very kind of you. But I have a meeting tomorrow morning, so I really have to get back to the city."

Michelle pulled up the weather app on her phone. "You see, Michael, there's going to be a thunderstorm tonight. The mountain roads are very muddy when it rains, so it's not safe for you to return tonight."

I realized there was no possibility I would be returning to my apartment that night. "I see. In that case, thank you for letting me stay."

Michelle smiled at me. "You're very welcome. By the way, how are your Chinese lessons going?"

I froze and scanned her expression, which was perfectly neutral—no emotions at all behind her watchful eyes.

"Last time we had dinner together, you mentioned you were taking Chinese lessons. How are they going? Have you found a good teacher?"

"Oh, yes. I think I'm making progress. Though I haven't been as committed to it lately as I should be, with all that's been going on."

"I see. One of the young men who works with Bo—I believe you met him at the AV Conference—said he spotted you with someone near Tsinghua University last week. He thought it might've been a lesson, so he didn't come say hi."

How would Bo's associate have known I was taking Chinese lessons? And if he did see me—how long had he stood there, and what had he heard? A woman emerged from the kitchen to let us know dinner was ready. We sat down at the marble dining table and she brought out a hot pot with slices of lamb and beef, fish balls, green vegetables, tofu, lotus root, and glass noodles. Bo decanted another bottle of red wine. My chair faced the window, and I looked out at the mountain ranges and the swollen dark clouds creeping closer. I wondered if my father's lab was somewhere in that view, obscured by rain, dusk, and canopy; whether he had even sat in my place at this very table.

Just then, a teenage boy joined us from upstairs. Michelle introduced him as their son Kevin, a rising senior at Beijing No. 4 High School. Kevin greeted me with a polite nod. Unlike his father, he had more of a sensitive look, with his pale, oval-shaped face, high nose bridge, and long haircut with the bangs covering his forehead. Bo started the conversation by telling Michelle and Kevin about my upcoming trip back to Princeton.

"I'm very envious of your upcoming trip, Michael. I spent a year as a young man studying in New York City. This was the year 1988—Reagan's last year in office when the movie *Die Hard* came out. You've seen it, right? The trip was too short and I promised myself I would return. Now thirty years have gone by."

I realized that Bo's account of his time in New York matched the timeline Scully gave me during our first conversation—he was telling the truth. "Why don't you join me on this trip? We could add you as a panelist for the Princeton in Asia panel. I'm sure the students would love to hear from you. Then we could spend some time in New York together before or after."

Bo put down his chopsticks. "But I'm not connected to the university in any way. You don't think that would appear a bit suspicious?"

"Not at all," I said, "we bring in outside speakers all the time. Selfishly, given your stature, it would make me look really good. And I'll admit I am eager to impress my former classmates."

He chuckled. "Now that I understand. I was very much the same when I was your age. Sadly, now is a difficult time for men in my position to visit the United States. Our friend Wengui made too much noise and ruined the party for everyone. I will have to live vicariously through you. And, if all goes well, Kevin, who we hope will study in the US next year."

Kevin stared down at his plate and shifted in his seat. I noticed he was barely eating.

"Yes, he's in the middle of it all now. College applications are due in just a few months. We've hired a consultant to help guide him through the process. But to be honest, I don't trust him. Despite his exorbitant fees, he promises nothing and insists no one else in the business can either. In fact, he tells us admissions officers will view Kevin skeptically because he's coming from China, since Chinese students have a reputation for faking transcripts and test scores. Essentially scamming their way to get in. But this is hypocritical bullshit. Michael, tell them what you told me about the thirteenth graders."

I told Michelle and Kevin about the thirteenth graders, and Michelle shook her head in disapproval. Then I offered to help edit Kevin's essays, which pleased Bo immensely. Now the conversation settled into a more natural rhythm. Predictably, the topics revolved around Kevin: we talked about his extracurricular activities, what he hoped to study in college, what it's like to attend an American university. Then Bo told several stories about his career as a venture capitalist, taking care to draw parallels between me and his younger self, which were so incredibly specific I had to remind myself he was making them up. It amazed me that neither Kevin nor Michelle seemed to register any reaction to Bo's made-up stories; was it possible they didn't know what he really did for work?

Kevin excused himself, saying he had to study for his SATs. As the sky outside darkened, I started to feel increasingly trapped. Now that Kevin was upstairs, Bo transitioned to work talk, praising my extraordinary early results and promise. I got the sickening feeling that he was manipulating me once again. Who was Bo to make me feel as if he saw only the best in me, only to lie to my face and use me? What about the promises that had been made and hastily forgotten? Did he think I wouldn't notice, when he swapped Christine for Vivian, or did he just think I would be too cowardly to say anything?

"Actually, there is something I wanted to ask you, Bo," I said. "Where is Vivian? Candidly, I've been wondering what's happened to her."

Bo's expression darkened in an instant. "Do you have reason to believe something has happened to her?"

"I just haven't heard from her since I arrived in Beijing."

Bo let the silence in the wake of my words hang in the air for a few seconds. "And you think I might have something to do with that?"

"No. I'm not saying anything happened. I just thought you might have a sense of where she is, given you're her uncle."

"I see. The two of you did seem close. However, I don't control my niece. Unfortunately, she's been known to disappear for months at a time."

"It's getting late," Michelle interjected. "I think we'd better let Michael get some rest. I asked Xiaowen to pick him up at 7:00 A.M. tomorrow."

"Yes. Come, Michael, let me show you to your room." Bo took me to a guest bedroom on the second floor and bid me goodnight. He was almost all the way down the hall before he turned again and added, "By the way, Michael, if you feel sleepless, see if the library has what you're looking for."

I took a hot shower and started to worry that I had been too aggressive in asking about Vivian. I gently pushed open the bedroom door and listened for any voices—I heard nothing except for the sound of typing from Kevin's bedroom, which ceased at one o'clock in the morning. After I was certain that the house was completely silent, I crept into the library next door and turned the light on. I saw it at once—the blackness of the camera lens peering into me from the canvas. I knew even before checking the artist's signature: the same painting I had seen at the gallery in San Francisco on my last day in America, hanging on the wall in Bo's library.

30

The next morning, Xiaowen picked me up at seven o'clock, and I met Ferris for lunch one more time to go over the plan for Princeton Reunions. There wasn't much to discuss since all the meetings would be fabricated anyway; we just had to chat through the plan for presenting the assets to Bo.

"One more thing, Michael," he said. "Agent Lim is actually going to be coming on the trip with you."

"Are you serious? Why?"

"He just said he wanted to meet. During the weekend, he'll be posing as your driver."

Fucking great.

I landed at JFK at around five o'clock in the afternoon. Stepping out of the gate in Terminal B, I wasn't surprised to see Agent Lim waiting for me.

"Fancy seeing you here," I said.

He put both his hands up. "Relax! Not here to handcuff you this time. Just giving you a ride."

Lim waved me past the immigration and customs lines and made a show of examining me from head to toe.

"You look good, Michael. New clothes?"

"A few."

"So they've been treating you nice, huh?"

I just barely stopped myself from rolling my eyes. We headed to the garage and got into Agent Lim's black Chevy Suburban.

"Where to, boss?" he said, dialing up the GPS.

"Nassau Inn in Princeton."

Agent Lim let out a low whistle. "Prime location—must be expensive this weekend! We've got a high roller. Let me know if the people you work for have an opening sometime."

"Look, now that we're in private, you can just go ahead and ankle bracelet me," I said.

"Michael, Michael. No need to be so uptight. Honestly, I'm here to protect you. You're a valuable government asset, remember? And, according to our files, not the strongest drinker; we can't afford any slipups with this crowd. Most importantly, we don't know who the Chinese may or may not have sent to tail you on this trip. That is, to verify you're representing your activities here accurately to Beijing."

That shut me up. Instinctively I glanced at the rearview mirror to see if anyone suspicious was tailing us on the highway. It was too dark to make out the faces in the cars behind us.

"Do you think that scenario is likely?"

"It's certainly not unlikely. Have you given them any reason to suspect you?"

I instantly regretted asking about Vivian a few nights ago. There were a few other moments, I thought, when Bo could have suspected me. Or when Michelle had casually inquired about my Chinese lessons.

"I'm not sure. Nothing comes to mind, but I know these guys are trained and I'm not."

"Sounds about right. How is our man on the ground, Ferris?"

"Holding up well. I've quite enjoyed working with him."

Lim nodded. "Well, he speaks highly of you. I'm not sure why. Candidly, I've been making the pitch to recall you for several months now. Don't get me wrong, if somehow you do deliver Bo, that outcome would more than justify your exoneration on acceptable standards of affirmative cooperation. I just don't think it's responsible for the bureau to put an untrained civilian in enemy territory like that. Particularly when said civilian has such obvious psychological complexes that could compromise the success of the mission—not to mention our overall strategic position in China, where we've been burned before."

I prickled at "obvious psychological complexes" but didn't want to press the point. The rest of the ride passed in silence. An hour later, we crossed the Washington Road Bridge and entered Princeton proper, the primordial soup of my neuroses. Past the bridge, the traffic on Washington Road was start and stop as both lanes were flooded with the cars of returning alumni. No one really needed a car to get around for the weekend, but people drove them in anyway, and those with convertibles pulled the tops down and waved presidentially as they cruised toward campus. On both sides, the uncannily pristine colonial and Georgian facades of downtown Princeton vaunted themselves from memory. We passed the winged glass silhouette of the Lewis Science Library, where I spent the greater part of my solitude; just about five hundred feet down the street, the Frist Campus Center, where I usually went for greasy fried food after a late night of studying. Frist was the town square where all walks of Princeton society collided at the end of the evening for chicken tenders and curly fries. I tried to avoid the 1:30–2:00 A.M. window there because that was usually when the eating club festivities ended and the formal-wear-clad

Nicks of the world poured in reeking of alcohol to bask in deep-fried social glory while continuing their conversations from the previous party. Whenever this happened I immediately felt like an intruder, my evident nonparticipation in their debauchery a conspicuous sign of unintended social disproof. Talk about obvious psychological complexes. I turned to the left and saw Agent Lim's observant gaze boring into my temple. I endured this slow-time tour of my undergraduate experience for fifteen agonizing minutes before we finally reached the Nassau Inn. Lim made a point of telling me he would be staying at the Holiday Inn in neighboring Trenton. He had my itinerary, so I should expect to see a lot of him this weekend.

I tried to get through check-in as quickly as possible in order to minimize the chance of unexpectedly running into someone from college when I hadn't had the time to mentally prepare myself.

"Welcome back, Mr. Wang," the receptionist said. "We have you in a King Suite on the third floor. Your bags will up shortly, and we hope you enjoy your stay."

When I got to the room, I found a black and orange windbreaker neatly spread out on the bed with a card on top of it.

Michael,

Welcome back, Mr. VIP! I figured you didn't bring your class of 2013 beer jacket to China but I managed to dig up a spare for you—hopefully it still fits! See you at the P-rade.

Jessica

It did not fit, but I was touched nonetheless. I had no idea how Jessica found out where I was staying—did she call every hotel in Princeton? Talk about making an effort. I thought about texting her but told myself I'd just thank her in person.

⟜

The next morning, I had a simple breakfast at the Nassau Inn, put on the suit Christine picked for me to wear during the panel, and headed toward campus. Princeton was blindingly sunny and humid this time of year. First I stopped by the check-in booths near the athletic fields to collect my class bracelet and the brochure for the weekend. I found the blurb for "Princeton in Asia" panel on page 2, alongside other events such as "Living and Working in Literary Fiction" and "Frontiers of Biotechnology." I found my own name printed under the "Princeton in Asia" header: Michael Wang, '13. I realized that I had missed the cheap thrill of seeing my own name in print.

By the time I got to Jones Hall, where the panel was being held, my shirt was already damp under the dark charcoal suit. I wiped the sweat from my brow and walked into the lecture hall. I'd arrived five minutes early, but only eight or nine seats in the hall were filled. Lawrence had set up a rather elaborate breakfast spread by the entrance, which made the room feel even emptier. The three other panelists and Lawrence were huddled together in a corner of the room catching up over coffee and orange juice; the other three were all white guys at least three inches taller than Lawrence, and for once Lawrence appeared less than calm and collected, as if embarrassed by the turnout for his event. I approached the group and recognized James Stacy, chair of the East Asian Studies Department. When I was a freshman I took his Business in China class, where he regularly invited CEOs of major Chinese corporations to guest lecture. I was awed by Professor Stacy's stature and visited his office more than a handful of times (though I ended up with a B+ in the class). Over the years, I began to form a deeper understanding of his career trajectory and the influence he'd had on the department and the university as a whole. As a scholar, he was nothing special—Lawrence was actually the one who told me that. What accounted for Stacy's meteoric rise at Princeton was raw ambition and political cunning. He'd started as an obscure professor of ancient Chinese history and made an unprecedented mid-career pivot to the field of modern China studies, a subject with a much more engaged audience. He then used his credibility as a China scholar to convince the university leadership that for Princeton to remain relevant in the twenty-first century, it had to establish a meaningful position in China; at the same time, he stoked fear by reporting on the expansionary moves rival universities such as Yale, Duke, and NYU were making in the region. The crux was that Stacy positioned himself as the only man who could guide the university out of the impending crisis. Like the Chinese elites that he studied, Stacy was supremely effective in cultivating powerful contacts that impressed the administration and, more importantly, generated healthy donor inflows. Rumor had it he'd even brokered the admission of a few Communist Party princelings, which brought in tens of millions of dollars to the department. His naked careerism sometimes attracted the scorn of more traditional colleagues—weren't intellectuals supposed to speak truth to power?—but in the end fear and the expansionist instinct won out. Over the course of five years, Stacy ascended from niche untenured historian to one of the most powerful figures at Princeton. Lawrence said the president of Princeton even allowed him to charter his own private jets—only for the purpose of entertaining the most important donors, of course.

"Hey, Professor Stacy!" I said.

He smiled and extended a hand. "Good morning, young man! I don't believe we've met."

"Actually, I was in your Business in China class the fall of 2009," I said.

He glanced at my name tag. "Ah, right. Michael Wang, of course! It's so good to see you again. Seems like you've been making some waves in China. I'm glad that my class had such an influence on you."

I just stifled a laugh. The extent of this man's self-centeredness was impossible to overstate. The way he had so transparently read my name off my name tag—I couldn't believe he was so well-received in China.

Obviously I wouldn't tell him that the following year I became disillusioned with the Woodrow Wilson School, switched to computer science, and resigned any ambition of being part of the world stage. And yet in spite of all that—or perhaps *because* of it—I had indeed ended up "making some waves" in China, or getting sucked into a whirlpool to be more accurate. When the irony of this occurred to me, I nearly laughed inadvertently in Professor Stacy's face.

Lawrence chimed in with a forced chuckle. "Hey, Michael! So grateful that you're doing this. Meet Tom Allen and Matt Dolan."

Tom and Matt were each about forty-eight years old and 6'3". They'd been roommates at Princeton, both East Asian Studies and Chinese double majors, now neighbors in Hong Kong. Tom was a senior partner at McKinsey and Matt a managing director at a large American investment bank.

"Neither of us were star students at Princeton, to say the least," Tom explained. "The recruiting standards in Hong Kong at the time were much, much lower. Demand was so high McKinsey was taking any Ivy League Chinese speaker with a pulse. Totally different story now, obviously, Tsinghua and Beijing Universities are our biggest feeders now, the locals have reclaimed their territory. But man, the first decade out there was a hell of a time. It was like the Wild West. I could tell you some stories."

It didn't occur to me until Lawrence asked us to take our seats on the panel that no one had asked me anything about my background.

Lawrence was seated at the end of the table with a microphone and a deck of notecards. He asked each of the panelists to introduce themselves, then invited James Stacy to provide some opening remarks on the state of governance and business in China. Stacy spoke off the cuff for about twenty minutes and it became very clear why he was so well-received by the Chinese elite. His narrative of the past twenty years of Chinese history had the veneer of academic nuance, but at its core could only be described as a celebration of the Chinese Communist Party's track record and an affirmation of its right to govern.

"Okay, now I'd like to turn it over to some of our panelists who have been living and working in the region for the last two and a half decades. Any general observations you'd like to share with this group? Maybe let's start with you, Tom."

"Thanks, Lawrence. As a firm, McKinsey has been active in China since 1994, just four years after the Shanghai Stock Exchange reopened. Our business in China has grown twenty to thirty percent since inception and now it's one of our most important markets. The opportunity for Princeton-trained talent has mostly been around professionalizing business practices. There was and still is a huge amount of inefficiency in their system that's inherited from centuries of graft and backwardness. I certainly don't expect that opportunity to go away."

"Thank you, Tom, very insightful. Matt, would you like to give some thoughts?"

"Yeah, of course. Look, as a firm we've really reaped the rewards of investing heavily and early in China. We saw the vision early—you know, great civilization, billions of people, tons of talent that needed to be unleashed. In the early days we were basically teaching these folks how to do double-entry bookkeeping, and not commit fraud. Obviously, now many of their businesses have taken off spectacularly, especially the tech companies. It's been a lucrative strategy for many of their savviest people, over the past several decades, to basically just copy American internet companies and roll it out to their huge population—shielded, of course, by the government's protectionist trade policies. But if you think that means the party's over, you're wrong. For entrepreneurs in China, there's still nothing that can replicate the cachet of an initial public offering led by a major US bank on the New York Stock Exchange."

"Wonderful, thank you, Matt. Michael, any thoughts for us?"

"Err, yes, happy to give some of my own thoughts," I said, backing away slightly from the mic because my voice came across louder than expected. I hadn't actually prepared any remarks. "So, I think everyone is here because we all know there is a lot of opportunity in China. We can take that point for granted. If I were sitting in your own shoes, I'd be wondering most about what working there is like and what makes someone in China successful. My main observation is that things move really quickly over there, and a lot—actually, even everything—can change overnight. So if you want to succeed, you need to be the sort of person who can adapt really quickly and deal with uncertainty."

"Good. Any questions?"

A slight brown man sitting near the middle of the room, probably a junior or senior, raised his hand. There was a ten-second delay as Lawrence climbed up the stairs to give him the microphone.

"Yes. This question is for Tom Allen. Tom, can you explain why McKinsey's Greater China office held an Arabian Nights–themed desert office retreat in Kashgar, four miles from a Uyghur internment camp? By serving the Chinese Communist Party as a client, isn't McKinsey complicit in the party's atrocities against Uyghurs?"

Lawrence instantly turned pale. Tom gave Lawrence an annoyed look, as if they'd had an arrangement beforehand that that specific question was not to come up. The student looked defiantly at Tom as Tom accepted the microphone from Lawrence.

"Thanks for the question. I believe you forgot to tell us your name?"

"My name is Hamza," the student said, but his voice sounded small and hollow without the microphone.

"Alright, Hamza. Thank you again for the question. First of all, I'd caution against the casual usage of words such as *internment camp* and *atrocities*. In my experience, defamatory language of that kind not only fails to describe the reality, which is always nuanced, but also deepens polarization on both sides of any issue. Which is not to say that we don't take the moral responsibility that comes with leadership in our industry seriously. As a firm we always evaluate the impact of our engagements on a case-by-case basis, and especially on aggregate, we are proud of the positive impact that our practice has had in the Greater China region, which has a population of over 1.4 billion people."

With that Tom passed the microphone back to Lawrence, who asked for the next question before Hamza had an opportunity to respond. For a moment it seemed like Hamza was going to rise from his seat, but a few seconds later the microphone was already on the way to the next audience member, a white guy in business casual attire who asked whether it was better for early career professionals to start in the US or Asia office of an international firm. This seemed to put Lawrence at ease. He fielded two or three more of these questions before announcing that the time for the session was up. Cue scattered applause.

After the end of the session, a couple of audience members hung around to mingle with the panelists. Most of them were huddled around Tom and Matt, while Lawrence and James Stacy held some sort of private sidebar. Unsure of where to put myself, I stood in the general vicinity of Tom and Matt's sycophantic orbit, watching as the students hurled canned questions about opportunities at their respective firms, hoping their names would stick. I suddenly became conscious of the fact that I was much closer in age to the students than to them. Ten minutes later, Tom and Matt announced they had to leave, abruptly ending the gathering; there was a general exchanging of business cards, then everyone filed out of the room. On the way out, Matt made a joke about Tom putting Hamza on the firm's "no fly" list.

Lawrence had insisted on debriefing the panel afterwards, so we walked together to Stephanie's, an American restaurant on Nassau Street, and ordered some brunch plates.

"So, how do you think that went?" Lawrence asked. "By the way, is that . . . your driver?"

He was looking through the window at Agent Lim's car waiting conspicuously across the street. Lim was just sitting there in his sunglasses staring straight ahead.

"Ah, yes," I said casually. "That's my driver Xiaowen. They sent him here from Beijing to accompany me. Don't mind him, please." Lawrence seemed impressed.

"Anyway," I continued. "I thought it went pretty well . . . maybe not as well attended as we would've liked."

Lawrence laughed. "Actually, the turnout today was better than I'd expected. The university likes to organize these events to give the whole thing a sheen of respectability, but the alumni are always too hungover to attend. Especially since they're so damn early in the morning. Tom and I were joking earlier that we'd be shocked if we got more than five people in the room. What I meant was, how do you think the panelists got along with each other?"

"Pretty good, I guess. Was a bit annoyed though not surprised that James Stacy didn't remember me—I went to his office hours at least six or seven times. Tom and Matt seemed nice enough."

Lawrence nodded. "James has a tendency to do that, yes. He was actually my senior thesis advisor; his name opens many doors in China. Though so far for me, sadly not quite enough. Anyway, my friend. You disappeared from San Francisco rather suddenly. What's the story? Give me the inside scoop."

I sighed. "Where to even begin? You remember the thing that happened at work the last time I saw you?"

"Yes. You made a breakthrough in self-driving car software and your boss snubbed you for a promotion."

I raised an eyebrow; Lawrence's memory never ceased to impress.

"Right. Well, after validating that what I'd invented was actually novel, I did some research and discovered that there were several promising self-driving car companies operating in China. I read some of their white papers and came to the conclusion that the Chinese companies were getting more traction than the American companies. So when a recruiter from Naveon reached out to me, I was well-prepared to seize that opportunity."

"Fortune favors the prepared mind, as Pasteur said. Out of curiosity, which headhunting firm represents Naveon? And how do you think they found you? For such an important role, it must have been a very wide search."

"Hmm. To be honest, I don't remember the name of the headhunting firm. It may even have been an independent headhunter. As for how they found me, they said they knew me from my portfolio of work on Samarkand."

"The coding freelancing platform?" Lawrence asked skeptically. I was surprised he was even aware of it.

"Well, yes," I said. "Not just the work I did for clients on Samarkand, though. I posted a lot of white papers on multinodal aggregation as well that generated a lot of discussion in the industry."

"Ah, so like a peer review of sorts. Interesting. And how's working there been so far? Seems like you've been promoted extremely quickly. I mean, a VP at the age of twenty-six. How many people are you managing now?"

"About forty or fifty engineers," I lied. "And the team is growing really quickly, so I feel like I'm learning a lot. Though now that the team is so big, I spend all of my time managing and I miss engineering."

"You and me both, old friend. It seems we are both hitting inflection points in our careers. For myself, the managing partner has sent me to Hong Kong to establish our Asia presence. So the nature of my work has changed as well. I'm not so much a lawyer these days as a salesman and a project manager. They've made it very clear I'll either build a successful Hong Kong practice or lose my chance of making partner."

"Sounds pretty stressful. But I'm sure your family can help you with introductions in China."

"Unfortunately it's not as simple as that. My family is well-connected within Hong Kong, but it's obvious now that all the real action is in the mainland. And in that world, I'm an outsider. A generation or two ago, it used to be easy for Westerners to break into the inner circle, but now that opportunity has passed. That's why I needed to make a good impression with Tom and Matt today. They established themselves in China about a decade before anyone there realized they didn't need foreigners' help. I'm hoping they might be able to introduce me to some of their advisory clients who need legal representation."

Lawrence took several large bites of his steak frites in rapid succession and washed it down with a swig of mimosa. I noticed his way of eating was a little more hurried and less elegant than I remembered. His face was a bit rounder as well.

"By the way, Michael, there might be a good opportunity for us to work together too and create a win-win situation," he continued. "Out of curiosity, I was looking through Naveon's patent filings. Some strange patterns emerge when looking at the picture as a whole. No surprise that your R&D team churns out dozens of patents each year, but in tech companies, patents are usually progressive and it's possible to trace a clear development path across multiple research initiatives. This isn't the case with Naveon's IP portfolio—discoveries seem to pop out of nowhere. As you know, tensions between the US and China, especially on the topic of IP, are at an all-time high. This could put Naveon at risk of DOJ investigation or worse. I'd suggest putting some defensive measures in place. If you'd like to introduce me to the CEO, I'd be happy to discuss how we can help with an overall IP strategy to protect Naveon in the long-term."

I looked over at Lim, who was still staring straight ahead. "Ah, I see. That is very troubling indeed. Let me speak to Peng and see if I can get him on a call with us. In the meantime, I'd appreciate your discretion on this matter."

"Of course," Lawrence said. "You have my absolute discretion! By the way, Michael, if I might say so, looking back now, I wish I had been a little more like you. You always had the courage to stand apart from the crowd.

My whole life I cared about nothing more than what other people thought of me. And that attitude led me to law school, where now I do paperwork for entrepreneurs like you. It's all just proximity to power, at the end of the day, all this meaningless chasing after prestige and credentials. By the way, did you get an invite to Jeff Bezos's barbecue tomorrow? Apparently invitations went out last night. Arche told me it starts at 10:00 A.M., but that seems way too early, right?"

I responded with a sort of knowing smile that I hoped implied I was in the know about Bezos's barbecue. Now we were wrapping up our brunch and the waiter came to clear the table.

"So, Michael, are you going to the P-rade later?"

"I think so. Starts at two o'clock, right? What are you doing for the next hour and a half?"

"Pre-drinks at Ivy, of course. What about yourself?"

I deflected the question, though not without giving him the opportunity to invite me to Ivy, which he didn't. Ivy was Lawrence's eating club—the most exclusive and historic at Princeton. *Good luck securing legal business from my fictional start-up*, I thought bitterly. When the check came, I insisted on paying, and was surprised he didn't fight me for the bill. Then Lawrence said he would catch me later this weekend and we parted ways.

I started walking in the direction of the quad like I had somewhere to be, attempting to appear to not notice the incredibly loud EDM music blasting from the walled courtyards of the eating clubs on Prospect Street. They wanted you to hear the party without being able to see it. Everywhere I looked, groups of attractive young alumni were spilling out of grand entryways and loudly deliberating on where they should "roll" next. So far, no one had spotted me. After about ten minutes of this I was feeling almost embarrassed enough to just wait things out at Nassau Inn.

"MICHAEL!"

I turned and saw Jessica on the other side of the street waving at me. She ran over and gave me a hug.

"Hmm, you look nicer than usual. Didn't wear the class jacket I ran around to find for you, though, of course. Where are you headed right now?"

"I'm pretty jet-lagged from the flight here. Was going to head back to the inn and take a nap."

Jessica rolled her eyes. "You've got to be kidding me. You're here for like twenty-four hours, there's no time for a nap. Okay, you're coming with me to TI. We can grab a few drinks there before the P-rade!"

TI, short for Tiger Inn, was Jessica's eating club at Princeton—the demographic there was primarily wrestlers and extremely extroverted Asian girls. Jessica was now leading the way and I had to pick up the pace a bit.

On the way over, she shot me a pouty look. "I'm still mad at you for ghosting me in San Francisco, by the way. But we'll talk about it later!"

Five minutes later I was waiting awkwardly outside the entrance of TI's massive Tudor mansion while Jessica had a word with the doorman. The house music from the courtyard was too loud for me to hear what she was saying. She kept gesturing back to me, then finally the doorman nodded and Jessica ushered me inside. We squeezed past a hallway of sweaty partiers to get to the courtyard, where they'd set up six tables of beer pong. Everyone seemed incredibly inebriated and once again the music was too loud to hear anyone talk. We found two Solo cups and filled them with beer from the keg. Jessica, perhaps sensing how uncomfortable I was, asked if I wanted a shot. I nodded and we went upstairs to a quieter floor of the club. Jessica took a bottle of tequila from the cupboard and we took one shot each. Feeling loose and pleasantly warm from the shot, we headed back to the courtyard and started to mingle. Everyone was already quite drunk and extremely friendly. I recognized a handful of distant acquaintances from college and managed to say hello. After about an hour or so the courtyard started emptying out, which meant it was time for us to go to the P-rade.

Jessica motioned for me to come join her group and introduced me as her friend from back home. I met four of her friends and we forgot each other's names instantly, but no one seemed to mind. We did one more round of shots and headed out onto the street.

By the time we arrived at the P-rade, the spectacle was already well under way. Vintage cars modded out in black and orange rolled down University Street, flanked by euphorically inebriated alumni of all class years. My ears rang with marching band music and loud cheering. Was this what they meant by school spirit? The whole thing was over about an hour after we got there, at which point everyone started clumping together to try and discreetly organize after-party plans. Since I had nothing to contribute to the conversation, during this part I just stayed within Jessica's general orbit and tried to maintain a facial expression of self-reliant nonchalance, which I hoped signaled that while I was happy to go to an after-party, I couldn't care less about whether or not I was included. There was some discussion, some open-market bartering on the question of passes and how many passes each person had for groups of varying hypothetical sizes. Finally, after five minutes of excruciating social limbo, Jessica tugged on my sleeve and said that a bunch of us were going to head to Tower, which was where the debate/theater crowd "partied." She didn't seem particularly enthusiastic about this plan, which instantly made me think that she'd lost some social currency by being attached to me in the pass-trading game just now. Our group walked to the austere brick clubhouse of Tower. It was definitely a more diverse group in there, and I got the vibe that everybody was applying to or headed to law school in the fall. They were serving nicer drinks, but everyone seemed to be having less fun than in Jessica's club. I noticed myself feeling more comfortable and confident in this definitively less attractive group of people than at the previous venue. Pretty soon I was three or four drinks in and had joined a group of recent grads that were having a spirited debate about the quality of living in San Francisco. I had just started delivering my take on the San Francisco homelessness issue when I felt a tap on my shoulder.

It was Hamza, the guy who asked the question about Uyghurs during the Princeton in Asia panel.

"Oh, hey man, what's up!" I said. "I'm Michael." I went in for the dab but he just stood there with his arms crossed.

"I know who you are," he said. "Are you a member here?"

"Well, no. I came here with my friend Jessica," I said, gesturing to Jessica, who was in a more fun bubble of the party.

"Don't know who Jessica is either. Anyway, I'm the President of Tower Club," he said. Then he turned to the group. "And you are a right-wing genocide apologist for the Chinese Communist Party."

There were a few scattered gasps from those standing within earshot.

"Hey man, I think you're confused. The guy you asked that question to isn't here. I was just *on* the panel. I wasn't even invited until the last second, actually."

Hamza sneered. "I'm going to stop you right there. If you don't think you had an obligation to speak up for marginalized communities while you had the platform to do so, then you're absolutely guilty by association. Silence is violence!" This drew nods of approval as well as some finger-snapping. I looked around nervously and saw that the commotion had attracted a small group of onlookers.

"I'm going to have to ask you to leave," he said firmly.

"Um, okay," I said. Then I turned to the group. "Just to clear things up, I'm not a genocide apologist. This is a misunderstanding. But I'll leave."

"What the fuck is going on here?" Jessica had just showed up and was slurring her words.

"Hi. I'm Hamza, president of Tower Club. Your friend here is a genocide apologist for the Chinese Communist Party, which is currently mass murdering millions of Uyghurs. So I'm sorry, he has to leave."

"I'm sorry, but do you know what the fuck you're talking about?" Jessica said. "This is my friend Michael, who is literally a software engineer. He has zero interest in mass murdering Uyghurs."

Now the people in the crowd looked very confused. Hamza uncrossed then recrossed his arms. "Well, maybe you should have seen him at this Princeton in China panel cozying up to CCP insiders. As club president, it's my responsibility to make sure Tower is an inclusive safe space for everyone. And your friend's presence is making it unsafe, so I'm going to have to ask him to leave."

"FINE!" Jessica said. "God, you guys are literally such pussies . . ." She gave Hamza the middle finger then took my hand and stormed out of the building with me.

"Thanks for that back there," I said, as soon as we were out of earshot.

"Well, I didn't help very much, did I? Whatever, it's fine. That party was so lame anyway."

"You looked like you were having fun."

"That's part of my thing, Michael, you know it is."

"Fair. Want to head back to Tiger Inn?"

"No, I don't think we can do that," said Jessica, without explaining why. "Whatever. Should we just go to Terrace? I think it's late enough."

I was surprised she suggested Terrace. Terrace was probably the closest thing Princeton had to an "alternative" (druggy, vegan, nonheteronormative) scene, once described by F. Scott Fitzgerald as "breathlessly freakish." It was also a "sign in" club, which meant anyone could join; there was no selective bidding process. And for that reason, I felt at the time there was no point in joining, which could only be read as an admission of defeat.

Jessica and I walked right into Terrace without being stopped by a bouncer. Everywhere we went we were surrounded by guys wearing leather pants and girls with purple hair and nose rings. There were also copious amounts of crushed-up drugs in plastic baggies strewn about in the open. Some of the baggies weren't sealed all the way shut and were spilling powder onto various surfaces. Frankly, Jessica looked more uncomfortable than I was.

Jessica said she thought there was live music in the backyard, so we went outside to check it out. Compared to the chaos indoors, the scene outside was almost idyllic. The music was just one undergrad playing indie folk originals without a microphone. We found a spot on the lawn not far from the house and sat in comfortable silence for a few minutes.

"By the way, where's Nick?" I asked, surprised I hadn't noticed his absence until just now.

"Not in the picture anymore."

"Whoa. You gonna tell me why?"

Jessica gave me an angry look.

"You remember my mom, right?"

Of course I remembered Jessica's mom. She was this tall, imposing woman from Beijing who spoke in staccato sentences and was always alone at school events because her husband was away pursuing business ventures in China. According to Jessica, her mom always blamed her for being the reason she was stuck at home instead of making a name for herself like her college classmates from China. She channeled all of this frustration into making Jessica a star and saw Jessica's accomplishments as her own, which was a constant source of resentment for Jessica. To be honest, Jessica's mom could often be a pretty unpleasant woman. I got the sense that she saw me as kind of a loser and a distraction for her daughter. But as soon as we got into Princeton, she completely flipped the script. Suddenly I was always welcome to hang out at her house, even alone with Jessica in her room.

During Jessica's sophomore year of high school, it came out that her dad had finally made it big in China—but he'd also started a second family there. To my amazement, her mother basically shrugged it all off and got a job at a small accounting firm the next month to support Jessica on her own, and eventually pay her way through college.

Jessica took a deep breath. "Right—of course you remember her. Anyway, ever since I moved away from home, I've been calling her once a week. You know, just to check in, since now I was so far away and she didn't really have anyone else. Around the beginning of this year, I noticed she was acting unusually forgetful. It was small stuff at first, like not being able to remember the names of my friends from high school. Then she started to forget things I just told her the week before. But one day when she called me in a panic because she'd gotten lost on her way back home from the grocery store, I knew I had to fly home to see her.

"The doctor told us it was early-onset Alzheimer's, but he couldn't predict how quickly her condition would deteriorate. What we knew for sure was that at some point, probably in the next year, she'd need to either have a full-time caretaker or move into a memory care facility.

"Of course, Nick was the first person I'd told. By this point we'd been dating for two years. My mom loved Nick, or at least the idea of him, and her face lit up every time I brought him home from Princeton to visit on the weekends. I assumed the feeling was mutual. At first we decided to hire a part-time helper for her to smooth things over while we monitored her condition. Then the late-night calls started, and it was like all of a sudden she was letting out all the anger she'd bottled up since my dad left, or maybe since I was born. She'd scream into the phone that the helper was stealing from her and that I was leaving her to die. She'd say I was just like my father, who could only think of himself, and that she'd always known the day would come when she'd regret moving to this country and starting this family. Sometimes she called three, four times a night, with no recollection of the previous conversation. Of course, Nick heard everything. Afterwards it was: 'Are you just going to let her speak to you like that? She's abusive, Jessica. Toxic. You need to establish boundaries. You don't owe her anything; you need to put her in a facility where she can get the specialist treatment she needs.' I told him I couldn't just put my mother in a home; even if they could give her the best treatment, there was no way to do it without making her feel abandoned. Then he said: 'When are you going to start making your own choices instead of just doing whatever your family expects from you?' That was it for me. I broke up with him, quit my job, and moved back to Tenafly."

I suddenly realized why she was telling me this now. I was there for her when her dad abandoned them in high school, and this exact scenario was something we'd talked through many times in the past: as the only children of single parents, what would happen if one of our parents got sick? The only answer, of course, was the promise that we'd be there for each other if and when it happened—no matter what happened between us. It was one of the last things Jessica said to me when she broke up with me freshman year: *I think of you as someone who's always going to be in my life.* Somewhere along the way, I had forgotten that promise. Now I could clearly see the pain on her face and felt ashamed.

"I'm so sorry, Jessica. I had no idea any of this was going on. I'm sorry I wasn't there for you."

"Maybe it's selfish of me to be telling you this," she continued, "but the whole time this was happening, I couldn't stop thinking about you. I just knew you'd understand exactly what I was going through, and make me feel okay no matter what I decided to do. It feels strange being back in Tenafly without you. That's why I tried so hard to get you to come back for Reunions. But when I looked you up, I saw that you left the country for good without even saying goodbye. You know, right before you left, I actually saw you once. You were walking around Pac Heights with this really pretty girl. She was so stylish too, looked like she was from somewhere really chic like London or Singapore. I figured that's what you always wanted. You left SF with her, right? If so, then I understand."

When I looked at her again, I recognized the same sincere, vulnerable girl I'd met in high school. Maybe she had been the same person this entire time. I couldn't remember how we had grown apart in the first place. It felt odd to be having this conversation with her at Princeton, only sixty miles and seven years from where we grew up together. In that moment, I wanted nothing more than to open up and tell her truth (or something close to it) about everything that had happened since I left San Francisco. But another part of me couldn't bring myself to shatter the new impression she had of me as someone who had gone on to greater things. At around two o'clock in the morning, I walked her back to the dorm where she was staying and we lingered at the door for a moment.

"Can I get something off my chest?" she said. I waited for her to continue. "It was my idea to invite you to the China panel. I asked Lawrence if there was any extra space, and luckily he said he had a cancellation. I knew you wouldn't have come all this way otherwise. That's how much I wanted to see you."

"I see," I said, but now there was a hollowness in my voice. Something in the space between us had shifted. I suddenly felt embarrassed of the expensive suit I was wearing, of my performative nonchalance leading up to the trip; it was the feeling of nakedness from being seen by someone who really knew you. "I think I should go. It was good to see you."

"Goodbye, Michael," she said, smiling and sniffling. "I'm glad you came."

Back in my hotel room, I was just about to turn the TV on when I heard a loud knocking at the door.

"Come on, let's go for a ride," said Agent Lim.

I followed him out to the parking lot and got into his Suburban. Lim deftly navigated us out of Princeton Township and soon we were on I-95 headed toward Manhattan. We coasted on the freeway for twenty miles, then took a right on exit 99 and stopped in front of a late-night Chinese buffet called Jade Empress right before the New Jersey state line. The place was decked out in many of the greatest hits of the genre: wall-mounted scrolls, plastic waterfalls, redwood panels, and beckoning cat figurine. The only other customers were four lonely old white guys sipping bottomless cups of coffee with hard eyes staring straight ahead waiting for morning. At the center of the dining room was the buffet trough, each chafing dish about one quarter to one third full. My mouth watered instinctively at the potent corn syrup and soy sauce scent of the spread, which lit up the nostalgic pathways of my brain.

Lim loaded his plate with a heap of orange chicken, egg fried rice, beef and broccoli, lo mein, and crab rangoon. I just got a cup of black coffee. We took seats across from each other in a corner booth with hard overhead lighting. It was nearly two o'clock in the morning and Lim still had his tie on. He rolled up his sleeves and started eating voraciously, creating an almost passive-aggressive silence for several minutes that told me he hadn't had time to eat all day because he'd been busy tailing me.

"So tell me," he said finally, "where do things stand with Bo?"

"We're getting close. He trusts me, I think. Or at the very least, he sees me as a competent, reliable aid. I did a good job for him in San Francisco a few weeks ago and he's really interested in what Yang has to offer."

Lim stopped eating and put his elbows on the table, appearing unimpressed with what I had to report. "That's all great, Michael. But unfortunately, we're out of time. That's what I came to tell you tonight. It's got to be now or never. Before your flight is supposed to leave tomorrow, you need to call Bo and see if he'll fly out to meet Yang."

"No, no," I said, trying my hardest not to sound frantic. "We really can't do that. Please, listen to me just this once. You don't understand how close we are now—I even had dinner with his family last week! We just need to wait a little longer for the right moment. Bo's said again and again that it's too dangerous for him to leave the country right now."

"And he's right. That's consistent with our best intel from Hong Kong. But like I said, we're out of time. That's coming from the US attorney. If you don't think you can deliver Bo, then I would suggest you surrender yourself to me."

He picked his fork back up and continued to eat leisurely. It was the middle of the night, and we were in no rush.

"What happened to the original plan?" I said. "Ferris said we'd still have another week after Reunions to make it work."

"Unfortunately for you, Michael, Ferris has gone dark. We no longer have anyone in the country to handle comms with you, and if you got caught, there'd be nothing we could do. The government doesn't want another Otto Warmbier situation. And I don't want to watch your tear-streaked face on CNN pleading for mercy from a Chinese prison. How humiliating. Think about what that would do to the image of Chinese Americans here, Michael. It wouldn't be fair to those of us who never strayed."

I focused on steadying my breathing and marinated in Lim's disdain. If he wanted to kick me while I was down, then so be it. "Ferris has been caught?"

"We don't know that. It's definitely possible. The alternative possibility is he's lying low because Beijing is on high alert. The last time he went dark, it was when we lost ten of our agents to a mole at the CIA. He made it through that alive, so I hope he can get through this one too. But here's what I know for sure—having you running around Beijing leaving breadcrumbs everywhere is not going to increase his odds of survival."

Lim was right: if I got caught, I took Ferris down with me. On a server somewhere in Beijing was dozens of hours of CCTV footage of Ferris and me walking together. If I ended up in custody, Chinese authorities would be on their way to Ferris in a matter of minutes. The inverse, I thought, was likely true as well: if Ferris had indeed been caught, my cover would've been blown as well.

Lim threw a twenty on the table and rose from the booth. "So, that's it, then. Get some sleep tonight and figure out what you're going to say to Bo tomorrow. I'll pick you up for the airport around noon."

After Agent Lim dropped me off at the Nassau Inn, I pulled out my phone and checked Ferris's status on WeChat. The account for the Haigui

Language Education Center had been deactivated two days ago, and the business hours said "permanently closed"—so I really was on my own.

I drew the blinds and paced my suite for two, then three hours, desperately trying to come up with a solution. Of course, none presented itself—how could it have? I hadn't conceived of a single original intervention this entire time; all I'd done was passively execute my handlers' instructions and telephone the information they'd fed me. Now the line was being cut on one side. I felt crushed by the obvious immovability of the situation. In a few hours, I'd be a prisoner, and there was nothing I could do to avoid it. Because of Chinese tariffs on American corn, the impending failure of the DOJ's China Initiative, and a "century of humiliation" that started 150 years before I was born. And also because of my own deep-seated flaws of character and judgment. I laughed uncontrollably when I thought about how trivial my problems at General Motors and dating life were merely a few months ago—and yet how grotesquely connected they were to this game of nations that had somehow found me at its center. Of course it had been me. I climbed out onto the fire escape and started smoking my last pack of FPMO cigarettes.

I didn't see Agent Lim's car in the parking lot. Maybe he was watching the front door from the inn's surveillance feed and didn't know about the fire escape. I could climb down to the parking lot and run out to Witherspoon Street. It was only a ninety-minute cab ride to the Chinese consulate in New York City. I could call Bo on the way and see if he'd make arrangements for me. I'd have to give him Ferris, of course—but he'd said it himself, didn't he? *A certain degree of betrayal is unavoidable.*

No—I wouldn't disappear into the night again. Not when there was so little left to lose. I climbed back inside my room and buried my head into the pillow. I hated this feeling of being cornered by Agent Lim. I hated the disdainful way that he looked at me, the way he casually alluded to my "obvious psychological complexes," as if he could read every shameful thought in my head. The only thing worse than feeling invisible, I thought, was being see-through. Not that he'd been alone in this. Vivian and Bo as well—hadn't they always known exactly what to say to me? To get me to betray my country, leave my life? How easy and cheap my eager cooperation must have appeared to them. The only difference was that they didn't tout their mastery over me in the open, which was somehow even more humiliating.

As I lay there convulsing in spite, a terrible thought came to me. Even while they slid me across their board with impunity, I hadn't been the passive piece they thought I was. I'd seen, as well. I registered quite a bit more than any of them realized.

31

Ten hours later, Agent Lim and I were sitting together in the interrogation room at JFK where he'd first detained me. I dialed Bo's number and he picked up on the third ring.

"Hey, Michael. How did your meeting with Yang Xujun go? Will he work with us?"

"Unfortunately, no," I said. "I did everything I could to convince him but he said it's too risky for him right now. Because of the witch hunt. One of his closest friends in the Computer Science Department just got placed under house arrest. You were right, everyone is on high alert."

There was silence on the other end of the line. I let Bo sit in his disappointment for a few seconds.

"That's too bad," Bo said. "Well, that's alright, come back to Beijing. We can talk about what to do next here."

Agent Lim shook his head. I gave him a hard look and paused for two seconds before continuing.

"Actually, I have another update for you that you might like," I said. "At the fifteen-year alumni tent I spoke to the head of the golf program, James Wilkinson. I brought up your son's case. He was impressed by Kevin's recent tournament performance and I messaged that you were interested in making a significant contribution to the golf program this year. Wilkinson said there might be a spot for Kevin on the team this fall and that he was willing to have a meeting with you and Kevin to discuss it. Unfortunately, this kind of meeting has to be in person, and he also said we'd have to do it before next week as we're already late in the athletic recruiting season. What do you think?"

For an agonizing three seconds, the line was silent. "Hold on, let me talk to my wife," he said. Bo covered the microphone for about a minute and I could hear rapid muffled Mandarin in the background. Then he came back on. "Well done, Michael. I will not forget this. I can be there the day after tomorrow. Will that work for Mr. Wilkinson?"

"Yes, leave it to me," I said. "Send me your flight details and I'll escort you to the meeting from the airport myself to make the introduction in person."

"How should I prepare for this meeting?"

"I would bring a copy of Kevin's highlight reel on a portable drive. And for the donation, I would come with a number in the nine digits," I said authoritatively.

"Sounds good. Thank you for making time for this." Then he hung up.

I looked over at Agent Lim, whose eyes were gleaming.

"Michael, Michael," he said, shaking me by the shoulders. "You absolute devil. Bringing the kid into this? I didn't know you had it in you."

Bo was on Cathay Pacific flight CX335 from Beijing to JFK, touching down at 2:58 P.M. At two o'clock, I sat waiting by the window in the

United Lounge. Agent Lim had told me I could watch what happened next from here.

At 2:55 P.M., three minutes ahead of schedule, Bo's plane touched down, then came to a stop in the middle of the runway. A truck towing a set of passenger stairs slowly pulled up to the front cabin exit. Then, a caravan of black Chevy Suburbans swarmed the aircraft on both sides. Agent Lim and Agent Reddy stepped out of the lead vehicle and ascended the stairs. Two minutes later, they emerged with Bo and his son handcuffed and loaded them into the back seat of the lead vehicle. Kevin was visibly shaking as Reddy guided him down the steps while Bo kept his head down. The caravan dispersed, and after a few minutes, the plane continued to taxi to the gate.

A few minutes later, I watched the arrest replay on TV in glorious helicopter footage. The headline read: CHINESE SUPERSPY ARRESTED AT JFK. Voicing over the clip, the newscaster announced that Yuanhong Wang, a top-ranking Chinese intelligence operative, had been arrested by federal authorities who had lured him to New York on the false pretense of arranging a "side door" admission to Princeton for his son, Kevin Song. Bo, the newscaster explained, was personally responsible for the theft of American secrets worth more than $100 billion over multiple decades. I wondered where they got that number from. Then the program cut to a two-panel view where a different reporter was interviewing Agent Lim on the runway. Lim had taken off his sunglasses and looked handsome on-camera in his dark blue suit with American flag pin.

"The arrest of Yuanhong Wang marks a significant victory in our multiyear campaign against Chinese state-sponsored corporate espionage," he said. "We want today to send a powerful message to all those who would attempt to steal American secrets. The FBI is opening a new counterintelligence investigation into China every twelve hours. If you have spies in our country, now is the time to bring them home, because we are confident we will catch every last one.

"Lastly, this was really a team effort involving multiple federal agencies. A special thank you to US Attorney Richard Scully from the Northern District of California for his visionary leadership here."

The segment ended and cut to a report on the subway system in New York City. I looked around the lounge; no one seemed to have been paying attention. I took a few shaky breaths and ordered a whisky sour at the bar. My cell phone rang from a 415 number and I picked up immediately.

"Well done, Michael," Richard Scully said. "Listen, you played your cards well, and my office is true to its word. Go on and enjoy your freedom. All your problems just rode off into the sunset with Agent Lim in the back seat of that Suburban. May I give you some unsolicited advice? Try to avoid traveling to China."

I granted him an awkward chuckle.

"Listen, the reason I'm calling you right away is to remind you that your participation in this plan is top secret. The Chinese will be investigating what happened here today and we don't want any loose ends. We'll need you to come to San Francisco tomorrow to sign an NDA. We can talk more when you're here, I'm happy to answer any questions that you have. Can you be on a plane in the next few hours?"

"Yes, sir, of course," I said.

At JFK, I found the clip of Bo's arrest on YouTube and watched it over and over again. On the fifth or sixth rewatch, the vengeful thrill of seeing Bo handcuffed and shoved into the back seat gave way to something else. Maybe it was despair. Because even though he'd condemned me and changed the course of my life forever, it still hurt to betray somebody. And I believed—and still, to this day, believe—that although the premise was false, there were moments of genuine connection between Bo and me. Nothing is ever completely real, and nothing is ever completely fake.

As the adrenaline wore off on my way to San Francisco, I became subsumed with anxiety over what life would look like in the aftermath of this case. In the extreme case, would I need to go into witness protection? How would I ever find another job? For some reason, the drastic stuff like witness protection filled me with less dread than just the prospect of returning to the directionless void of the way things were.

My flight landed at around eleven o'clock in the evening and I took an Uber to my old apartment in Chinatown. I walked through the moon gate of Club Mandarin and found the restaurant empty, no sign of Daniel, Tony, or Jeffrey anywhere. I opened the door and surveyed the landscape of the things I'd so easily left behind—the remnants of something that at this point felt more like a past life. The plants had died and everything was covered in a thin layer of dust. Something about the scene broke my heart; maybe it was the impossibility of mentally inserting myself back into this space, of simply going back to the way things used to be. There'd been a splintering in my soul I couldn't suture. In the kitchen, I found a carton of purple FPMO cigarettes still sitting on the counter. I took out a pack and smoked them by myself in the alley outside of Club Mandarin.

After a fitful night of sleep, I met Scully the next morning at his office in a modest two-story government building in Potrero Hill. He came outside personally to get me from the waiting room, then shook my hand warmly and asked me to take a seat.

"Congratulations again, Michael. These things usually don't work out so well. Now, what questions do you have for me?"

I started by asking whether or not I would need to go into witness protection, and how I would ever find another job. Scully laughed.

"Oh, Michael. You've been watching too much *Narcos*. Things aren't okay between China and the US right now, but they're certainly not sending assassins over to murder civilians. I wouldn't worry about that. As for job stuff, you're in luck. Here's what you'll put on your resume . . . "

He slid over a piece of paper that looked like an excerpt from a fake resume. The main bullet read PALANTIR TECHNOLOGIES: SOFTWARE ENGINEERING MANAGER, JUNE 2017–JUNE 2018.

"We're giving you that promotion you always wanted!" he said cheerily. "The FBI partners with Palantir to provide job references for people like you who have helped us out in various unmentionable ways. You'll find the names and email addresses of your references, real Palantir employees with top-secret clearance, at the bottom of the page. We've instructed them to speak vaguely but glowingly. Are you planning on jumping right into the job search?"

"Not really. I need a bit of a break to process everything that's happened."

"Fair enough. Makes sense. What are you thinking for your time off?"

I thought for a second about how much I should tell Scully. "When I first went to Beijing at the beginning of this ordeal, one of my goals was to find my dad. He disappeared around the time I was nine or ten years old. Somehow I just knew in my gut that if he was anywhere, he'd be in Beijing. And then Bo told me that he'd actually recruited my dad many years ago to work at a secret research facility in the mountains outside of the city. I know I can't go back to China, but I'm hoping there's still some way for me to look for him."

Scully looked at me blankly and blinked several times. "Michael, I don't think that's a good idea."

"Why not?"

"It's true that Bo recruited your father in the year 1997. But he's not working in some top-secret Chinese government research lab. He's an inmate at the Santa Rita Jail in Dublin, 35 miles east of here."

I shook my head. "No, that can't be right. Are you sure?"

"Of course I'm sure—I put him in there myself. Your father was found guilty of economic espionage in 2002 and sentenced to seventeen years. I was an assistant US attorney at the time. To be honest, the similarities and differences with yours are fascinating. From the interviews, I got the impression that your father was motivated primarily by some bizarre desire to help his birth country, and only secondarily by the titles and recognition Bo used to tempt him. In fact, he never made any money off of this. I do remember he asked me during his sentencing not to share the story with you or your mother; I guess he wanted to spare you the shame. Look where that got us, eh? I guess the apple really doesn't fall far from the tree. It's good you weaseled your way out of this one, otherwise we could've been in store for quite an awkward family reunion in Santa Rita."

Scully had a bemused look on his face, like he'd been waiting to drop this information on me since the first time we spoke. I wouldn't give him a show. I clenched my jaw and my knuckles whitened over the armrest.

"Alright then," Scully said. "Anything else you want to ask me?"

"No, not at this time," I said icily. "Thank you for arranging the references. I'll be on my way now."

A sly smirk spread across Scully's jowly face. "Really, Michael? Aren't you wondering about what happened to Vivian?"

For a few seconds, it felt like every cell in my body was screaming for oxygen.

"I don't blame you for not being upfront with us about Vivian," he said. "I can see how from your perspective, it could seem like something that would be embarrassing to admit. Though I've got to say, we did ask you pretty directly to tell us everything about what happened up until that point. That definitely docked you a point or two in integrity. But no matter, all's well that ends well.

"So let me tell you what we know, or think we know, about Vivian before you spend the rest of your life looking for her too. She isn't some rich heiress or art collector. And Bo certainly isn't her uncle; he's her commanding officer. Needless to say, Vivian isn't her real name, which we don't actually know. What we do know is that she's a rising star at the MSS, part of a new guard that sees things in a fundamentally different way than Bo's generation. Bo and his inner circle are committed to the original strategy of unscrupulous IP theft to advance development at all costs. The new guard believes, I think correctly, that this strategy will eventually result in armed conflict between the two most powerful nations in history. Therefore, a courageous few have established a secret channel between the agencies to try and facilitate a sort of détente and slow the escalation of hostilities.

"Vivian is a key leader in this effort. And so is Ferris Guo, your handler. The two have been in contact since at least 2008. We believe Vivian was the principal reason why Ferris survived the purge of CIA assets in 2010; she found a way to take his name off the list.

"The long and short of it is, Bo's imprisonment will create a vacuum, which gives Vivian an opportunity to increase her influence within the MSS and shift the agency toward this new strategy. Spying will always be a fact of life in international relations, and we don't know if we can fully trust her, but she's someone we can at least work with to prevent tensions from spilling over into something disastrous. So I suppose what I'm saying is that you can feel good, Michael, about playing a role in making the world a safer place."

"So where is she now?"

"That I can't tell you," Scully said. "Obviously the strategy she just pulled off came at enormous risk to herself. If Bo's inner circle found out, they'd probably have her court-martialed for treason. For her own safety, we're no longer in contact with her. In fact, she cut off contact with us the moment she flagged you to us."

"She flagged me?"

"Yes, of course she flagged you," Scully said, a strain of impatience in his voice. "Like we told you from the very beginning—the technology that you 'stole' on behalf of the Chinese had no scientific or commercial value whatsoever. And we're opening up a new case every twelve hours. How do you think you jumped right to the top of the queue? Vivian insisted for some reason that you, of all the contacts she'd developed, had the potential to lure Bo out of hiding and catch him in a mistake. I'm going to be honest, Michael, at first I didn't see what she was talking about. I still don't. But thankfully for all of us, it looks like Vivian's faith in you wasn't misplaced."

Of all the contacts she'd developed. Given the totality of the new information, I'm not sure why that phrase stung so much. I excused myself and headed to the door.

32

I walked out of Scully's office into the foggy San Francisco morning and started retracing my steps.

I started at the Powell-Hyde station and waited for the trolley. I imagined myself turning back but got on anyway. The trolley peaked on top of Lombard Street and started its descent into Fisherman's Wharf. I knew where this story was going and felt myself pulled forward by its inertia.

I got out early. I went to the Club Mandarin, but something stopped me from breaching the moon gate. I wandered around Chinatown for another hour or so. A new-looking storefront in the neighborhood caught my eye; I nearly passed it before realizing it was Daniel, Tony, and Jeffrey's new barbecue shop. They looked busy and happy behind the counter, arguing loudly with each other as always. I stood outside the window for a minute or so but they didn't see me; I couldn't bring myself to walk in. I took a last look at the neighborhood and left through the Stockton Street Tunnel.

The final leg of my journey took me back up to Aquatic Park Cove, where I found the cluster of telescopes that looked out at Alcatraz.

Vivian was right about one thing. It was too painful to live on memories alone. And that's when I knew what I had to do. If this was the last time I'd look out from this side of the Pacific, then so be it. If I was going to be a ghost, I was going to be a vengeful one. There was no way I would go gently.

33

Weirdly enough, the only one who wanted to help me after everything was Christine. We spoke on the phone two days after Bo's arrest made the news.

According to Christine, while Bo and his son awaited trial in the United States, Bo's wife was under house arrest in Beijing. Rumor had it that Bo's capture was tantamount to exile, since the investigation was sure to uncover evidence that would implicate him in corruption back home. All of his assets had been frozen. And that's when she told me about the apartment.

Like many Chinese elites, Bo had been stockpiling property all over the world for several years as a way of transferring wealth out of the country. Opera Residences in Sydney's Bennelong Point was a new development that had just been completed in March, and Christine had furnished it herself. Christine said cautiously that if I wanted, it was possible for her to give me remote access to the unit through the property manager's iPhone app. Within twelve hours, I was on a one-way flight to Sydney. As I puzzled over why she was helping me, I felt a pang of regret: not once, I realized, had I taken the time to think about what Christine wanted.

Over time, I found a few ways to make the place my own. For example, I installed an identical unit of the La Marzocco GS3 espresso machine I'd had in San Francisco. I missed the high-pressure showers from my old apartment in Beijing, so I had Bo's taken out and replaced with a replica. One afternoon, at an antiques market in Surry Hills, I came across a scholar's rock that reminded me of the one in Bo's backyard in Beijing, so I bought it and had it put up on a mantel in the living room.

At first it felt weird to watch the news about Bo's trial from the air-conditioned comfort of his own living room, but very quickly I found a sense of satisfaction in it. I never missed a broadcast. It was Richard Scully versus the attorney Bo had hired, a guy who looked like a senior version of Lawrence, while Bo sat stone-faced and mute at the front. He looked like he hadn't slept in days, but even so managed to bear his lot with a shred of dignity, which is more than I could say for myself. Bo was very telegenic and there was something about his demeanor that commanded respect; it was clear this wasn't the first purge he'd been through (though probably his last). Every now and then, my presence would indirectly insert itself into the trial, when Scully presented evidence collected by "anonymous government witness." During these moments I'd feel a sharp and sudden moment of pride, always hoping the camera would pan to Bo so I could register his reaction to learning the role I'd played in his downfall. Was it insane to think a small part of him would even be proud of me?

Ferris was right—one of the best things about Chinese people is that they always want the best for the next generation. Ultimately it was this insight that provided the key to my "freedom." At first it felt sick to use his parental instincts against him, but then I wondered if he'd gotten my dad on a similar strategy. My dad was a man who'd always seen science as a gift to the world and not something to be jealously guarded by nations. Something for the next generation. Something to help me.

Why then had I accepted Christine's offer to live at Bo's apartment in the first place? At first I couldn't tell if I was getting revenge or punishing myself. In the end, I figured it just felt fitting. I started to consider the possibility that maybe the state of betrayal was something that suited me.

I monitored my dad's release date on the state of California's public incarceration records. To my surprise, it was coming up in three months; he'd be free just a few days after my twenty-seventh birthday. I wondered what he'd do when he got out. Unfortunately, there was no government bailout deal with fake references waiting for him. But he was the sort of man who could make peace with his circumstances and wouldn't think twice about moving into a motel and finding a job at a Chinese restaurant.

I wondered if he would try and find me. At first I tried writing him a long letter explaining everything that happened, not just in the past few months but in the years that had gone by since he disappeared, but this felt too self-indulgent or confessional, and in the end I decided the picture I'd created of myself was too embarrassing to show him. I realized at some point that all I wanted was to somehow convince him that I turned out this way of my own accord, that he wasn't at fault for the person I became, and that on some level perhaps things were always fated to turn out this way for me—but then I realized there wouldn't be a need to explain any of this if he never found out about what happened in the first place. So I stopped writing the letter. It struck me that the irony of all this was that when my father "disappeared" all those years ago, he probably performed a similar calculus.

I'd made enough money in China to live comfortably for a few years, but partially out of necessity and partially out of boredom I started freelancing again on Samarkand. *Boredom* maybe wasn't the right word. I had no visitors and no activities; this state of idleness worked my anxious imagination to a fever pitch. What Scully had said about Vivian and Ferris's decade-long partnership often woke me up in the middle of the night. It took me a while to place the feeling, but then I realized it was how I felt when Vivian had told me the story about Vincent, the painter from Beijing whose romance she'd kept from her watchful father. The first time I heard that story, I worried about how I could possibly take the place of someone like that in her heart—now I'm struck by how naïve I was to believe it all in the first place. I pictured Vivian and Ferris celebrating their respective promotions together at some secret resort in Switzerland, toasting with champagne glasses. Would they mention my name? My face burned when I thought about Ferris and the loyalty and warmth I'd once felt for someone I thought of as a brother.

It was a couple months before I started to attempt to create a life for myself in Sydney. I knew that getting a job was key, would serve the purpose of putting me in real-life situations with real-life human beings. What I ended up doing was getting a job as an instructor at a coding boot camp in Gore Hill. I had one section that was for high school–aged kids and another that was for adult "career switchers." My students in the latter section came from all over the world and had ended up here because of some sort of large-scale career or life frustration. One woman had been a diplomat in the State Department but became disillusioned with the lack of control and moral ambivalence of her work. Another was a retired Finnish football player who'd gotten injured in the last season and lost his ability to play. Some people were sketchier and clearly running from something. This crossroads was almost like a hostel environment of sorts. Because I couldn't say anything about my past life, I learned how to become a really good listener, and to my surprise, people opened up. As one of the "fixtures" of this space, over time I started to see the first green shoots of a real life: one with other people and a concept of a future. Compared to other futures I had imagined previously, this one was more limited in scale. I didn't have dreams of greatness anymore; in fact, I didn't want to attract any more attention than necessary and took solace in my invisibility. I started to spend less and less time on Samarkand, at least the social forum part of it, though I still took jobs from the marketplace. If things continued in this way, I figured, at some point (presumably) I would meet a woman, maybe even start a family several years down the line. And for my children, this way of existing in Sydney wouldn't be some weird purgatory, it would just be normal life. After about six months of this I came to the conclusion that I was, in fact, an immigrant, just like my mother and father before me.

It didn't take long for me to convince myself that the life I had in Sydney was a completely new one, that the memories from San Francisco were from a past life. This was easy because the social connections tracing me back to America were so few. I'd let down and shut out so many people over the years that pretty soon the outreach stopped entirely. Even Jessica had given up on me. I guess at a certain point, you do lose people forever.

The one exception was an unexpected email from Daniel, my friend from Club Mandarin. He was writing from his new laptop to tell me that the barbecue shop was finally a success. They couldn't agree what to call the place between the three of them, so they'd named it Mike's BBQ. In fact, he'd gone through the trouble of getting my email from Madame Suyi to figure out how he could transfer me $3,241—my share of the shop's profits from the first year. When I read the email, I wept for the first time in months.

I continued to monitor the state of Bo's trials in the American news. Since it had now been a year, coverage was slowing down, but I had Google news alerts set up to update me on new developments. There was never anything exciting. But every time I started to feel too comfortable in my new life, the old fears would come creeping back. Maybe Bo would reemerge or one of his lieutenants would show up to avenge him. What would I do then? Pick a new country and start over? I never could stop looking over my shoulder.

A full year after I moved to Sydney, I felt settled enough in my own life that I decided to shut down my Samarkand account for good and move all my funds off the platform. So one Friday evening, after going out for dinner with my new friends, I logged into the platform for the last time. That's when I noticed that the status sticker next to viv798 had turned green again—active as of two days ago. Something told me she'd know where to find me.